HARD AND FAST

"*Hard and Fast* hit me like a ton of bricks and didn't let up until I finished the last word . . . A great second installment from Erin McCarthy! I was captivated and completely enamored of both characters and the love they shared."
—*Romance Junkies*

"McCarthy has done it again! This follow-up to *Flat-Out Sexy* is a thrill ride that's unexpectedly funny, sentimental, and thoroughly entertaining. It's full of real women and sexy men, and these authentic characters, their unexpected love, and a few twists will make you a stock car racing fan."
—*Romantic Times*

"A wild ride. This delightful tale entices the reader from page one . . . The passion is as hot as a fire cracker . . . Buckle up, ladies, this is one fun read."
—*Romance Reviews Today*

"This is Erin McCarthy at her best. She is fabulous with smoking-hot romances! *Hard and Fast* is witty, charming, and incredibly sexy." —*The Romance Readers Connection*

continued . . .

"A runaway winner! Ms. McCarthy has created a fun, sexy, and hilarious story that holds you spellbound from start to finish . . . A must-have book for your bookshelf!"

—*Fallen Angel Reviews*

HEIRESS FOR HIRE

"If you are looking to read a romance that will leave you all warm inside, then *Heiress for Hire* is a must read."

—*Romance Junkies*

"McCarthy transforms what could have been a run-of-the-mill romance with standout characterizations that turn an unlikable girl and a boring guy into two enjoyable, empathetic people who make this romance shine."   —*Booklist*

"Amusing paranormal contemporary romance . . . Fans will appreciate Erin McCarthy's delightful pennies-from-heaven tale of opposites in love pushed together by a needy child and an even needier ghost."   —*The Best Reviews*

"One of McCarthy's best books to date . . . *Heiress for Hire* offers characters you will care about, a story that will make you laugh and cry, and a book you won't soon forget. As Amanda would say: It's priceless."

—*The Romance Reader* (5 hearts)

"A keeper. I'm giving it four of Cupid's five arrows."

—*BellaOnline*

"An alluring tale."   —*A Romance Review* (5 roses)

continued . . .

"The perfect blend of sentiment and silly, heat and heart . . . Priceless!" —*Romantic Times* (4½ stars, Top Pick)

"An enjoyable story about finding love in unexpected places, don't miss *Heiress for Hire*." —*Romance Reviews Today*

A DATE WITH THE OTHER SIDE

"Do yourself a favor and make a date with the other side." —Rachel Gibson, *New York Times* bestselling author

"One of the romance-writing industry's brightest stars . . . Ms. McCarthy spins a fascinating tale that deftly blends a paranormal story with a blistering romance . . . Funny, charming, and very entertaining, *A Date With the Other Side* is sure to leave you with a pleased smile on your face." —*Romance Reviews Today*

"If you're looking for a steamy read that will keep you laughing while you turn the pages as quickly as you can, *A Date With the Other Side* is for you. Very highly recommended!" —*Romance Junkies*

"Fans will appreciate this otherworldly romance and want a sequel." —*Midwest Book Review*

"Just the right amount of humor interspersed with romance." —*Love Romances*

"Ghostly matchmakers add a fun flair to this warmhearted and delightful tale . . . An amusing and sexy charmer sure to bring a smile to your face." —*Romantic Times*

THE
CHASE

erin mccarthy

BERKLEY SENSATION, NEW YORK

THE BERKLEY PUBLISHING GROUP
Published by the Penguin Group
Penguin Group (USA) Inc.
375 Hudson Street, New York, New York 10014, USA

Penguin Group (Canada), 90 Eglinton Avenue East, Suite 700, Toronto, Ontario M4P 2Y3, Canada
(a division of Pearson Penguin Canada Inc.)
Penguin Books Ltd., 80 Strand, London WC2R 0RL, England
Penguin Group Ireland, 25 St. Stephen's Green, Dublin 2, Ireland (a division of Penguin Books Ltd.)
Penguin Group (Australia), 250 Camberwell Road, Camberwell, Victoria 3124, Australia
(a division of Pearson Australia Group Pty. Ltd.)
Penguin Books India Pvt. Ltd., 11 Community Centre, Panchsheel Park, New Delhi—110 017, India
Penguin Group (NZ), 67 Apollo Drive, Rosedale, North Shore 0632, New Zealand
(a division of Pearson New Zealand Ltd.)
Penguin Books (South Africa) (Pty.) Ltd., 24 Sturdee Avenue, Rosebank, Johannesburg 2196,
South Africa

Penguin Books Ltd., Registered Offices: 80 Strand, London WC2R 0RL, England

This is a work of fiction. Names, characters, places, and incidents either are the product of the author's imagination or are used fictitiously, and any resemblance to actual persons, living or dead, business establishments, events, or locales is entirely coincidental. The publisher does not have any control over and does not assume any responsibility for author or third-party websites or their content.

THE CHASE

A Berkley Sensation Book / published by arrangement with the author

PRINTING HISTORY
Berkley Sensation mass-market edition / April 2011

Copyright © 2011 by Erin McCarthy.
Excerpt from *Slow Ride* by Erin McCarthy copyright © by Erin McCarthy.
Cover art by Craig White.
Cover design by Rita Frangie.
Interior text design by Kristin del Rosario.

ISBN: 978-0-425-24014-4

BERKLEY® SENSATION
Berkley Sensation Books are published by The Berkley Publishing Group,
a division of Penguin Group (USA) Inc.,
375 Hudson Street, New York, New York 10014.
BERKLEY® SENSATION and the "B" design are trademarks of Penguin Group (USA) Inc.

PRINTED IN THE UNITED STATES OF AMERICA

10 9 8 7 6 5 4 3 2 1

THE CHASE

CHAPTER
ONE

"I bet he's as bad in bed as he is on the track."

Kendall Holbrook looked at her friend Tuesday Jones cautiously as they sat on the boards in pit road watching Evan Monroe lapping the track on a test run. This was one particular driver's sexual prowess she did not want to discuss. "Do you mean bad-good or bad-bad?"

"What?" Tuesday cocked her head and frowned. "There is no bad-good."

"Yes, there is. You could have meant that he's a badass. That kind of bad."

Her friend shook her head, making her dark hair slide forward. "No. No badass. Bad is just bad, as in he sucks. I mean, he can't drive for shit, and any man who can't drive certainly can't f—"

Cutting her friend off, Kendall said, "Okay, I get it!"

"Which is really too bad because he is phenomenally cute. What a butt. That's not a bad ass. That's a good ass. A delicious ass."

"I never noticed." Liar. She was a huge, jumbo, giant liar. Not only had she noticed Evan's butt, she'd seen it naked a decade earlier when she'd been young and stupid and had thought dating him made an ounce of sense. It hadn't.

But she could definitely say that Evan had not been bad-bad in bed. He had opened her eyes sexually, or technically had rolled them back in her head, the first man—boy, really—to have done that.

"You must be talking about his butt, because you can't deny that you've noticed his driving is less than stellar this season."

Kendall waited until Evan's car roared around the track in front of them. "Oh, that I've noticed. This is the worst season of his career."

Speaking of which, would it be considered evil if she admitted that a small part of her was just a little gleeful that the man who had broken her heart was down on his luck? Nope, she didn't believe it would be. Just ask any woman who had been burned by a two-faced man and she'd be on her side. Besides, it's not like she wanted him to die or anything.

Wait, did she?

No, no, definitely not. She just wanted him to not be the successful golden boy for once.

"I feel sorry for him," Tuesday said. "It's like he's so used to being good, he doesn't know what to do with himself."

"I don't feel sorry for him." God's honest truth there. Kendall had fought and clawed to get where she was, and Evan had just breezed through life, the son of a racing legend, sponsors falling in his lap. "Have you listened to the man? His ego can stand a hit or two."

"Yeah, but I wouldn't mind comforting him." Tuesday pushed up her sunglasses and gave a naughty grin. "Come

here, sweetie, let me comfort you with my hands on your
bare butt and your—"

Again, Kendall cut her off because she knew Tuesday
had no barriers or concern for the fact that a dozen people
were milling all around them. But then again, Tuesday was
in the media and didn't have to answer to the same public
relations czars.

Not that image was first and foremost on Kendall's
mind. She just didn't want to hear Tuesday's graphic description of fictional sex with Evan. Why, she wasn't sure.
It wasn't like it mattered anymore who Evan slept with. It
hadn't for ten years. But still. Just still.

"I thought you said he probably sucks in bed."

Tuesday dangled her feet, her boots scuffing the wall.
"Oh, I would just make him lie there while I took whatever
I wanted. My submissive sex slave."

"Oh, Lord." Kendall rolled her eyes. "If you think Evan
Monroe is down with being a submissive you need to start
wearing a helmet."

"Wearing a helmet when? I'm not a driver."

"Wearing a helmet when you're walking because clearly
you banged your brains up somehow if you think that man
would just lie there and do what you say."

"And how do you know so much about what Evan Monroe
would or wouldn't do?"

Kendall couldn't see Tuesday's eyes behind her sunglasses but she recognized that tone. Her friend was suspicious and tenacious in ferreting out secrets. It's what made
her an amazing racing journalist and gossip blog writer,
known online as Tuesday Talladega.

Striving for nonchalance, Kendall fought the urge to tug
on the front of her jacket. "Come on, it's obvious. He's a

walking egomaniac alpha male. Like every other driver in the series."

"Umm-hmm. If I didn't know better I'd think there was more to this story."

God, she was going to blush. Twenty-eight years old and she was going pink in the cheeks. "No story! And don't you dare write me into your blog speculating about me or I will egg your house. I know where you live, you know."

Tuesday just laughed. "Please. You would not. And you know I won't gossip about your personal life. Unless it's really, really good."

"That's reassuring." Kendall had read Tuesday's blog many times. Her friend was snarky and biting and raised questions that got people thinking, and not always in a positive way. Kendall did not want to be on the receiving end of that wicked pen. Or keyboard, as the case may be.

Shifting on her feet, Kendall gave in and yanked at the front of her fire retardant jumpsuit. She was starting to sweat. Glancing at the track, she noticed Evan was coming in to pit and talk to his crew. His brother, Elec Monroe, was already pulling onto the track in his number 56 car.

"I'm kidding," Tuesday said, waving her hand in dismissal. "I do talk about your career, but I have to. Everyone would notice if I omitted discussing the most intriguing bit of news to hit stock car racing in years. A *female* driver in the cup series, hello, it's a major sound bite. But I'll never trash you, Scout's honor. I am a loyal friend."

Tuesday didn't sound offended, but Kendall still felt guilty that she had implied she couldn't trust Tuesday. "I know. You are a good friend, and I'm damn grateful to have you around to keep me sane. But I don't want to be the biggest news to hit stock car racing just because I have a uterus."

"I don't think it's your uterus most men are concerned with. It's your vagina. Va-jay-jay. Your man hole."

Nothing like saying it like it was. Kendall was about to tell Tuesday exactly what she thought of the expression "man hole," when she heard a strangled laugh from behind her. Great, someone had heard them.

"Is this what happens when we let a woman driver into the cup series? Instead of chassis and boiler plate restrictors, we talk uterus and va-jay-jay?"

Oh, freaking fabulous. That wasn't just any someone. That was Evan goddamn Monroe. Right behind her. Making her feel stupid and small and furious. It was a curse that of all the people milling around, it would be him that would overhear their conversation. Why, why, why, why?

Whirling, she glared at him. "I don't believe we were talking to you, so *we* are not talking about anything that is any of your business."

Evan fought the annoyance that always flared when he was within ten feet of Kendall Holbrook. The woman drove him insane, and not in a good way. Why she always had to be antagonistic was beyond him. If memory served she was the one who had dumped him all those years ago. He'd been a nineteen-year-old idiot rushing into love, on the verge of popping a certain question to her, when she had disappeared, not returning his calls and totally avoiding him. After a few weeks that he would like to erase from his memory banks, involving desperate voice mails and pounding on her front door begging her to talk to him, he had given up and crawled away to lick his wounds.

So where did she get off being hostile when he was the one who had been wronged? And here he was, just trying to be friendly and joke around with her.

"Furthermore," she said, her finger coming up.

Furthermore? Good Lord. She was about to rant. He could see it brewing in her. For a woman as tiny as she was, she'd always managed to be good at getting worked up. Kendall stood five-two on a tall day, with a petite body and long blond hair. She looked like a high school cheerleader, not a stock car driver.

At the moment her hair was in a ponytail, and it occurred to him that she looked kind of cute in her fury.

"I was remarking on the fact that my gender is all together too much a topic of conversation around the track, which you proved by coming over here and dropping that appallingly sexist comment."

"I was teasing you," he said, enunciating carefully to drive his point home. "It was a joke. We do that around here, give each other a hard time."

"You don't know me well enough to be tossing off comments about my vagina."

Evan's eyebrows shot up. "Oh, really?"

It might have been a while, but Evan knew every inch of Kendall's body, including all her female parts. In fact, if memory served, he had been the first one to explore that particular stretch of highway. Kendall seemed to realize her error, too, because she immediately started to bluster.

"I mean, you know, we're coworkers, that's it. Not friends. I highly doubt you talk to the other drivers about their penises."

Evan went from annoyed to amused. Her cheeks had turned pink when she said "penis." He felt his face split into a grin. "No, we don't talk about penises. That would be awkward. But we definitely mention dick now and again. Bragging about our own. Mocking someone else's. It's all standard guy talk. You know, dicks. Cocks."

Her blush deepened to a deep shade of red and her eyes widened. "You're just trying to unnerve me. It's not going to work. You can talk about all the . . ." She hesitated then threw back her shoulders and said, "*dick* that you want. Just leave my body out of it."

"You're the one who brought up your va–jay-jay, not me." Feeling more in control because he got the distinct feeling Kendall wasn't feeling in control, Evan just smiled complacently at her. "Who's your friend, by the way?"

He stuck his hand out towards the brunette who had been watching their exchange with obvious interest. "I'm Evan Monroe."

"Tuesday Jones. Nice to meet you."

"The sports reporter? Bob's daughter?" Kendall's friend was attractive, wearing jeans, boots, and a long coat. Her skin was fair, lips vibrant red. He couldn't see her eyes behind the sunglasses, but he would guess they were a deep brown. Attractive, but not his style. He leaned more towards stubborn blondes.

"That's me."

"Tuesday is an interesting name. I bet there's a story behind it."

"Yes, there is." She tilted her head, her demeanor very confident and almost remote. "And I'll tell it to you when you buy me a drink tonight."

Very smooth. A lady who knew how to play the game.

Unlike Kendall, who gave a snort to his right.

Evan didn't feel any burning desire to go out with Tuesday, but she was a good-looking, clearly intelligent woman coming on to him, and that had potential. Plus, he couldn't help but enjoy the fact that this flirtation was going down in front of Kendall. Proof to her that some women found him attractive.

"Sure. How about I meet you at the wine bar at seven?" She looked like a wine bar type.

"Excellent. See you then."

It was a dismissal. Again, Tuesday was very smooth.

"Looking forward to it. Have a good afternoon." He gave a smile to Tuesday, then a brief nod to Kendall. "See you around, Holbrook."

"Yep."

That was her answer. Yep. Evan fought the urge to "what the hell?" her. But it didn't matter. The past was the past and Kendall might be in his present, but like she said, they were coworkers. Competitors. Not friends.

So Evan walked away, strolling towards his buddy Ryder Jefferson, who had just recently remarried his ex-wife. Why the hell anyone thought that made sense, Evan couldn't imagine. He wasn't even going to get married once, let alone twice.

"What's up, Jefferson?"

"Not much." Ryder bent over and pulled his shoe off, frowned at it, then put it back on. "Saw you poking the bear over there."

"Huh?" Evan didn't even want to think about poking. It brought to mind all manner of inappropriate images for daylight at the track. Especially since for the first time in years, the star of his mental video was a petite blonde. Good God.

"Kendall Holbrook. Saw you talking to her, which is a brave thing to do. Most of us have tried to be friendly only to have our heads bitten off and rolled down the track."

"Really?" Evan glanced back at Kendall, who was pulling her helmet on.

"Don't tell me you haven't noticed. That girl has a major chip on her shoulder."

"I don't think about Kendall Holbrook." Liar.

Ryder gave him a skeptical look. "Really? That's funny considering she got pulled up out of the truck series to drive for our team, securing a fantastic sponsor and getting media coverage like we haven't seen the likes of in years. So you're telling me you haven't been watching her?"

"I watch her driving, not her. And she can have a boulder on her shoulder for all I care. That's her problem, not mine."

"She's going to need to learn to smile if she wants to make the suits and the fans happy. Doesn't matter if she doesn't want to be pals with any of us, but she needs to play the game smarter with her image."

Evan glanced back at Kendall thoughtfully. She'd only been driving in the series since Daytona and he had been abiding by a policy of trying not to notice she was around. He knew she was getting a lot of media coverage because his sister Eve, his PR rep, was complaining about it, but Evan hadn't watched any of it. Was Kendall really pulling attitude?

If the way she had spoken to him was any indication, yes. But that was different. They had a history.

"Well, isn't that what her PR person is for? To tell her to smile pretty for the camera?" And why should he care? It was her career, her life. None of his concern.

"I'm sure. But I have to say, I'm curious how all of this is going to play out."

"I'm not," he declared, in a voice he knew was short and clipped and bordering on childish.

But he couldn't help it. He was already having enough problems getting around the track each week. He didn't need Kendall Holbrook distracting him, too.

"Didn't you used to date Kendall?" Ryder asked casually, tossing his helmet in his hands.

Was nothing a goddamn secret in this town? Everyone was always in everyone else's business, and Evan was tired of it. "For about a minute a hundred years ago."

"You still have any feelings for her?"

Evan lost patience with the conversation. He did *not* have feelings for that woman, other than a lingering annoyance that she'd been such a total wimp about breaking up with him. The least she could have done was have the decency to tell him what he'd done wrong.

"What the hell is this, *Dr. Phil*? You get married and suddenly you want to talk about feelings? I don't have any feelings."

Ryder laughed. "For a guy who doesn't have feelings you sound pretty riled up. Hey, I'm just offering an ear, man. And since I'm a guy who knows a thing or two about taking a second chance on a relationship, I figured I'd throw it out there that I'm around if you want to talk."

What he was feeling was damned uncomfortable with the direction of this conversation. "Thanks, but I'm good. But I'll call you if I need someone to go get a mani/pedi with."

"Douche bag. Don't be crying in your beer to me then."

"I won't." He had nothing to cry over other than the sorry ass state of his career.

Which come to think of it, was bad enough to shed a tear or two.

Evan looked over and caught Kendall's eye. She made a face and turned away.

Feeling the need to kick a tire, Evan spotted his sister Eve. Perfect. She was always willing to go a round with him, and he needed someone to fight with.

"Hey, Eve," he called when she was within a few feet of him. "Were you planning to work today or just stare at your reflection in your BlackBerry screen?"

"Shut up or I will cut you," Eve said as she halted in front of him, her eyes flashing right back at him.

His tepid comment hadn't brought that on. Eve was primed to go a round herself.

Evan tensed his shoulders and glanced over at Ryder, who just shrugged his shoulders and moved out of firing range.

"What's your problem? Besides lack of sex and a nose that could use plastic surgery." It probably wasn't wise to go at his sister when she was clearly in a mood, but it was a defense mechanism he'd perfected with her over the years. Insult first instead of waiting for the strike.

"My problem is that we're in deep shit, Evan. No joking, no smiling, no blustering, or prancing around with a blonde on your arm is going to fix this."

The irritation he'd been feeling all morning was suddenly replaced by the first niggle of fear. Eve was overdramatic, but this was a little much even for her. "What's going on?" he asked cautiously.

"Your sponsor pulled out."

For a second Evan's vision went black, like it had when he'd hit the wall at 120 miles per hour and given himself a killer concussion.

He couldn't have heard her right. That couldn't be right.

Trying not to panic, he spit out, "What? What do you mean?"

Eve reached up to smooth back her ponytail, and he saw that her hands were shaking. "I mean you lost a major sponsor. Five hundred thousand a race, gone. We're fucked."

"Jesus Christ." Evan stared at her in disbelief. It was unbelievable. Incomprehensible. A total fucking disastrous hideous awful nightmare.

His career was in the goddamn toilet.

With a growl, he stomped down the track to the exit before he actually did kick a tire and got fined on top of all the other problems he had.

Of course, he had to walk past Kendall Va-Jay-Jay Holbrook, who didn't even spare him a glance.

His career was spiraling down with the speed of a felled plane, and hers was rising equally as fast.

And worst of all, he did still have feelings for her.

Ryder was right, he was a douche bag. A stupid, sponsorless, unlovable, easily dumped douche bag.

CHAPTER
TWO

TUESDAY was going on a date with Evan. Kendall stared at her friend and pondered exactly how she felt about that. Glancing over at Evan, she caught his eye. She couldn't help but pull a face.

She knew that for the past ten years he'd been dating a revolving door of women. Blondes, brunettes, redheads—it didn't seem to matter. As long as they were beautiful and dumb, with a substantial rack, they had been on his arm. She looked away, unable to deal with the intensity of his stare. It didn't matter who he dated, and she was pathetic that she still let him get under her skin after all these years.

Hell, she should be grateful he had spent the last decade parading models around in front of the cameras. It only proved he was shallow and that he commodified women, which was why they hadn't worked out.

She'd been over it almost from the beginning of the end. There were no feelings there other than disdain.

But that didn't mean she wanted her best friend grabbing a beer with him.

"Why did you just ask Evan out?" She paused while a car went around the track behind them, drowning out any words she might have spoken. "I thought you said he would be lousy in bed."

Tuesday shrugged. "Doesn't mean I don't want to find out for myself."

"That doesn't make any sense."

"I'm like the girl that has to touch the fire even after I've been warned it's hot." Tuesday pushed up her sunglasses. "It's a terrible personality flaw."

"It sounds like a waste of time."

"Besides, why would one date equate with sleeping with him?"

Because that's what Kendall would do. Did. Only with Evan Monroe. It had been something about their chemistry together. One date and she'd been gone. Falling hard for him and naked.

Feeling the urge to sigh, she said, "You're right, it doesn't. But it still seems like a waste of time to me."

"Some of us like to date," Tuesday said pointedly. "Some of us like to go for a drink or to dinner or the movies with some male company. Some of us don't think that going years with the only flirtation in our lives being romantic comedies from Netflix is acceptable."

You know, Kendall had to say she resented that. "I've been building a career. There hasn't been a whole lot of time to date. I travel all over the country."

"Mmm-hmm."

"I date," she insisted.

"When? When was the last time you dated?"

"Uh . . . like two years ago." Damn. That was kind of a

long time when she was forced to say it out loud. "But I could date if I wanted to. I just don't want to."

"But the real question is, do you want to date Evan Monroe?"

"What?" Caught totally off guard, Kendall felt her cheeks burning again. Twice in fifteen minutes. A new personal best, and not one she was proud of. "Why the hell would you ask that?"

"Because normally you don't pay any attention to the other drivers. And normally you would never question my asking one of them out for a date."

Was that true? Probably. "That does not mean I want to date Evan. Because I don't."

Now Tuesday stared hard at her, so intently Kendall had to break eye contact.

"What does it mean?"

Damn it. She was going to have to come clean. "I just don't think you're going to enjoy yourself with Evan, because the truth is, I dated him myself a long time ago, and it was miserable."

Which wasn't entirely true. Most of their relationship had been pure moony-eyed bliss, until they had crashed and burned. That had definitely been miserable.

"What?" Tuesday threw her hands up in the air. "Why the hell didn't you tell me before? Great, I'm scum. I hit on my best friend's ex-boyfriend."

"One, you're not scum. You didn't know. Two, you didn't know because I didn't tell you because I didn't know you were going to ask him out." If any of that made any sense at all. "It's no big deal. It was a long time ago."

"Well, I'm going to have to cancel the date." Tuesday looked around the track. "Where did he go? I'd better find him and cancel now since I don't have his number."

Kendall panicked, grabbing Tuesday's arm. "No! You can't cancel. If you cancel he'll think it's because we talked and I admitted to you that he and I used to date."

Tuesday's eyebrows shot up over the top of her sunglasses' rim. "That *is* what just happened."

"Yeah, but I don't want him to know that because he'll think that means I care that you're going out with him, which I don't. I totally don't care. I mean, he and I, that was a hundred thousand years ago and totally irrelevant to now or to the future. If you want to date him and get married and have children, and think that makes any kind of sense given the kind of man he is, well, that's your business and I support you."

What she was doing was over-talking and incriminating herself.

At the end of her ridiculous speech Kendall sucked in a breath and tried not to wince.

There was a pause, then Tuesday said, "Fine. I won't cancel the date because you don't want me to, and I see the logic in the first part of what you were saying. The second half was just nuts. But there won't be a second date. I don't date my friend's ex-boyfriends, under any circumstances."

"It doesn't matter—"

"If you say 'it doesn't matter, he meant nothing to me' one more time, I'm going to write in my blog that you're a hermaphrodite."

Kendall felt all the blood drain out of her face. "You wouldn't."

"Of course I wouldn't, but what the hell, Kendall, be honest with me. This was clearly more than a couple of dates ten years ago."

Because she was superstitious and she was testing her

car again the next day and didn't want any slipups, Kendall crossed her fingers behind her back before she lied through her teeth. "That's all it was. I swear."

"Pinky swear?" Tuesday's finger came out.

Damn it. "No." Kendall gave up the good fight. "Okay, he sort of kind of broke my heart. But I was eighteen and naïve. Everyone gets their heart broken at eighteen."

"Why? What happened?"

"Nothing. That's what happened. One minute we were together, then we weren't. It's no big—"

"Deal. Yes, so you've said. Are you sure you don't want me to cancel?"

"No! I really don't." The last thing in the world Kendall wanted was Evan thinking she was still carrying a torch for him. The very thought of how humiliating that would feel made her break out in a sweat under her driver's jumpsuit.

Though she had to admit, she wasn't thrilled with the idea of Evan flirting with her best friend. Not because she had feelings for him still. But because he was a jerk and Tuesday shouldn't have to suffer through that. No other reason than that.

"Don't worry, I won't make out with him or anything, I promise."

The feeling that rose up in Kendall was small and green, hot and tight, but she refused to acknowledge in any way that it might be jealousy. Swallowing hard, she managed to force out, "It doesn't matter if you do."

TUESDAY stared at her best friend with a fair amount of speculation. In the five years she'd known Kendall, there had been only one serious boyfriend, and Kendall had been thoroughly calm and content in that relationship, and equally calm when they had broken up. Emotion was something Kendall reserved for driving, and even then that was off the track, not on. To see her normally determined and in control friend blushing and blustering and panicking was bizarre. Unnerving.

She knew that Kendall had some deep-seeded insecurities, but she always covered them with that steel determination. This wasn't like her at all.

And it was something Tuesday was going to get to the bottom of. She'd go out on this date with Evan Monroe. And use her journalism skills to get a full confession of what had gone down between him and Kendall.

"I'm not going to make out with him," she repeated. "I'll just talk to him. It's no big deal. It doesn't matter."

She intentionally echoed the words Kendall had been spouting repeatedly for the last ten minutes, to see if it would get a reaction. It did.

Kendall made a face. "I'm done for the day. Are you leaving, too?"

"Yep. Last chance to tell me to cancel or explain to me what really happened between the two of you."

"There's no story, Tuesday, so save your digging for something newsworthy."

"Sure thing." Tuesday glanced at her cell phone. Digging would commence at the wine bar at seven o'clock.

EVAN should have canceled his date with Tuesday Jones. If he had her number, he would have. But he didn't, and he wasn't going to stand her up, so he was sitting in the wine bar waiting for her, halfway to drunk already.

His day sucked. His career sucked. His life sucked.

And how in the hell he was supposed to make small talk with a total stranger was beyond him.

This was all Kendall Holbrook's fault. He wouldn't even have agreed to meet with Tuesday if he hadn't been pleased with the idea of annoying Kendall. Which he wouldn't have been if she hadn't dumped him on his ass all those years ago.

That might be screwed-up logic, but it was his, and he was going to back it. Sitting at the bar, Evan tugged at his shirt-sleeve. He'd gone the striped button-up shirt with jeans route, and he felt underdressed in the chichi place. He was definitely a jeans and a beer kind of guy, and this place was trendy, the patrons were dressed expensive, and the wine list was about seventeen pages long.

He'd ordered a rum and coke instead of the beer he'd really wanted so he wouldn't really stand out like a sore thumb, and now he was just feeling stupid sitting there by himself. The day had made him feel inadequate enough, he didn't need some damn pretentious wine bar adding to his insecurities.

What the hell was he going to do about his career?

Eve had been freaking out, and rightly so. It was bad. Losing a sponsorship meant he was seen in the industry as a poor performer. It meant his fan base was dwindling. It meant his team owners were going to be scrutinizing him and wondering if he was worth their financial investment.

He had to drive better. Plain and simple.

But the real question was why he was sucking so bad out there on the track.

He didn't know the answer to that.

Which was a problem.

"Can I get another drink?" he asked the bartender.

"Sure, no problem."

"I see you started without me. Am I late?"

Evan turned to see Tuesday slip onto the bar stool beside him, setting her purse down on the bar. She gave him a casual smile before shrugging her trench coat off.

"I was early," he assured her. "It's good to see you. Can I get you a drink?"

"Absolutely." She plucked the giant binder menu off the counter and started perusing. "Hallelujah for the return of the cocktail. I never was a beer drinker."

Figured. Just looking at her, beautiful and thin and bordering on exotic, her jewelry all expensive-looking and her shoes spiky heels with very pointy toes, Evan knew this was not his kind of woman. Not that he really knew what woman was his type. While he had dated a series of party girls in his twenties, he hadn't really had a serious relationship since . . . that person. Damn it.

"I'm a beer guy," he told her.

"Then why are you drinking . . ." She picked his drink up and sipped it, making a face. "Rum and Coke?"

"It seemed like a faster way to get drunk," he told her honestly.

Tuesday laughed. "Meeting me requires reduced sobriety?"

He hadn't meant that to sound quite the way it did. "Of course not. No, it's just been one of those days that has kicked me in the teeth, you know?"

"I think everyone has had those. But generally speaking getting drunk doesn't help the situation."

Everyone knew that. He knew that. Didn't make it any less appealing. "So you followed in your father's footsteps with sports reporting," he commented. "Guess I did the same."

"Yeah."

He waited, but she didn't elaborate. "So . . . how did you get into the blogging?" From what he'd heard, her website was always accurate, but focused on the gossip in their sport instead of stats.

"It seemed like a void I could fill."

Well, that was helpful. Evan took a sip of his drink. "Yeah?" He tried to think of something else to say, but he was running on empty.

"Which is it, business or personal, that has you reaching for the glass?" Tuesday flagged the bartender down. "Can I have a lemon drop, please?"

Evan thought about that. "Mostly business. But maybe some personal." Like why the hell Kendall still got under his skin. And why did everyone else around him seem to have some sort of secret to happiness with a woman that he had no knowledge of. His brother was happy. Ryder was happy. Even Ty, who he would have thought was a confirmed bachelor for life, was following Imogen around with a stupid grin on his face. Hell, those guys were carrying their women's handbags and getting couples massages.

He had yet to find any woman who even came close to inspiring him to that kind of dorkiness.

Kendall wasn't the massage type.

Damn it. "No, not personal. Never mind that. It's just that my career isn't going exactly stellar at the moment."

Tuesday waved her hand. "Oh, we all know your driving sucks this year, so what? Everyone has a bad year. The fact that you're in the cup series means you are technically at the pinnacle of your career. So quit whining."

Evan turned and stared at her. She was one ballsy chick. He kind of liked and hated her all at the same time. "Well, thanks for the sympathy."

"I mean, seriously. You know how many guys would kill to be in your flame retardant shoes? I don't think that's what's bothering you at all. I think it's personal."

Would it be totally tacky if he paid for her drink and got the hell out of there? "It doesn't matter."

"Who is she?"

"No one!"

"There has to be someone."

He was starting to get irritated. This was a shitty date. Shitty day, shitty date. He felt like he was being grilled on a witness stand by the prosecutor. "There is no one. I'm not dating anyone."

"But it's someone you used to date, right? Maybe someone you thought you were over but who has suddenly popped back into your life?"

No. Maybe. He didn't think so. "This is totally not first-date get-to-know-you chatter."

"You're right." She took her drink right out of the bartender's hand and took a healthy sip. "I'm just going to be straight up with you here. I asked you to meet me for a drink before I realized that you and Kendall have a history. She says it's cool with her, but I can't fathom dating my best friend's ex, no matter how long ago it was."

"Well, I can respect that." And maybe he could leave now and go sulk in private. "I probably should have declined your invite, but it was over a long time ago with Kendall and me."

"When did you two date?"

"About ten years ago. I was nineteen." And stupid. Evan shifted on the bar stool, a headache starting behind his eyes. God, he didn't want to talk about any of this.

"Was it serious?"

He could have lied. Could have blown off the question.

But he was tired of pretending like it was no big deal. It wasn't anymore, but it had been at the time. She had broken his goddamn nineteen-year-old heart. "It was to me. It was very serious." He stopped just short of admitting he had loved her. "I can't speak for her feelings though."

"How long did you date?"

"About three months. It wasn't that long, but we spent a lot of time together. Damn near every day."

"What was your favorite thing about her?"

Evan was just buzzed enough to actually contemplate the question. He let his mind drift back a decade to when he and Kendall had been sharing most of their time and affection with each other. What had it been about her?

"It was her smile. When she smiled, it went all the way to her eyes, and I felt so proud that I'd made her happy." Evan caught himself. "Man, how stupid does that sound? I think I need to chill on the rum."

"You don't need to chill on the rum. What you need to chill on is this idea that you have to be a big man driver who can't show any emotion other than cockiness."

He shrugged. It was what it was. It wasn't a career for crybabies. And he wasn't sure cockiness actually qualified as an emotion.

"So why did you and Kendall break up?"

"Beats me. One day she just stopped returning my calls. One minute we were hot and heavy, the next she totally shut me out. I never understood what happened."

"Really?" Tuesday looked at him thoughtfully. "Did you have a fight or something?"

"Nope. We'd spent the night together and I snuck out of her room like I did a lot of nights because she was still living at home. We were supposed to go to the movies the next day. But she wasn't at home when I went to pick her up and she wouldn't answer my calls. I must have called her like a hundred times that week. Nothing."

Evan wasn't exactly sure why he was spilling his guts to Tuesday, considering he'd spent ten years trying to pretend he hadn't been humiliated quite so thoroughly. Maybe it was needing someone to know that he'd been wronged. Maybe it was needing Tuesday to go home and report to Kendall that he had no clue what he'd done wrong. Maybe it was needing to just say that he hadn't done anything wrong at all, and that it wasn't cool for Kendall to have dumped him without a word.

"Really? That's interesting." Tuesday frowned at her lemon drop. "Maybe it was just a miscommunication or something. Do you think you would have stayed with her if that hadn't happened?"

"Well, I can't guarantee it would have been forever, but that was my plan." Evan tossed back the rest of his drink, the ice clinking against his teeth violently enough to jar him into realizing he just might be drunker than he'd thought. "I was set to ask her to marry me."

Tuesday choked on her drink. "Holy crap, are you kidding me?"

"No." He sort of wished he were.

"And you've never gotten married?"

"Nope."

"Huh. That really is very interesting."

He wasn't sure it was as interesting as it was just sucky.

"Can I step down off the witness stand now?" he asked. "I think I need to go home and pass out."

He wanted to sleep for the next twelve hours and forget this day ever happened.

"Sure, but I reserve the right to call you back to the stand for further questioning." She grinned at him. "And don't leave the country."

"I can't afford it," he told her, taking a moment to indulge in self-pity.

"Oh, my God," she said, rolling her eyes. "Give me a ginormous break. There is no way you're hurting for cash unless you've spent your substantial earnings on hookers and blow."

No. He hadn't really spent much of his money, to be honest. He'd been saving it for a dream house. A big, empty dream house that he would have to live in alone. Solo. By himself.

Definitely less disgusting than sex for hire, but decidedly more lonely.

"Can I get another drink?" he asked the bartender.

Tuesday excused herself to go to the restroom, but Evan barely heard her over the deafening volume of his own pity party.

CHAPTER
THREE

KENDALL was trying to watch TV, but all she kept doing was glancing at the clock to see if it was possible that Tuesday would be done with her date with Evan yet. Given that it was only seven-thirty, it didn't seem likely. She grabbed a black toile pillow off her couch and hugged it. Her mother always said she didn't understand how a woman who could break down an engine could also have a thing for French toile, but Kendall didn't see why it had to be one or the other.

Couldn't she dig racing and gilded sconces all at the same time?

Not in her family. It was one or the other. You were either a domestic goddess or a grease monkey, and never the two shall meet or cross gender lines.

Normally HGTV held her riveted, but tonight she could barely focus on the screen in front of her. 7:32. Good Lord.

Her cell phone rang and it was Tuesday's ringtone. Kendall dove for it and answered, practically screaming, "Hello?" Why was she calling her so early?

"Okay, I have five minutes because he thinks I'm in the restroom, so just listen to me and answer my questions without wasting time."

That was frightening and weird. Why had Tuesday ditched him to call her? What the hell was going on in that bar? "Okay." Kendall bit her fingernail, caught herself doing it, and made a face.

"Why did you and Evan break up?"

That was not what she'd expected Tuesday to ask at all. Caught off guard, she answered truthfully. "Because he thought it was stupid that I wanted to be a driver. He laughed at me when I told him my dream." It had been the ultimate betrayal to her at the time. It had hurt that he hadn't respected her desires or believed she could achieve her goals.

"So you had a big fight about it?"

Kendall bit her lip instead of her nail. "Well . . . not exactly. He laughed and I changed the subject."

"And then you broke up with him?"

"Yes." Sort of. It might have been more like she had just stopped talking to him.

"And explained why you broke up with him?"

Fighting the urge to squirm, she said, "I don't think I said that in so many words."

"Did you say any words?"

Damn it. Why did hearing it spelled out like this suddenly make her feel so bad? It had been childish to dodge his calls. "Not really. Probably not. No. I think I sort of just stopped answering the phone."

"Oh, my God."

"I was eighteen!" she said in defense of her actions. "And I was hurt. He laughed at me!"

"And now ten years later you're both still hurt and harboring resentments. This is stupid. You owe him an explanation.

He owes you an explanation. Get your ass down to this wine bar and resolve this so you can both stop glaring at each other and get back to the real business of your careers."

"What makes you think he even cares one little bit?" If he had cared, he wouldn't have laughed at her.

"He has no clue why you broke up. It bothers him, it's obvious. Give him an explanation and an apology and give him the opportunity to apologize to you. It's time to move on. You said it yourself, you were eighteen, and you were clearly insecure. Hey, I get that, it's normal at that age to have doubts. But you're twenty-eight now and it's time to deal with the past so you can tackle the future."

"When did you become my therapist?"

"A friend is by definition an unpaid therapist. Trust me, both of you will thank me and sleep a lot better at night. This is called closure."

"I don't think this is a good idea."

"Don't make me bring him to your apartment."

Kendall balked. That would be awful because then she would be trapped there until he decided to leave. Not to mention that it was far too intimate.

She knew Tuesday wasn't bluffing. Unlike her, Tuesday never bluffed. "Fine. I'll meet you there."

"Ten minutes, that's all you get."

"I still don't think this is a good idea."

"You'll thank me later. By the way, how was he in bed?" Tuesday asked curiously.

Kendall didn't say a word, suddenly thrust back in time to hot nights with the boy who had made her understand all the wonderful things her body was capable of.

"That good, huh?"

"That good," she agreed.

Then she hung up the phone and went to throw on jeans

that didn't make her butt look too big and to run a brush through her hair.

EVAN couldn't shake Tuesday. Every time he hinted that maybe it was time to call it a night, she launched into some huge and meandering story that had him nodding politely and wondering when this hell was going to end. She seemed like a nice enough woman, but there was no chemistry between them. Not to mention she had pressed him about Kendall and he had confided in her about their breakup, which was not hot for a first date.

He was heading from buzzed to full-on drunk.

He wanted to go home.

Shifting on his stool, he pushed his drink away and tried to focus on what Tuesday was saying.

"So then I did one of those simulation drives and I have to say I get the thrill you experience when you go around the track. Speed is sexy."

What was sexy was what had just walked in the door. Evan's foot slipped off the rung of the bar stool as he spotted Kendall standing in the doorway, scanning the room.

It had been a long time since he'd seen her in anything other than a sponsor's golf shirt or a racing suit.

She looked better than he remembered, jeans hugging her in all the right places, a V-neck sweater displaying a fair amount of cleavage. Her hair was loose and flowing down her shoulders, over the white coat she was wearing. As she scanned the room, her fingers played with a necklace dangling above her breasts.

The scary thing was Evan was just as attracted to her as he'd been all those years ago, and maybe it was the liquor, but he had a weird sort of longing taking up residence in his chest, like indigestion, uncomfortable and hopefully temporary.

It was a day that just got stranger and stranger, and he turned to the bartender. "Can I have a water please?" It was time to kill the buzz and go home before the day went from suckfest to total irreversible disaster.

If his brain had been moving a little quicker, he would have ducked out of the bar before Kendall laid eyes on him.

But it was already too late for that. Kendall had spotted them and was heading towards them. "Okay, awkward alert," he told Tuesday in a low voice. "Kendall just showed up and she's seen us. It's too late to make a run for it."

"Why would we make a run for it? I'm the one who invited her."

Evan stared at her. "You invited your friend to join you on your date with her ex-boyfriend? That's fucked up."

"You and Kendall clearly need to talk and clear the air. You're both dragging around ten-year-old baggage and that's just stupid." She gave a cheerful wave to Kendall.

Evan wanted to crawl under the bar. Right after he strangled Tuesday Jones. It was one thing to make two-minute small talk with Kendall, it was another to be set up to talk about their past.

"This is none of your business," he told Tuesday, completely irritated. "And I'm not going to—"

"Hey," Kendall said, coming up to stand in front of their respective bar stools.

Her arms instantly went across her chest.

Good to know she wasn't feeling this little Oprah moment either. Though she had shown up. Evan wondered what that meant. "Hey," he said, sure his smile looked more like a psychotic grimace.

"Okay, I'm heading out. Be civil and you'll be surprised

how much better you feel tomorrow." Tuesday threw down some money, scooped up her purse, cheek kissed Kendall, and breezed towards the door.

"Your friend is nuts," Evan told Kendall, taking the water the bartender handed him.

"What's nuts is that I actually listened to her and came down here." Kendall plunked herself down on Tuesday's abandoned stool. "Though she did threaten me."

"With what?" Evan felt a little more at ease knowing Kendall wasn't any more on board with this than he was.

"She always uses her blog as a threat. But this time she threatened to bring you to my apartment if I didn't show up."

"How would she have managed that? I'm not really that maneuverable."

A hint of a smile crossed Kendall's lips. "But you are a man, and probably not one to turn down sex. I think her devious plan was to let you think you were going to her apartment."

Evan's eyebrows shot up. "She is nuts. God, I pity the man who finds himself in her clutches." He sipped his water. "And I would not have had sex with her. I'm not that easy."

Kendall snorted. "Sure."

He felt defensive and more than a little offended. "I'm not some man whore. I don't just sleep with anyone." Though he was remembering a particular campsite incident a few months back with Nikki Strickland's maid of honor and felt a twinge of something that he was not going to call shame.

"I think you're protesting a little too much."

He would not rise to the bait, he would not . . .

"I'm a born again virgin," he told her. "I haven't had sex in years."

That would show her.

There was a pause, then she started laughing. "So who

are all those women you've been prancing around with over the years? Your abstinence counselors?"

It occurred to Evan that she wouldn't have known who he'd been with if she hadn't been paying attention to him. "You noticed, huh? Jealous?"

"Of what? Silicone? Hardly."

"But you've clearly noticed them. That says jealousy to me." Which felt mighty good, he had to admit.

"How could I not notice them? They all have breasts the size of Rhode Island. It's a little hard to miss that crossing the stage at drivers' intro."

"I never took a woman across the stage at drivers' intro. That's for wives and fiancées and serious girlfriends." He wasn't sure why it was important to clarify that, but it was.

"And you're allergic to those apparently."

That felt a little below the belt. Evan scrutinized Kendall, noting the high color in her cheeks. She was nervous and agitated being with him. Ten years was a long time to wonder and he was feeling a little tired of it.

"Why do you think that is exactly, huh, Kendall?"

"I have no idea. You're shallow?"

He had thought about confessing, thought about telling her that he had planned to propose marriage to her, that her sudden cold shoulder had had more impact on him in the last ten years than he'd like to admit. But that snarky comment stopped him.

"Exactly," he told her, scooting his water closer in reach on its cocktail napkin. "How did you guess?"

Kendall sighed. "I'm sorry, that was bitchy." She fingered her necklace again and gestured for the bartender's attention. "I think I need a beer."

"Look, just tell Tuesday we talked and we'll call it good. There really isn't any point in digging into the past. We had some good times and then we didn't. No big deal." Evan worked pretty damn hard to inject total nonchalance into his voice.

And he was not sneaking shots at Kendall's cleavage. Much.

But Kendall suddenly blurted out, "How could you laugh at me?"

He had to admit, the rum had his engines cranking over slowly, but he had no clue what she was talking about. "Huh? I've never laughed at you. I was just teasing you today, honestly, I wasn't trying to be a pig." Because he suffered from the need to get the last word, he couldn't stop himself from tacking onto his apology, "And you brought up girl parts first."

She waved her hand impatiently, then ordered a beer from the bartender, which is what he should have done. Screw what other people thought. If he'd stuck with beer, he wouldn't have felt like his head was floating in Jell-O.

"I don't mean today." Kendall turned and stared at him intently. "Do you remember that last night we were together? How you snuck into my room and spent the night?"

"Yeah, of course I remember. It was a good night. We made love then just lay there talking about the future." A future he had assumed included her.

"I told you I wanted to be a driver in the Cup series and you laughed at me."

Evan frowned at her. "No, I didn't. I admit you caught me off guard. I mean, I knew you liked racing midget cars and that you saw it as a hobby, but you'd never talked about driving pro. It startled me."

"Why, because a girl can't drive?"

"No," he said slowly, wondering where this was going. "I knew you could drive. I went to a bunch of your races, remember? What surprised me was it seemed like an ambition that came out of nowhere. I wasn't expecting it, that's all. Nothing more, nothing less."

Kendall frowned, her forehead wrinkling. She took a long swallow of her beer, opened her mouth to speak then shut it again.

"What?" he asked her.

"Did you think it was a stupid goal? That I was setting myself up to fail?"

Shifting on his chair, he turned so he could see her fully, his legs entrapping hers. "No. I was young and confident, both in me, and in you. I went home and fantasized about you and me finishing one-two in the series. I knew you could do it. I even made plans for you to hit the track in one of my dad's cars later that week."

"You did what?" Kendall's eyes were as big as saucers.

"Yeah. I figured you'd want to get behind the wheel of a stock car, and my dad was cool with it. I thought maybe someone would see you burning up the track and take an interest in your career."

There was a moment of silence, then Kendall clapped her hand over her mouth in horror, a mumbled "Oh, dear God" coming out from behind her fingers.

"Why did you break up with me?" he asked, unnerved by the conversation and her reaction. "I called you a hundred times and you never answered. What the hell happened?"

"Because you laughed at me. Because I thought you were patronizing me and wouldn't support my dreams."

Evan needed a second to pick his fucking chin up off the bar. "Are you *serious*? That was the reason?"

Kendall winced as Evan gave her a stricken look of horror. "It seems maybe I was wrong," she said, her heart pounding and her stomach clenched in nausea. "I don't know, it seemed totally logical to me at the time. I mean, I was hurt, really hurt. Devastated by the thought that you were calling me a moron."

"I didn't laugh at you!"

"Yes, you did!" She could regret and apologize for her overreaction, but she had not imagined that startled guffaw he'd given her. Which he said had been just that—startled.

"This is insane." Evan ran his fingers through his hair. "Why didn't you just talk to me about it? We could have worked this out in a five-minute conversation."

"I don't know. I was eighteen. And totally defensive because you know my dad got me into racing. I was his substitute son, the only tomboy out of three daughters, so he pushed me into all of that. Then when I said I could drive pro, he basically told me that was nuts." Kendall reached for her drink. God, this was an appalling confession of her clear daddy issues. "I thought you were doing the same thing, betraying me the same way."

"I wasn't." Still looking like he'd been smacked a half dozen times, Evan reached for his drink, paused halfway to his mouth, then put it back down and picked up his water instead. "I stood there on your front porch and begged you to come out and talk to me."

She remembered. She remembered the pain, the raw, brutal agony of wondering if she were doing the right thing, but feeling so hurt, so devastated, so duped. "And I stood in the house crying, thinking that the boy I had given my heart to didn't respect me or believe in me."

"You . . . you gave your heart to me?"

"Duh." Kendall sucked half of her beer down. "I told you I loved you. You *owned* my heart."

"I told you I loved you, too," he said defensively. "I cried, Kendall. Okay? I fucking *cried* when you wouldn't talk to me."

There was something about the way he said it, like he wanted credit for the extra visual of his emotion, that made her press her lips together to keep a giggle from slipping out. This was a strange and almost farcical conversation.

Fortunately, Evan realized she was about to laugh, and his mouth split into a grin. "God, that sounded overdramatic. Listen to us. We're as big of drama queens now as we were at eighteen."

Letting her laughter out, she nodded. "Seriously. Maybe if we had both laid off the drama and just talked, we wouldn't have hurt each other."

"You more so than me." He grinned. "You set the drama in motion."

Kendall nudged his leg with her foot, smiling back. "Fine. You're right. I was putting my issues with my dad onto you and that was stupid. I should have listened to you, should have taken your calls, should have given you a chance to explain. I'm sorry." She really was. For the whole damn debacle.

God, it was like a huge weight had been lifted off her shoulders. Ten years of imagined betrayal gone, just like that, with ten minutes of communication. It was insane.

"And I'm sorry if I didn't have the right words to let you know I was proud of you. That I supported you."

"Thank you." Kendall let out a sigh of relief. Her shoulders even physically relaxed down a few inches. Tuesday had been right, this talk needed to happen.

Turned in his stool, Evan's legs were on either side of hers, and she suddenly became aware of how close he was sitting to her. How the denim of his jeans was scraping along hers, his upper body leaning towards her. He was as attractive to her now as he had been at nineteen, and he'd been leaner then with youth. Now he was all hard-packed muscle, and Kendall swallowed hard. It had been difficult enough to pretend she wasn't attracted to him when she had thought he was a raging jerk, but now, well, getting into the Cup series had been easier than denying her feelings now.

She was so attracted to him.

"Wow," he said. "This is funny and horrible all at the same time, isn't it? I mean, we really tore each other up and for what?"

"Stupid," she agreed.

"So what do we do now?" he asked. The corner of his mouth tilted up. "I'm used to hating you for breaking my heart. I think I need to do some mental recalculating."

"Me, too."

Was it her imagination or was he looking at her differently? Not with a "gee, glad we worked this out" kind of look. It was something a little more curious than that, like he was studying her face, her lips, her chest.

Maybe she was doing the same thing, for all she knew. Maybe it was just a normal reevaluating, changing the lens through which you viewed someone after you realized you'd been wrong, but personally hers felt a lot more like plain old lust. Which was a stupid response and one she needed to squash immediately if not sooner.

"So that's it? We're just good now? Friends?" Evan asked, his expression a little bemused.

"Being friends would be nice." And so would having him take her hard up against a wall.

Yikes. Where had that thought come from? Kendall crossed her legs in between his. Tuesday was right. She needed to get out more.

"Okay, so fill me in on the last ten years. What have you been up to?"

That question was easy. "Umm, let's see. Driving with single-minded determination. That's about it."

"No quickie Vegas weddings? No trips around the world? No moment where you walked away from it all and decided you wanted to be like a pastry chef or something?"

"No, no, and no. I wanted to be a driver."

"And now you are."

"And now I am."

He smiled softly, a smile that went all the way to his rich chocolate eyes. "Good for you, Kendall. I'm happy for you."

"Thank you," she said, mortified when she realized how breathy her voice sounded. Clearing her throat, she added, "What about you? What have you been doing?"

"Same thing as you. Though it's safe to say I lack the single-minded determination."

"What do you mean?"

"I don't know. Just that I haven't been driving well. Some days I just wake up and wonder if this is it . . . strug- gling and never getting that championship win, that holy grail of racing."

"Some drivers never get that. It doesn't mean you weren't successful." Kendall paused, wondering what else she should say. The truth was, she and Evan didn't know each other any- more, and she couldn't tell if he was really discontent or just expressing frustration.

But while she gathered her thoughts, he shrugged and grinned. "Listen to me whining. Guess I don't have much to complain about. I wouldn't have made a good pastry chef either."

So he didn't want to go deep. That was fine. Kendall was just so glad they were talking like this, normal, relaxed, that she wasn't about to push it. "Oh, I don't know. You made me a cake for my eighteenth birthday, remember? It was chocolate and it was awesome. A little lopsided, but it tasted like heaven."

The gesture had been as sweet as the chocolate.

But Evan gave her a sheepish look. "I have a confession to make. I tried to bake you a cake, and it was a disaster, so I bought another box mix and paid Eve twenty bucks to do it for me."

Kendall laughed. "Are you serious? Well, damn, and here I thought you were a whiz in the kitchen. But I think I'm flattered. At that point in our lives, twenty bucks was serious cash."

"Very true. And the kitchen is not a room I excel in. On the other hand . . ."

Oh, she knew that look. Kendall held her breath, her heart ramming against her rib cage. "Yeah?"

When the hell had his hand dropped onto her knee? And why wasn't she shifting away from it?

"I definitely know my way around the bedroom."

CHAPTER
FOUR

THE minute the words came out of Evan's mouth he figured he had just veered into scumbag territory, but he was drunk, and Kendall was smiling at him, and it had just flown out before he could stop it. Here they were, having a friendly conversation for the first time in years and he had to go and ruin it. But that was precisely why he had said it . . . it had been so long since he'd seen her in anything more than passing, and that had always been laced with animosity.

Sitting here, legs close, chatting intimately and openly, he had just been overcome by how beautiful she was, and the flirt had just popped out.

Drunk or not, he knew he needed to apologize.

But before he could, Kendall said, "I remember that even more than I remember your chocolate cake."

Damn.

"In those days I probably had more enthusiasm than skill, but being with you made it easy, Kendall."

"It was definitely easy, alright." Her tongue moistened her lips. "I didn't know I could feel that kind of pleasure until you."

"I was scared to screw it up since I was your first . . . I wanted it to be good for you."

"It was."

Her eyes had darkened with the same lust he was feeling, but also with tenderness. The combination had Evan's gut twisted up, feeling like he'd landed squarely back in the past, when they had been together and he had been happy. Being loved by this woman had been a damn fine thing.

"I have never regretted it was you. Not even after the way it ended."

Evan swallowed hard against the emotion that was crawling up his throat. "Thanks. I needed to hear that. And trust me, I never regretted it either. Even when I was pounding on your front door, I wouldn't have traded that for never having met you."

"I guess that's good at the same time it's tragic, huh?"

Yeah. But he'd spent enough time wondering, regretting. It was time for a new chapter in their story. "We can only go forward, not backwards. No sense in beating ourselves up any more than we have."

"Oh, I can always find ways to beat myself up." Kendall gave a slight smile then shifted her leg so it was alongside his.

Evan knew he probably shouldn't be this close to her, shouldn't be stroking her thigh right above her knee, but it felt so natural, the expression on her face triggering his response. That was the way she'd always looked at him, like he was the only person in the room, and while he knew he didn't have the right to still touch her, it felt like he should.

"Don't beat yourself up about this or anything else. We

were kids. It was overdramatic and dumb. Just remember that I loved you."

The minute those words left his mouth, Evan suddenly realized that he needed to get the hell out of there. Needed to put distance between himself and her dewy pink lips, her cleavage, which had matured in the last ten years, and her tender, lust-laced eyes.

Especially when she said in a breathy voice, "Oh, I loved you, too."

That wide gaze, the warmth of her body, the sexual tension in her voice had him leaping off his bar stool. Time to go before he said or did something totally and completely stupid.

"That's probably a good place to leave this, Kendall, before we manage to find a way to irritate each other again. I should go. Thanks for coming out. I'm really damn glad you did." Evan pulled out his wallet and dropped some cash on the bar.

"I'm glad I did, too, but I don't think you should drive home, Evan. You have had quite a few drinks."

He wanted to deny it, but it was the truth. "I'll call a cab." He sucked down the last of his water and pulled out his phone. "I'll just look up the number."

"I can give you a ride. I only had one beer."

Damn it. Evan gripped his phone hard and fought temptation. It was the polite thing for her to say, right? It didn't mean anything at all. Nothing suggestive or sexual or anything beyond casual friendship. Just that she didn't want him to die or get cited with a DUI. She'd offer any idiot she knew a ride, including this idiot.

"It's not a big deal." It wasn't. He needed to not make it one. Punching buttons on his phone, he tried to focus on finding the cab company's number.

"Don't be stupid. I'm giving you a ride." Kendall stood up, grabbing her purse off the bar. "I just need to pay for my drink."

Evan paused and gave her an incredulous look. "I already paid for your drink. And I guess you calling me stupid means that little moment we had a minute ago has passed. I didn't get out of here fast enough before the good feelings went to hell."

"Well, you are being stupid. It's way easier for me to give you a ride than for you to sit around waiting for a cab. And the reason the moment passed is because you decided to bolt."

Bolt? She thought he was capable of bolting? That was a surefire way to put his back up. "You calling me chicken?"

"I think we're both chicken. That's why we wound up not together in the first place."

Evan drew himself up to his full height and looked down at the little spitfire in front of him. "I don't back down from anything. On the track or off."

"Oh, yeah? Then let me drive you home."

She had crossed her arms on her chest and tilted her chin to meet his gaze defiantly, and Evan knew precisely what he was going to do. "I will if you give me a kiss."

Her mouth dropped open. "I don't think so!"

Evan fought the urge to smile in triumph. "Chicken."

"I'm not chicken on or off the track, either."

"Then kiss me." He had her neatly cornered and felt damn smug about it.

She, on the other hand, looked furious. "I could just let you get a cab after all, you know."

"But you won't because that would be like letting me win."

Kendall stood silent for a second, clearly weighing her options. Then she nodded. "Okay, if that's the way you're going to be. I admit that I can't let you finish something I started. It's a character flaw."

Evan grinned. "One I'm about to enjoy."

Kissing Kendall was like playing with matches and a big old vat of moonshine, but he was the first to admit he wasn't exactly known for slow and logical. He was the poster child for speaking without thinking.

Her arms were still crossed and she did all but purse her lips as she stood there waiting. Evan tossed his phone onto the bar, and took his time moving in closer to her, studying her jawline, her pert nose, her luscious lips, her rich amber eyes watching him nervously. It pleased him to think that he could make her nervous, that the thought of a kiss just might have her insides twisting the way his were. When he lifted his hand to her face, she jerked a little, her backside bumping up against the bar.

"What are you doing?" she asked.

"Touching you," he murmured as he cupped her cheek and leaned down over her.

The palm of his hand slid against the smoothness of her skin, while his fingers tangled into her hair, his lips drawing closer and closer to hers. Evan had positioned himself one leg on either side of hers so she was surrounded by him, a small but sexy nod to submission.

"Just get it over—"

Cutting Kendall off with his lips, Evan stifled the rest of her sentence, with the only goal making her forget to want any kiss with him to end. But the second his lips touched hers, he forgot whatever it was he was trying to prove. The second his mouth caressed hers, it was like he was nineteen all over again, hot and flushed and excited and in love. His mouth remembered Kendall, even after a decade, and he knew exactly how to tilt and touch her.

Desire shot through his body, aching shot through his heart, understanding shot through his mind. Gripping his hand in her hair tighter, Evan pulled her closer to him, pressing her chest against his as she opened her lips and surrendered to his kiss. What started out as one soft press of his lips to hers turned into a series of long, delicious, demanding kisses, his tongue slipping inside to taste her.

Past and present collided, sensory memories assaulting him, yet the desire was very much real and now, the tension between them new, their touch wary and mature instead of reckless and fumbling. She moaned, a breathy little sigh against his lips, and Evan followed suit when she dropped her belligerent stance and threw her arms around his neck.

She'd gone up on her tiptoes, and Evan moved his hands down her back, down to the curve of her ass, and squeezed. It felt so good, all of it, so good, that he forgot where he was, who he was, and what he was. Nothing mattered but tasting her, taking her mouth over and over and owning it.

But Kendall dropped down to the balls of her feet and pulled back when his hand slipped to the inside of her thighs. Definitely disappointed, definitely grateful that at least she'd had the sense to call a halt given that they were in public, Evan stared down at her, an erection that could cut glass straining against his jeans while he waited for her to ream him out. She was breathing hard, wiping her dewy lips, her eyes ginormous.

"Told you I wasn't chicken," she said.

Evan grinned. "Neither am I. Now I guess you should give me a ride home, huh?" And if he had his way, they'd be making a little pit stop en route and trying that kiss on for size a second time.

* * *

KENDALL just about stripped her gears pulling out of her parking space, she was that unnerved. She drove a Corvette, a good old American sports car, full of speed and detailing and country sass. It had over 620 horsepower, and while its front weight bias might mean it would have a hard time beating out some of the other super sports models head-to-head on the open track, it was a damn fine car. It had been what her father had always wanted, and Kendall had bought one for him and one for herself. Her dad had wanted black. She had gone for the cobalt blue, that perfect shade that landed somewhere between royal and midnight, and it made her happy.

A symbol of success.

But at the moment, she was taking no pleasure in driving it with Evan Monroe riding shotgun. Because over the years she had thought about thumbing her nose at Evan, about rubbing his face in her success, just a little.

Now she was sitting here with him next to her realizing that the past decade had been a ridiculous gigantic misunderstanding and that everything she'd thought and felt needed to be shoved through the do-over machine. All that was confusing enough, but when you added in that killer kiss, well, she was as jumpy as a cat in a room full of rocking chairs.

Evan had dared her into that kiss, knowing full well if he had just tried to kiss her she would have balked. He knew her well enough to know that if he challenged her, she wouldn't back down. It was scary to realize he still knew her that well, and mortifying to think that she was so competitive she couldn't walk away from something stupid when she was dared.

It had also been a shock to realize that the second his lips pressed on hers, it had been like nothing had ever changed.

It was like she was eighteen all over again, and she had flung her arms around him and kissed back for all she was worth.

And yet, even while she saw how potentially dangerous that was, she couldn't bring herself to regret it.

"Alright, where do you live?" she asked, turning down the heat. It might only be March and still crisp, but she was burning up from the inside out.

"In those town houses off of Singleton Road right by the Harris Teeter. Where do you live?"

Kendall thought it was a damn miracle they'd never run into each other at that grocery store. Not that she cooked. "I live across the street in that apartment complex. Literally right across the street."

"It does have a small town feel here, doesn't it?"

"It's more like you can't go five feet without tripping over someone involved in stock car racing one way or the other."

"Does your family still live here?"

"Yep. My parents are in the same house out in the sticks. My sister Kyle is a nurse, and my sister Kaylynn is a kindergarten teacher. They have six kids between them." Enough kids to keep Kendall from feeling the urge to procreate herself, and enough kids to keep their mother off Kendall's back for that very same reason. Sort of. Well, not really.

"Damn. It has been a while. Your sisters were younger than you."

"As my mother reminds me as often as possible. How are your parents?"

"Good. Great actually. They're having a grand old time being stepgrandparent's to Tammy's kids. I guess it was no surprise to any of us that Elec got hitched first, but his bride came with a ready-made family. My mother better enjoy it. I don't see Eve or me following suit any time soon. Or ever."

Kendall refused to question why his anti-marriage stance would bother her, but it did. "I've seen Elec with the kids at the track. He's a good stepfather."

"He took to it like a fish to water." Evan suddenly tapped her hand on the gearshift as she drove. "Nice car, by the way. I like watching you drive."

Lord, she was blushing in the dark. "You've seen me drive plenty of times. And this isn't even a race car."

"No, it's sexier than that. It's you relaxed, yet in charge."

She had no idea what to say to that, but she couldn't help but press the gas pedal just a little harder to feel the speed, show off just a touch.

"Hey, you remember how we used to race on that old dirt track on Route 3? God, I haven't been there in years."

"Of course I remember." She remembered every minute of every day she'd spent with Evan. They had laughed a lot racing around the track, and they had fooled around a lot as well, in the back of his old Ford. Funny how she thought back and they both seemed so young, so free, so immature, yet at the time she would have sworn she was all grown and then some. "It's no surprise you haven't been there. You've been a little busy."

"We should go there. Right now."

"What? Why the hell would we do that?" Kendall chanced a glance at him. She recognized that sound of enthusiasm. Evan had been an impulsive teenager, and it seemed he hadn't changed in that regard.

"For old times' sake. We'll take a spin around the track. This car can handle it." He gave her a charming smile. "Come on . . . What are you, chicken?"

"That only works once a night."

•

Kendall braked at the intersection and told herself to hold firm. It was idiotic to go running off to an abandoned dirt track at eleven at night with Evan Monroe.

"Come on, please? It's been a really shitty day, Kendall."

Something about his tone had her turning to look at him.

"I lost my sponsorship today."

Her hand jerked on the gearshift. Holy shit. "Are you serious?"

He nodded. His eyes were unreadable in the darkness, but she could see his jaw was set, even as he shrugged in nonchalance.

"Oh, God, I'm so sorry. That sucks. What happened?"

"Underperformance. Tough economy. Don't worry, I'll work it out. But today is a bad day. And I'd like to go sit on that dirt track with you if you don't mind."

Like she could say no to that? "Of course." She changed lanes and turned right, heading away from the storefronts and condos. They drove in silence for a minute, then she asked, "Does anyone know?"

"Just you, me, and Eve. And of course, the suits who pulled the plug. But by tomorrow everyone will know."

Kendall was touched that he had shared that with her. She knew how she would feel if she were in his shoes. Defeated, frustrated, like she were going backwards. It was a tough business, with very few at the top. "Sponsorship is a rough aspect of this business. We need it, yet how much of it controls us? I mean, it was inevitable that I got a female deodorant as my sponsor. I'm a woman, they want me to sell product for women."

"Calling attention to the very thing you're trying to avoid."

"Exactly."

"No one is going to forget that you're a woman, Kendall.

You might want to consider embracing the edge it gives you."

Part of her bristled instantly, but then she thought about what he was saying. "Don't you think that's a sellout?"

"We're all sellouts. We have to be. And I will take the next sponsor who offers to pay my way, even if its diapers or sexual lubricants. It's business, not personal."

Kendall snickered. "I don't think we're going to see a lube car anytime soon. Though if we did, I would probably get it. A hot pink and purple car with a giant phallic-looking bottle all over the side."

"And I'll be driving the adult diaper car."

"Not even baby diapers?"

"Hell, no. This is my horror fantasy. Totally the incontinence car." He laughed. "Maybe I shouldn't say it out loud, I'll bring it on myself."

Kendall pulled into the track road, her car hitting ruts and bouncing hard. "It will all work out, Evan, I know it will."

There was a pause, then he said, "And if it doesn't?"

That vulnerability in his voice squeezed her heart. "It will," she said firmly.

He didn't answer, just looked out the window and pointed. "Park it right along there, and let's have a sit."

Kendall parked, and they climbed out and moved around to the front of her car.

"Can I sit on the hood?" Evan asked.

She appreciated the respect. "Sure. This isn't a special car. Just my everyday car."

"It's kind of flashy for an everyday car." Evan sat on the hood, his legs spread wide, forearms on his thighs.

Kendall tried not to find that attractive, but failed miserably. She also tried not to look at his crotch, and bombed out there, too. Not that she could see anything, given the angle, but just knowing what was there had her feeling warm despite the cool night air.

"I'm a flashy kind of girl," she told him, which was a total lie.

"That's a total lie. You're a tomboy, always have been."

The truth, yes, but it didn't sound particularly flattering out loud. "Gee, what every girl dreams of hearing."

He grinned. "A sexy tomboy. Always have been."

She crossed her arms over her chest. "Uh-huh, thanks."

He patted the hood next to him. "Sit down. And you don't need to be so defensive about not being a girly girl, you know. Everyone is their own person. So your sisters have traditional female jobs and you drive a race car. So what? And you can break down an engine and take a turn at one sixty and swear like a sailor. Doesn't make you any less female."

"I know that." Kendall climbed onto her car, feet on the fender. "Damn, this hood's cold. I do know that. I can wear a dress and feel feminine after an afternoon in the garage. By the way, transmission fluid makes an excellent conditioner, which I found out after letting half my head get soaked by accident. My hair was soft for a month."

Evan laughed. "I'll keep that in mind. So what's the problem then? So you straddle two worlds, two traditional ideas of gender roles. A lot of women do."

"It's not like I want to be a guy, or even one of the guys. I just want gender to not matter."

"Well, guess what? It does. So just own it. Use being a hot chick to your advantage."

Kendall sighed. She wasn't even sure what was bothering her, really. She was just tired of always fighting to get ahead and then feeling like it had been handed to her out of pity or curiosity because she was a woman. But intellectually she knew no one was handed a damn thing in this sport. She had earned it, or she wouldn't have it.

She also knew Evan had a point. She could rail against the ways of the world all she wanted or she could learn to live with it. "When did you get to be so smart?"

"What? I always thought you were a hot chick."

One glance over at him told her he had known exactly what she had meant and it wasn't about her looks. But if he couldn't take a compliment, she could. "Oh, yeah? Am I a super hot chick?"

"Definitely. Because you're the chick who can look beautiful in a dress, who can be a lady, yet at the same time is not afraid to get down and dirty. You like speed, and that is so goddamn sexy."

Kendall went still on the hood of her Vette. That was how she saw herself, a girl definitely, yet a girl who liked to drive fast and get her hands dirty. That Evan saw that so clearly and thought it was sexy was, well, hot. He was hot. She'd always thought he was damned attractive, and here in the chill night air, in the silence of the empty track, with him looking at her like he thought she was the only woman who had ever existed on the planet, she wanted him the way she hadn't wanted a man since she was eighteen.

It had been him then and it was him now. Which was a very strange and overwhelming feeling.

"Thank you," she murmured.

"No. Thank you." He leaned closer to her. "I'm going to kiss you again and you have about ten seconds to stop me."

Throwing caution to the wind in her personal life wasn't usually Kendall's style. Really not even on the track. She was methodical and aggressive, but not impulsive or a daredevil. But at the moment, she was perfectly willing to toss over common sense and let Evan Monroe lay his lips on hers just one more time.

"I'm not going to stop you."

"Hallelujah."

She didn't. In fact, Kendall leaned forward and eliminated that final sliver of air between them.

God, he felt so good. He was warm and strong and familiar, even after all these years. It was like her body, her senses, her heart remembered every taste, touch, scent of his, knew how they fit together.

And fit together well, they did. One touch of their mouths, one brush of a kiss, and Evan had pulled her closer, practically onto his lap on the hood, his lips claiming hers with hard, demanding kisses that took her breath away and took the chill right out of her body.

"God, you feel good," he said, his hands rushing over her sides, down to her thighs, her backside.

Kendall had nothing to say in response, her mind a total blank, filled with nothing but desire and raw need, so she let her actions do all the talking. She plunged her tongue into his mouth, her own hands gripping the lapels of his shirt, her breath hot and anxious, one leg hooking over his. She kissed him with all her pent-up frustration, ten years' worth of sadness and worry and anger over how she thought he had perceived her. She kissed him out of relief, out of lust, out of concern for his immediate future, out of fear for her own. Out of passion and aggression and intensity.

For the memory of her first love, the man who shared her need for speed.

A kiss wasn't enough to contain, control all those chaotic thoughts and emotions.

Kendall reached her hand for his thigh and found a burgeoning, encouraging erection jutting towards her.

Thank goodness. She was hot and wet and she was taking a ride whether he liked it or not.

Evan was drowning in lust, Kendall kissing the hell out of him, her tongue everywhere, her warm little body getting closer and closer with each touch of their lips. His hands were racing over her tight backside, and he was working on a painful throbbing erection, knowing it was destined for a letdown, when she dropped a hand right onto his junk.

"Oh, damn," he said, before he could stop himself. "Kendall, don't, you'll kill me."

He meant that sincerely. While he wasn't celibate like he had claimed earlier, the way his body was reacting now he might as well be. A couple of strokes and he'd be so hard he wouldn't be able to sit in the passenger seat. She'd have to lay him out in the backseat so he didn't suffer any injuries.

"Shh," she said, which was a sure indicator he was about to be tortured.

He was right. Kendall unzipped his pants.

"What are you doing?" he asked, because he had to know how tight of a rein he needed to have on his control.

She gave a soft laugh as her finger worked down the zipper then moved to his button. "What does it look like I'm doing?"

"Unzipping my fly. But to what purpose?"

"I'm going to get on you and ride you."

Evan's ears rang with a dull buzzing. His vision blacked out. Every muscle in his body constricted.

Sweet Jesus. Was she serious?

"If that's okay with you, that is."

He nodded, rapidly, mouth too full of anticipatory saliva to respond. Not that his brain could form words anyway. He no longer had a brain. He was just a giant cock, standing up at attention, waiting desperately for her to do something with him.

"Are you sure this is okay?" she asked again, stroking up and down on him.

Finding his voice, he said gruffly, "Hell, yes, I'm sure." To prove it, he reached out and undid her jeans, a little tit for tat.

Somewhere in the back of his mind it occurred to him this might be a bad idea. He and Kendall had just started talking again after a decade and their newfound friendship was fragile at best. Sex would complicate that. But the tiny corner of his brain that had any sense whatsoever was drowned out by testosterone flooding into every nook and cranny of his consciousness.

"Oh, good," she said, and her voice was breathy and excited, which spurred him into action.

Undoing her pants, Evan pushed up her shirt at the same time he exposed her panties. Kissing the soft skin of her belly, he flicked his tongue along the top of her panties, stroking back and forth on the warm flesh. She shivered, her fingers pressing into his shoulders.

"Are you wet?" he asked.

Now it was her time to just nod.

"Let me see." Evan slid into her pink panties, cupping her mound, before pushing his index finger inside her. She was slick with want and deliciously tight. "Oh, yeah. Very wet."

And damn if she wasn't moving her hips in rhythm already, forcing his finger deeper. A glance up showed Kendall's eyes were half-closed, her head tilting back, hair sliding across her face. Sexy didn't even begin to describe it. He let her move for a minute, pumping faster, her breath coming in urgent pants, before pulling his finger out.

She protested with a whimper. But Evan was already shoving her jeans and panties down to her knees.

"Are you on the pill?" he asked, suddenly aware that he had no condom, and even if he did, he didn't want to wait to unwrap it. He wanted her now. Before now. For the last ten years now.

"Yes." Kendall wasn't looking at him, but was staring down at his cock, which he had freed from his pants and boxer briefs.

He thought she might hesitate, change her mind, but she just put her foot on the bumper and said, "Help me with the physics involved here."

"My pleasure." Evan grabbed her ass and hauled her right onto him. "Just bend your knees on the hood. Gravity will actually be our friend."

He leaned back just a little, then when her legs were in place, he settled her right over his erection. Teasing with the tip at her hot, slick entrance, he closed his eyes and swallowed hard against the desire rushing up inside him.

While he would have just sat there savoring, gathering control, Kendall didn't pause for more than a beat before she drove herself down onto him.

She moaned in his ear, an exhalation of the same ecstasy he felt.

Knowing she was going to have limited movement, Evan grabbed her hips and thrust up inside her welcoming body.

Damn it.

This was crazy good. This was unreal. This was wild and fast and intense.

Her little cries rang in his ear and he pushed into her harder, wanting to take that sound and own it, hold it. He pumped and she groaned and he didn't hold back at all. Just gave it to her with all his pent-up frustration and feeling.

When she came almost immediately, Evan felt the most profound satisfaction he'd encountered in a long-ass time.

"Oh, my God," she whispered. "That was . . ."

"Amazing?" he asked, slowing down just slightly to give her a second to catch her breath.

"Embarrassing."

Evan stopped altogether. "Excuse me?"

"It took you sixty seconds to get me off. That's embarrassing."

Reassured, he kissed her earlobe. "We just have good chemistry, that's all. Now be quiet."

Kendall stuck her tongue out at him, but drew it back immediately on a moan when he lifted her hips and dropped her down hard on him.

Aware that he was probably squeezing her hips a little too hard, Evan eased up. But it was hard to stay loose, in control. Kendall was sitting on his cock on a Corvette and he was condom free. This was a freaking dream come true. This was a calendar. A video.

The thought of being able to watch a replay of Kendall doing this to him, over and over, made him groan. Still feeling a bit of a rum buzz, Evan wasn't as cool as he'd have liked to be. Her breasts were brushing his chest, her fingertips digging into his shoulders, her lips dropping feathery kisses on the corners of his mouth, and he was gone. The way she wrapped around him, legs, hips, sweet hot insides around the length of him, he gave in and exploded.

FIVE

KENDALL felt the unbelievable sensation of a second orgasm sweep over her as Evan came deep inside her, his grip tight on her waist, his guttural cries ringing in her ear. She never came twice. Not this close together and not from penis. To pop off a second time she always needed oral sex. But there was no denying that she was coming, and she clung to him, her legs awkwardly bent but not even bothering her.

It was just pure pleasure, just fast, stripped down, raw ecstasy.

And it was embarrassing, she hadn't been lying about that.

One kiss, and she was jumping on him on the hood of her car.

Thirty seconds and she was having an orgasm.

Two minutes and she was doing it all over again.

Breathing hard, her body quivering with aftershocks,

Kendall clung to Evan, her head on his shoulder. Swallowing hard, she tried to think of something to say, but there was nothing that came to mind. He didn't seem inclined to talk either, and they sat like that, his hands holding her from sliding off and hitting the dirt road, until her heart rate returned to normal and she was altogether too aware of the fact that there was a biting wind and where it was biting her was on the butt.

"Guess we should move," he murmured in her ear. "Your legs are shaking like Jell-O."

That, too.

But part of her wanted to stay that way indefinitely. Stay wrapped in his arms in the aftermath of an explosion of passion. Once she moved, it would turn awkward, and regret would wrap around her like a scratchy wool blanket.

"When you drop me off, why don't you come on inside with me?" Evan said, his fingers brushing her hair off her cheek in a gesture she found both sexy and tender. "I'd like to try that again on a bed, where I can taste you. All of you."

"Yes." Kendall said it without hesitation, then wondered if she was being too easy. If she should make him work a little harder.

Then he shifted her off of his body and she decided she didn't give a rat's hooey. It wasn't like she hadn't just been easy, and if straight shooting got her some more of that sooner rather than later, she was all for it.

"Mmm," he said, in a deep, rumbling voice that felt as intimate as his finger stroking inside her had been. "You feel amazing. I hate to let you go."

Suddenly terrified at the unexpected longing those words had bubbling up inside her, Kendall managed to slide off the car hood and readjust her panties and jeans. Evan was right, her legs were trembling. "All good things must come to an end."

Evan was still sprawled out on the hood, propped up by his forearms, his pants open and disheveled. He gave her a lazy grin. "Is that so? That seems cynical to me."

"Says the man who has resigned himself to driving the incontinence car." She nudged his foot with her boot. "Let's go. I'm freezing my buns off."

"We don't want that." Evan gave a terrific sigh and peeled himself off the car. "Where are your keys? I'm driving."

As if. "I don't think so."

"I am. And I'm taking your car around this track, just once, for old times' sake." He buttoned his pants and came towards her, his hand outreached. "Give me the keys."

"No. You're smoking something, Monroe. You are not jacking my car up on this track. And no one drives my car but me." Not even her father drove her car. That's why she'd bought him his own. She was territorial about her mirrors and her seat and her engine.

Evan's hand fell. "Please? Not even today? This could be the beginning of the end of my career, you know."

Shit. He looked so hangdog. Guilt twisted inside her.

"Alright." Kendall pulled her keys out and dropped them into his hand. "But don't take this track too fast, it's all pitted."

He grinned at her and kissed her forehead. "Damn, you are such a girl, tomboy or not. No guy would have fallen for that line of bullshit I just handed you."

She had been had. Outraged, Kendall smacked his arm. "Give me the keys back!"

"Nope." He dangled them in the air above his head, and way out of her reach. "Unless you want to jump for them."

"I guess some things don't change. You're still a jack-ass." But she wasn't really that annoyed. It was hard to be irritated when her inner thighs were pleasantly humming still and he was grinning all adorable-like.

"You know what else hasn't changed? It's still stupid that you and your siblings all have K names and me and my siblings all have E names. In fact, it's even dumber now that we're all grown up. What the hell were our parents thinking?"

Kendall laughed. "That it was cute. And you're still as random as ever."

"Was that random?" He shrugged. "What isn't random?"

At the moment, her entire night could be classified that way. She followed his lead and climbed into the car, trying not to panic at being in the passenger seat. It was possible she had some control issues when it came to driving. But hell, driving was her job, of course she liked to be the one behind the wheel.

"You nervous?" he said to tease her. "Don't be, I have it all under control. Except I can't find the ignition."

Terrified, she whipped her head over to see if he was serious. He wasn't.

"God, you're gullible."

She was. Of course he knew where the ignition was. Just because there wasn't one in a stock car didn't mean he didn't drive a regular car. Duh. She was losing it. Gripping the dashboard, she tried to relax as he pulled out. What was the worst thing that could happen?

Evan hit a pothole hard. "Whoops."

"You did that on purpose."

"I did not. Visibility is poor here."

"And you're full of shit. You drive under the lights going

damn near two hundred all the time. You're not like that guy I dated who didn't know the clutch from the brake."

Realizing that it was true, Kendall relaxed and settled back into her seat. Evan had been driving practically since birth. Taking her Vette around an empty track was not going to damage her car in any way.

"Which guy was that? He sounds like a loser." Evan drawled out the word "loser" with a heavy twang, so it sounded like lose-uh.

"It doesn't matter." He wasn't important. None of the men she had dated had been particularly important. Which at times had scared her. Here she was cruising up to thirty and she hadn't even come close to falling in love. Not since the teen puppy love she'd felt for this annoying man next to her.

Except he wasn't particularly annoying to her at the moment.

He was making her smile, with his own quick grin and casual charm.

And he was turning her on, with the way he sat so confidently in the driver's seat, his hand gripping the gearshift loosely. Those fingers, that had just been inside her, worked to shift gears with fluidity and strength. He had opened the engine up so that her car was eating up track. Evan was owning it without hesitation, taking the first turn smoothly, his eyes facing forward, but his mouth turned up at the corner.

"Not bad," he told her.

No, it wasn't bad at all. In fact, she was getting hot in her jeans all over again watching him. He was inherently sexy, powerful, masculine. The hard edge of the second turn threw her towards him and she brushed against his arm. The muscles beneath his shirt were bulging from the position of his arm on the gears.

"I'm going to make your car my bitch," he told her, shooting a grin her way.

The hell he was. "My car is a guy. And that was totally sexist, by the way."

"How do you know your car is a guy?"

"Because it's strong and fast, but it lets me call the shots. This is *my* ride."

"That was sexist, too. But so fucking hot I'm willing to overlook it." Evan turned the wheel and eased up on the gas as he left the track.

The jolt as he nailed a pothole at eighty miles an hour rattled her teeth, but Kendall didn't care. That tone of voice he had used, that matter-of-fact willingness to admit he wanted her, had her shifting on her seat, inner thighs moist. "I wasn't trying to be hot."

"Well, it was. You are. And I'm taking you home."

"So you said." Kendall cleared her throat, a tightness, an anticipation, closing it off. "And I believe my answer was yes, so get the lead out, Monroe. My grandma drives faster than you do."

He laughed. "Oh, little girl, you are asking for trouble."

"I already got me some trouble, and it's driving my car. What I'm asking is for you to hurry on up so I can get laid." Much as with her car, she felt the need to show Evan who was boss.

Not that she was in control of him or herself or anything else for that matter. One hour and a smoldering kiss and she was letting him nail her on the hood of her car, but why make it any easier for him than it already was?

"Yes, ma'am." Evan slammed on the brakes as he approached the main road, and barely glanced left before jumping her car from dirt to the pavement.

Knowing she had no business saying anything after

she'd just urged him to speed, Kendall bit her lip and tried not to consider the damage her shocks might be sustaining. It didn't matter. The truth was, she was having a great time. A few hours earlier, she wouldn't have thought she could spend five minutes with Evan without wanting to choke the life out of him, and yet he was making her laugh and loosen up more than she had in months.

This was the way she remembered what it was like to be with him— a lot of teasing and laughter and joy. And the heat. The sexual tension that had always been taut between them like a high wire.

It was all still there and it was exciting. Exhilarating. Scary as hell.

Maybe it was just the high of relief. The giddy sensation of knowing that Evan had cared about her. That he hadn't been some kind of misogynist insulting his girlfriend.

Whatever it was, when they cruised past the grocery store and into the town house complex, Kendall was anticipating what was ahead for her in Evan's bed more than she was looking backwards at the past.

EVAN tried to keep it under the speed limit, but it was damn hard. He was enjoying both driving Kendall's car, and the bold looks she was shooting him. Combined, they had him eager to get her home and in his bed, and he found his foot pressure increasing repeatedly, before he got a grip and eased up again.

Thank God it was a short ride.

This was nuts. A complete twist on his day that he could have never anticipated, but he wasn't one to turn down a golden opportunity. Not just to have sex. He was damn glad he and Kendall had cleared the air. It eased the hurt, the bitter rejection he'd felt, to hear her apology, to understand that she'd been hurt, too, and had reacted immaturely. The fact that she could admit that it had been on the childish side gave him a respect for her. If you couldn't look back at your mistakes and take responsibility, then you were never going to grow and change. Evan could see now that he had wasted a lot of time taking his hurt over Kendall out on other women or, more specifically, on the concept of relationships in general.

That had occurred to him somewhere on turn two of that old dirt track, as Kendall had sparred with him and he'd found himself enjoying her company in the way he hadn't enjoyed a woman's company in a very long time.

Tomorrow meant nothing. He knew that. He knew enough about women, and Kendall specifically, to know that tomorrow she would wake up and regret that she'd had sex with him so quickly, and she would go weird. She would say they'd gotten swept up in past feelings and that they had both needed the closure.

But they'd already had sex once, and she hadn't balked yet, so he was determined to enjoy her while it lasted. Hell, maybe those things were true. Maybe he was getting carried away. Yet when he pulled into his drive and she put her hand over his, her fingers cool and soft, gripping his fist as she shifted gears with him, he really wasn't sure.

"Don't trust me?" he asked. "I know how to put it in park."

"I know. I'm just reasserting my equality. My way of saying we got here together."

Something squeezed inside his chest at the word *together*. That shit had to stop if he was going to stay cool and in control. Evan took her hand, lacing his fingers through hers and lifting them to his mouth. He brushed his lips across her knuckles, watching as her eyes went wide.

Pausing for a second while he nibbled at her flesh, Evan raised an eyebrow and told her, "Nice try. I was driving."

Her mouth dropped open, then her eyes narrowed. "So that's how you want to play? What if I just dump you here in your driveway and go home."

"You won't." He hoped like hell she wouldn't.

"I think I will."

But Kendall's plan to achieve this had her leaning right across Evan to try to open his door in some futile effort to kick him out.

Which meant that she was splayed all across him, her arms brushing his chest, her chest brushing his thighs, her hair tickling his arm. Her position was remarkably similar to that of a woman going down on a man, and Evan felt an erection spring to life instantly.

This was not her brightest move yet.

"Kendall?" he told her, running his hands through her hair as she wiggled and grappled with the door handle. "You do realize you're in danger of getting your eye poked out."

"Huh?"

She glanced up at him, then down. Suddenly going still, Kendall gave a little cough, and he could actually feel the warmth of her breath through his jeans, which didn't help his problem at all.

"You don't really want to kick me out, do you?" Shifting slightly, he bumped her arm. Unintentionally, of course.

Kendall lost her balance and her face fell in his lap. He really hadn't meant for that to happen, and the unexpected contact, her mouth and nose bumping him, had him groaning before he clamped his lips closed.

"You're a jerk," she muttered into his crotch.

"I swear, I didn't mean to do that." He had his moments of being a sex-driven pig, he could own that, but he really hadn't meant to toss her face into his dick. That went against all the rules of having a good time and respecting each other. "Let me help you up."

Trying to scoot away from her, and having no success, Evan tried to lift Kendall up by her waist. That wasn't working either. She was a tangle of limbs and outerwear, with the gearshift jabbing her side and the steering wheel impeding his attempts to right her body. Feeling uncomfortable, like she was going to think he wasn't trying, Evan leaned forward, his plan to at least send the seat backwards to give them more room to maneuver. But Kendall put a hand on his chest to stop him.

"Since I'm down here," she said.

And then she yanked his zipper down in one smooth motion.

Oh, no she didn't.

Evan just stared down at her, his brain unable to process what he was seeing, hearing, feeling. His erection, on the other hand, had no problem figuring out what to do and jumped a little in her direction, rock solid and raring to go.

"I . . . I . . ." Evan cleared his throat and tried again. "You don't like to do that." She hadn't. It had made her uncomfortable, and after a few aborted attempts where she had tried just to please him, Evan had given up on oral sex. He hadn't wanted her to do anything she wasn't totally into.

"I'm not eighteen anymore."

The desire to feel her mouth over him warred with the

sudden annoyance that she had learned to like it with some other guy. What had he done that Evan hadn't? Or was it just an age and maturity thing?

"We're in the driveway," he said, though a glance in both directions showed no one was around. It was late and dark and her car was low. Someone would really have to be bending over and looking to see anything.

But it seemed like he should protest.

"You don't want me to?" She started to pull away, shrugging as she struggled to sit up. "Okay."

Evan's hand flew out without any hesitation and grabbed her shoulder to stop her. He wasn't fucking stupid. "No, no, of course not. Just making sure you're cool with this."

"I don't start what I'm not willing to finish."

Well, that was debatable, but he wasn't going to get into it with her. Not when her mouth was hovering over his naked cock, her breath hot and teasing on his flesh.

"Then I'll stop talking and let you do your thing."

When her lips touched his skin, Evan clamped his lips shut and concentrated on breathing. Flexing his fingers, he decided he just needed to lift them off of her altogether or he was going to end up squeezing her, pumping her up and down on him. That wouldn't be cool. This needed to be her show.

Which it was. Kendall flicked her tongue across his head before sliding it down the length of him. Just that little tease had him clenching every muscle in his body. He reached out for the door handle for something to hold on to as she fully closed her slick mouth over him and took him deep.

Damn. Damn. Damn. Evan closed his eyes for a second to just savor the tight, hot feeling, but then he opened them again. He wanted to see Kendall over him. She was moving faster now, her blond hair falling forward over her cheeks, surrounding him. With her fingers she encircled him below her mouth, squeezing tightly.

"Oh, shit," he said, before he could stop himself. "That feels good."

Pulling off of him with a juicy pop, she gave him a sly smile. "That's the point."

Yeah, she wasn't eighteen anymore. For which he was suddenly really grateful. "Then I won't state the obvious." Evan lifted his arms and folded them behind his head in a posture of relaxation. "I'll just enjoy it."

Not that he was even remotely relaxed. But something about having his hands off her as she slipped her tongue over him again made the pleasure all that more intense. When she started moving faster, her mouth and fingers working in tandem, Evan did close his eyes. This was serious ecstasy. This was the kind of desire that had his whole body tightening, his mind emptying, his heart racing. This had all of him concentrated right there, in her hands and under her slick, hot mouth.

It went on and on, a delicious base rhythm, tripping every nerve ending from head to toe, driving him closer and closer to the edge.

But somehow, and without biting his own tongue off, Evan managed to keep from coming. He didn't want this to end, didn't want to finish before he could drive her to the same madness.

"Kendall, let's go inside."

She didn't speak and she didn't stop. She might have shaken her head no, but he wasn't sure. Evan tried to back up, but there was nowhere to go. "Kendall."

There was no pause. She just kept sucking him, and Evan was feeling a little desperate. This was not going to happen. He was a grown man and he was going to make this last all fucking night.

So he took her head and pulled her off him, gently but effectively.

She panted, her cheeks squeezed between his hands, her lips puffy and shiny, eyes dark with lust. "What?"

"We're going inside." Evan managed to haul and nudge her up into a pseudo sitting position. Then he kissed those beautiful lips that had just been driving him insane. She tasted salty and aroused and eager, her mouth greeting his enthusiastically.

"Oh," she said, her arms coming up around his back. "Evan."

It wasn't a question, it was a statement. His name spoken on such a heady sigh of delight had him feeling that unpleasant twist inside his chest again. Ignoring that, he concentrated on what a giant turn-on it was that she was so aroused herself.

"Baby, inside, come on, now. Let's go." Shoving his erection back into his pants, for the most part, Evan turned the car off and opened the door.

Kendall looked floppy and sexy and disappointed, but she threw her hair back and opened the passenger door.

Evan shut the door, then came around the front of her car, holding the keys out for her. "I don't think I make a very good chauffeur."

She gave him a smile, snatching the keys. "Not if this is how you end your nights after driving people around."

"Only with you, baby."

"The name is Kendall."

He laughed as he hit the code to open his garage door. "Is 'baby' sexist?"

"I think almost everything that comes out of your mouth is sexist."

Evan would have been offended except he knew Kendall wasn't serious. If she were, she would have pulled out of his driveway already. "Then I might as well just call you what I really want to. I have my heart set on a new nickname for you."

"What is it?" She shot him a suspicious look as she followed him into his garage.

"Nope. Not telling yet. A nickname this good needs the perfect moment to reveal it."

The scowl that crossed her face almost made him forget about the need to have sex immediately if not sooner. Teasing Kendall was a whole lot of fun. She rose to the bait every single time.

"You don't really have one, do you?"

He did, but there was no way he was saying it out loud. "Believe what you want." Evan took her hand, small yet calloused by all her years of driving and working on engines. It was a real woman's hand, not the soft perfection of some of those Hollywood-type chicks he had dated. He and Kendall had a lot more in common than he'd ever had with any of those women. "Just come on inside."

Instead of answering, she leaned around him and opened the door to his town house, brushing past him and flicking on a light as she entered.

Evan said a prayer of gratitude, followed by another hoping that he hadn't left his place too disgusting that morning. But he knew that more likely than not his living standards didn't meet the expectations of a perfectionist like Kendall. Even before Elec had gotten married and moved out, Evan had been something of a slob. Now it had only gotten worse without his brother nagging him.

The only solution was to rush her past the kitchen and get her naked in bed.

"Bedroom is to the right, up the stairs, first door on the left."

"Aren't you even going to offer me a drink or anything?" Kendall walked past his kitchen towards the stairs, but her eyes swept curiously over his place.

Even in the dim light from the hall, Evan could see he'd left dirty dishes all over the counter. He'd have liked to say it was because he was exceptionally busy at the moment, but the truth was, he was always messy. Nothing gross, just . . . cluttered. Sometimes it took him a while to clean up, which was no big deal.

Why he suddenly felt the need to apologize for any of that was beyond him. "Would you like a drink?"

"No, thank you."

Evan didn't even try to prevent an eye roll from happening. "Smart-ass." He moved towards her and took her hand, intertwining her fingers with his. "Now, come upstairs with me." Dropping a soft kiss on the corner of her mouth, on her ear, he added, "Please."

Kendall shivered. "You always were good at talking me into sex."

Something about that gave him pause. "Did I talk you into something you weren't ready for?" That would bother him, if he had pushed her into sex before she wanted to.

Evan held her hand, and his lips brushed over her temple, inhaling the scent of her fruity shampoo.

"Of course not. I think you know me well enough to know that I don't do anything I don't want to. I was scared, nervous, sure, but when we made love for the first time, I wanted to. And it was beautiful."

Emotions that he wasn't about to name surfaced rapidly, one by one, little bubbles popping up and exploding, but the only one that he was willing to acknowledge was lust.

Kendall's voice was a sexy slide across his flesh, like teasing fingers.

Stroking her hand in his with his thumb, he murmured, "It was beautiful. You're beautiful. Then and now."

"Take me upstairs."

"My pleasure."

CHAPTER
SIX

KENDALL barely had time to glance around Evan's bedroom before he had her splayed out on his bed. The room was dark and he was just a shadow over her, the only sounds the rustle of their clothing and the in-and-out of excited breathing. Why was it that something so simple as having him near her caused the extreme reaction it did? She felt excited, pleased, aroused, just from his body over hers, totally clothed, his hands reaching for her.

She wasn't going to think about it. She was just going to enjoy it.

Evan pushed her coat off her shoulders and she wiggled out of it.

"I want to see you," he murmured, moving off the bed and across the room.

When a lamp came on, bathing the room in a soft glow, she felt the need to warn him. "I'm not eighteen anymore, you know. I have cellulite."

Which was such a mood killer. Annoyed with herself,

she sat up, planning to take her shoes off. And maybe knock herself in the head with one of them.

She expected him to crack a joke or tell her to shut up in that playful banter they had. But as he approached the bed, Evan bent over, his arms on either side of her, his face level with hers, his brown eyes serious and warm.

"Hey. We all fear we're not perfect. But to me, Kendall, you've always been perfect."

Oh, God. She was drowning. She was completely and totally drowning in his eyes, his words, his body. Suddenly there was no past, no future, no outside world, there was just this bed, this dusky room, and him.

Because she didn't know what to say, she reached up and kissed him. They had always had good chemistry, a steamy connection, and it flared up all over again, that passion that had driven her a decade ago to do things she had never imagined. Things that had made her blush then, and things that she just greedily wanted now.

Evan stepped back and pulled off his shirt, dropping it to the floor.

His body had changed, too, in the last ten years, only he had filled out. What had been lean and lanky at nineteen was now muscular and toned at twenty-nine. She reached out and stroked his bare chest, enjoying the heat of his skin and his firm flesh. "Very nice."

He dropped down into a squat and pulled off her boots. They hit the floor with a thud. Then he peeled off her socks, quickly and efficiently.

"I get cold without my socks on."

He shot her a look of disbelief. "I'm not making love to you with your socks on. It's warm under the covers, and in five minutes you'll be so hot it won't matter."

"Then hurry." She was half teasing, half serious. She

didn't want to be distracted by the fact that she was shivering. She got cold easily, what could she say?

Evan stood up, moving in between her legs. He pushed her knees apart. "Hurry? You're going to eat those words."

Kendall wasn't sure what that meant, but she was looking forward to finding out. Though she had to admit, with the bulge in his pants right in front of her, she was contemplating pulling him out and sucking again. That had felt so damn good, to have him in her mouth, his moans ringing in her ears. Knowing that she was giving him that much pleasure had totally turned her on, too.

But before she could act on her thoughts, Evan had leaned forward, so that she was forced to lie back on the bed. Then before she could pull her legs onto the mattress, he had popped the button on her jeans and stripped them down the length of her, turning them completely inside out. The cold air hit her flesh and gave her goose bumps, but Evan was right—she didn't care. Not when he hovered over her, kissing the inside of her thighs, his tongue trailing along her panties, his lips softly pressing against her mound.

She sighed, grateful for the contact. It had been a long time since she'd dated, and she'd missed this, the running of hands over her flesh, the soft feathery kisses of a lover. She'd missed orgasms, too, but those she could create on her own. The skin on skin was irreplaceable.

Did it matter that it was Evan? Probably, if she were being honest with herself. When she was feeling so relaxed and sensual and languid, she just might be inclined to admit that truth.

He petted and kissed and teased her until delight shifted to discontent and she wanted more, wanted her panties off, and him to touch her more intimately. "Evan . . ."

"Yes?"

"Take my panties off."

"Eventually."

Just pulling her panties slightly to the side, Evan ran his tongue along the crevice of her thigh, the hot wet sensation making her squirm. She wanted him there, inside her, but he just teased, his tongue making one brief flick over her clitoris before retreating.

He stood and she stared up at him, wondering what the hell he was doing. Then he popped his pants open and took down the zipper. Good plan. Kendall lifted her backside and shoved her panties down to her knees, then wiggled her feet until they dropped off. This way she didn't have to wait around for him to do it.

"Your panties fell off," he told her as his own pants went south, boxers included. Seeing Evan standing in front of her fully naked had saliva pooling in the corners of her mouth. He was gorgeous, no doubt about it. Hard and yet pretty, all at once, with broad shoulders, a strong jaw, and a quality penis. All in all, a heck of a package.

"Whoops," she told him. "And I think my shirt's about to fall off, too."

"No, I got it." He bent over her and flicked his tongue inside her belly button, tripping off a low ache deep inside her womb. "Sit up a little."

She did, and he had her sweater off in a second and tossed God only knew where, fully exposing her to him. Kendall had a chest that was disproportionate to her frame. She was short and for the most part petite, but since the age of thirteen she'd had breasts that dominated her figure. They had always annoyed her, getting in the way and making her the object of scrutiny she didn't appreciate.

But at the moment, Evan's scrutiny made her think they weren't such a bad thing after all. Women paid major money for breasts like hers, and given the way his eyes were darkening and his jaw clenching, she understood why.

"Oh, honey." He reached behind her back and undid her bra.

He might as well have said, "Let me at 'em," the way he tore her bra off and sent it flying, his mouth and hands descending on her breasts.

Kendall relaxed, already enjoying the attention with the first brush of his fingers on the underside of her breast, and the moist enclosure of his mouth over her nipple. That suck and tug were amazing, sparking a desire that raced out from her nipple to every part of her body. She was achingly and desperately wet, her legs spreading farther without any awareness on her part. She caught a glimpse of ceiling, a quick view of Evan's short hair, but mostly her eyes were closed against the assault.

He moved to the other breast, and when his spare hand wandered down her stomach and slid into her slick heat, they both groaned.

"You're so wet," he said.

Men had said that to Kendall in the past and she'd always felt like it was an accusation, like she should apologize for her arousal, but with Evan, it was different. He sounded pleased, in awe, seriously hot and bothered, and she didn't hesitate to lift her hips a little to drive his finger deeper.

"You got me wet."

"Then I should get you off, too."

Evan's mouth abandoned her nipple and his tongue trailed down past her ribs, over her belly, pausing for one torturous second over her clitoris before plunging deep inside her where his finger had just been.

She almost vaulted off the bed into his ceiling fan. "Oh,

holy shit, Evan." She hadn't expected that. Hadn't been pre-pared for that. Hadn't known how good it would feel to have this thick, hot tongue inside her. "You need to stop." She didn't want to come again. Couldn't come again. If she did, then she wouldn't be able to with him inside her, or with his tongue on her clit, both of which would be more intense. She couldn't waste an orgasm.

But he kept at her, in and out, in and out, his hand teas-ing at her nipples, plucking and strumming, his nose tick-ling her clit.

"No. No." Heels digging into the mattress, she tried to back up, tried to push his head away with her sweaty palms, but he didn't go anywhere and she came on his mouth in a hot gush of fluid and desire, a massive, rocking orgasm that had her back off the bed and her moans silenced in shock.

It felt so hot and erotic and dirty, in a good way, like she was fucking his face, and she felt her cheeks flushing with heat at her thoughts, her reactions, even as she reveled in them, gripping his head and grinding every last ounce of pleasure out of her orgasm.

Then she fell back, spent, gasping for breath, her legs trembling and her vaginal muscles still quivering as he pulled away. But with barely a pause, Evan pushed her legs up so they were bent at the knee and wide apart, and then he sank inside her.

Swollen and sensitive and still achingly aroused, Ken-dall moaned at the way it felt to have him push deep, filling her completely. Evan stopped, his eyes closed, his breathing ragged. Then those dark eyes popped open and he stared down at her as he started to move, a mid-speed rhythm, hard but not too slow or too fast. Kendall found herself grappling to hold on to his shoulders, needing something to ground her, both physically and emotionally. The weight of his gaze, the push of his body into hers, felt so good, so intense, yet almost too much, like she wasn't herself. It was too free, too explosive, too passionate, and the sounds that flew out of her mouth shocked her.

She had lost control and didn't mind. He was driving her pleasure and she was reveling in it. Evan stroked, his arms solid and muscular on either side of her, his expression intense and unreadable. Kendall felt herself spiraling out of the rational, into a place where this was real, where this passion between them mattered, where she wasn't eighteen and stupid, but a woman who had more sense. A woman who knew how good this feeling was, how rare even just this kind of sexual satisfaction was. The way he moved inside her . . . Kendall squeezed his arms tighter.

Then she came again, everything from her center out shuddering in shock and pleasure. This time, she made no sound, her throat closed off, her cries silenced by the shattering luminosity of the moment.

"Roll on top of me," Evan urged.

Kendall couldn't even answer. She had no ability to speak, think, move.

But Evan flipped her over, their bodies still intertwined when she ended up splayed over top of him.

For a heartbeat, Evan thought Kendall was just going to lie there on him, content, maybe even fall asleep. But as he thrust up inside her, gradually she stirred, her hips meeting his. He couldn't believe how unbelievably amazing watching her orgasm had been, how seeing her shatter like that beneath him had almost done the same to him. Changing positions had been to prevent that happening too soon and yet, he was already enjoying this too much. Feeling the length of her body draped over him, the press of her breasts, and the warmth of her flesh, he was beyond aroused.

When she peeled herself off of him and sat fully up, Evan was surprised, but damn grateful. It was a hell of a view, and with her legs wide open and the pull of gravity, it brought her more fully down on him. All in all, a fucking fabulous combination, and he lay there and let Kendall do her thing.

Do it she was. There was no hesitation or shyness or excessive bounce. It was languid and sexy and confident, her eyes half-closed, her mouth open on soft sighs.

Evan wasn't a man who had beautiful words or creative descriptions or an understanding of fine art or literature. But as he watched Kendall moving over him, her hands in her hair, her breasts rising and falling with the tempo of her strokes, her swollen lips open in ecstasy and her back arched in a graceful curve, he thought it was moving poetry. Perfection. All things beautiful combined in that woman, this moment.

Gripping her hips, he matched her rhythm, thrusting deep up inside her with tight urgency. Then he came inside her, a hot explosion, his teeth gritted against the pleasure as her eyes widened. She did that girl thing, where she flexed her inner muscles on him, dragging his orgasm out longer, and as his convulsions slowed he let out a low groan.

"Sweet Jesus, Kendall."

"No shit" was her reply.

Her hands fell out of her hair and did a slow stroll down her neck and chest, cupping her breasts. The sight of that made his cock jump again and she gave a little cry, an orgasm aftershock.

Then she lowered herself onto him, her hair falling across his face. Evan stroked her smooth back and swallowed hard. He was hot and sweaty and out of breath, but he felt awesome. Like he'd won at Daytona. Twice.

Her chin was on his chest as she looked up at him. "Umm. So what's my nickname?"

Evan grinned. "I was thinking Jay would be a fine nickname for you."

"Jay? What the hell does that mean?"

"Short for Va-jay-jay. After all, if you hadn't said that, we wouldn't be here right now enjoying this evening together."

Her mouth dropped open and she looked like she might just tear him a new one, but then she laughed softly. "That is so completely offensive. Yet somehow funny."

"That's how it's meant." Evan slid his fingers up the curve of her waist, along the side of her breast. "I'm a funny guy."

"And I'm reiterating that I don't need a nickname."

He laughed. "You come up with a better one. Bet you ten bucks you can't."

"How about Goddess? That works for me."

"Huh." He made a noncommittal sound. "That's so typical."

"And Jay is better?"

"Yeah, I mean how many women can have a nickname that's so personal? Tailored right for them, instead of some generic one?"

"You're a pig," she said, yawning, her words completely without malice.

"You're probably right." Evan held Kendall close to him, very much aware that this could be it. All the time he was going to have with her, intimate and close and warm like this. So he kissed the top of her tousled head and wondered why he felt so content . . . why he felt so natural and normal with Kendall. Complete.

Which sucked.

Evan lay awake staring at the ceiling long after Kendall had fallen into the soft, even breathing of a deep sleep.

KENDALL woke up stiff and confused, her backside cold, her front sticky. Prying her eyes open, she realized she was still lying naked across Evan's chest.

And he was staring at her.

Good God. What the hell had she been thinking? There was nothing smart about sleeping with a fellow driver, history or not.

"What time is it?" Mind racing through her schedule, she tried to remember what time her test drive was. She had to meet her crew chief at the garage before, at ten, and then . . .

"Good morning to you, too."

Lips pursing, Kendall stopped trying to push herself off of Evan and looked down at him. He looked put out, and she instantly felt guilty, which pissed her off. "Good morning." She wasn't going to ask again, but her mind was spinning, and she realized she'd left her purse in the car. "Seriously, what time is it?"

Evan sighed, but he leaned over and turned the clock on his nightstand so she could see it. "Eight twenty-two."

"Shit. I have to be at the track at ten." Vaulting up, she tried not to feel hugely self-conscious that she was buck-ass naked as she climbed out of bed.

But failed as miserably as she had calculus when Evan let out a wolf whistle. Feeling her cheeks heat, she tried to figure out how to retrieve her panties without bending over a mere foot from Evan's face. Not that she knew where her panties were. There seemed to be a whole mess of clothes scattered all over the floor, none of which were hers. She did spot her sweater and bent at the knees to pick it up, smacking one of them against the bed frame in the process.

"Ouch."

"What the hell are you doing?"

"I'm getting dressed, what's it look like?" As she held the sweater up in front of her, making sure to cover all her important girl bits, she tried not to shuffle. Her mouth was dry and she was blushing and she just wanted out of there.

God. Sleeping with her first love, who happened to drive for the same team as her, and was her competition. That had been just brilliant.

"If I can find my underwear, that is."

Evan was lounging on the bed, fully naked and sporting a giant erection.

Kendall tore her eyes away from it. There was no point in checking out his package. She'd come, she'd seen, she'd come again.

Time to take her very happy hoohah home and concentrate on her career, not nailing Evan Monroe.

Ignoring the sudden betrayal of moisture between her legs, she scanned the floor and found her bra. Evan shifted and pulled her panties out from under his leg. "Here you go."

She snatched them so fast her speed would have done a kung-fu master proud. His eyebrows shot up.

As she knelt down by the bed so he couldn't see her and wiggled into her underwear, he propped himself up against the headboard. "So am I going to see you later?"

"Yeah, if you're doing test runs today. I'll be there from ten until probably two or so."

"That's not what I meant."

Of course it wasn't. Shit. "What did you mean?"

"I meant am I going to see you again. Naked or otherwise."

Awkward. And this was where Kendall was totally lacking in the sensibilities of the majority of her gender. She didn't always know how to be delicate. Or maybe tactful was the better word. But she was going to try. "Evan . . . I'm really glad we had a chance to talk last night. I owed you a real apology for my behavior when we broke up, and I'm so glad to hear that I was mistaken about what had happened. But last night . . . it was just closure for us. I don't think it's a good idea for us to see each other—like this—again."

Evan's hands were behind his head and he sighed before nodding. "I had a feeling you'd say that. If that's what you want, Kendall. I'm not going to chase you. I chased enough ten years ago."

Not sure how she felt about that, or what that really meant, Kendall frowned as she finished hauling up her jeans. "I mean, I hope we'll be friends now. That the sniping is a thing of the past."

He nodded. "Sure. Of course."

That was it?

Kendall stood up, fully dressed, boots on but unlaced. "Okay. Great. Awesome."

Awkward. Now what did she say? This was what she got. She was a slut who had forced him to have sex with her and now any potential friendship that could have blossomed was buried under her boobs and his boner.

"Do you need a ride to the bar to pick up your car?"

"Nah. I'm going back to sleep." Evan stretched lazily, making his erection jerk a little.

Not that she was looking.

"Are you sure?" Not that she wanted to drive him anywhere. In fact, she'd have liked to move to a hemisphere where Evan Monroe and his stellar penis didn't exist.

"Yep. I'll call a cab." He yawned.

Clearly he wasn't having the same emotional tornado tear through him that she was.

"Perfect. Okay. See you around." Kendall gave him the thumbs-up and turned to leave.

Dear Lord. She had given him the thumbs–fucking-up. Could she feel any stupider?

"Bye, Jay."

Yes. Yes, she could.

Kendall just waved over her shoulder and kept going, not trusting herself to turn around. Her cheeks were burning, and she decided that she still hated Evan Monroe just a tiny small bit.

CHAPTER
SEVEN

"WHAT exactly do you have to smile about?" Eve said.

Evan sat in the office that his family used to manage his and Elec's driving careers and tried to squelch the grin on his face. "Nothing." Just the most amazing sex of the decade, that was all. He could still picture Kendall on top of him, feel her body sluicing over his . . .

Something pinged him on the arm, knocking him out of his reverie. "Hey!" Eve had thrown a paper clip at him. "What was that for?"

"For wearing a shit-eating grin when you just had the biggest setback to your career. I mean what could you possibly be smi—"

Eve's crossed leg fell down onto the floor. "Oh, my God. You had sex last night, didn't you? That's why you're Mr. Happy this morning."

There was no point in denying it, so Evan just remained silent. He'd let Eve have her rant for a minute or two then he'd rein her in.

"What is it with you men? Does sex trump everything?"

What planet had she been living on? "Yes."

"Pretty much," Elec agreed from his position on the couch. He had been thumbing through a magazine but piped in with his support.

"Not that I'm saying I had sex. But I had a date." It wasn't his style to kiss and tell.

"Did anyone see you with her? Are there going to be pics on a blog with some barely legal stripper?"

"I resent that. I have never dated a stripper. Or anyone barely legal once I was past twenty-one myself. Neither appeals to me in any way." There were limits to the insults he'd take. But then he realized claiming a stripper would probably earn him less grief from Eve than the truth.

"Well, thank God. Is she anyone I know?"

Evan coughed. "I think you might know her, yeah." And normally he wouldn't admit a damn thing, but for all he knew there was a blog going up right now about Kendall and him being in that bar. Written by Tuesday Jones, probably. He could deny it, but that would just piss Eve off more.

His sister tucked her hair behind her ear and narrowed her eyes. "Who is it?"

"It might have been Kendall Holbrook."

Eve's jaw dropped. Elec gave a low whistle from the couch.

"You had sex with Kendall Holbrook?"

"I'm not admitting anything, only that I went out for a drink with her last night."

"Are you crazy?" Eve's voice had shot up two octaves. "When did you become the mayor of Moron-ville?"

Trust his sister to find an insult that infuriated him, even when he vowed to stay calm. "What's the big deal? It was one drink!" Then a whole night of naked.

"Do I need to remind you that your very existence in the cup series is in jeopardy? And that Kendall Holbrook is this season's novelty? She has the media crawling up her ass twenty-four seven."

Well, not quite.

"And drivers like her are the reason you lost your sponsorship. She has siphoned off attention from all of you guys in the middle of the pack, and for that reason alone she could be the enemy. But more to the point, if the two of you are seen together, it looks bad. You look like a boot licker."

"I don't know about that," Elec said. "I don't think anyone would see it as anything more than just a juicy piece of gossip."

"Great, thanks." Evan felt the warm fuzzies he'd woken up with evaporating.

"Everyone loves a good track romance."

"They do?" Evan never paid attention to that kind of stuff. Mainly because he'd been avoiding the whole concept of relationships, jealous of other people's happily ever afters.

"Of course they do. But the bigger issue here is distraction. If you're feeling the love for Kendall, is your competitiveness going to be compromised?"

Evan didn't hear anything past love. "What? What love? It was one drink!" And a night of hot monkey sex.

But the L word scared the crap out of him.

"I remember when you and Kendall broke up the first time around," Eve said, leaning back in her chair and sticking her legs up on her desk, her shiny black boots moving up and down like she was wagging her finger at him. "It wasn't pretty."

"We were kids then. Everything was drama. We're just hanging out, getting to know each other as adults." As equally horny adults. Evan shifted on his chair, feeling a little uncomfortable with the erotic memories dancing through his head. If he got a boner in front of his sister he was going to be embarrassed as hell. Plus she would mock him for the rest of his natural life.

"Yes, there was drama. You were awful, moping around, calling her every five seconds, crying. I wanted to smack you to make it stop, but it would have been like kicking roadkill."

Evan felt a little kicked right now. "Your sympathy is overwhelming, as always."

"Ease up, Eve," Elec said, his voice mild but firm. "You had your share of heartbreak when you were a teenager. That shit hurts."

His brother had always been the softer touch, and right now he appreciated it. "Thanks, bro."

Eve sighed. "God, I hate it when you deflate my anger. Can't you just let me be pissed at you?"

Grinning, Evan flicked the paper clip back at her. "No one can stay mad at me. Look at Kendall. It only took ten years, but now we're talking again. No one can resist my immense charm."

His sister snorted. "Seriously, stay away from the cameras. Don't let this get turned into a big deal. Be careful not to be photographed. And most of all, do not, I repeat, do *not* let this turn into drama. Do not let it affect your driving, your focus. And do not engage in some kind of nasty public breakup with Kendall."

"There's nothing to break up. We're just friends." If he told himself that enough, eventually he'd start to believe it. The truth was, he wasn't sure they were even friends, but he knew that he wanted a repeat of last night as soon as possible. Eve didn't need to know that.

Sighing, she said, "You're going to be the death of me. Either that or responsible for my slow slide into alcoholism."

"Why so serious, Eve? Maybe you need to get laid, too."

Her feet hit the ground and she pointed her finger at him. "You did sleep with her! I knew it! Damn it!"

Shit. He had just outed himself. Elec started laughing from behind him.

Nothing to do but grin and own it. "Don't worry. It wasn't in public and there were no cameras."

"How do you know? There are surveillance cameras at every decent hotel."

"Why would we be at a hotel? We were at my place. And I'm not telling you anything more than that because it's none of your business."

He certainly wasn't going to tell his sister how amazing Kendall had looked coming, or how delicious her nipples had tasted, or how he had let her walk out that morning without a fuss because he fully intended to see her naked again soon.

"Your career is my business, so don't mess it up."

"It's all good." Well, maybe not his career, exactly, but he and Kendall . . . it was all damn good.

"YOU did what?" Tuesday paused in the process of raising her press pass badge over her head. "I don't think I heard you correctly."

Kendall looked uneasily around the garage, making sure no one was in earshot. "I slept with him. It's not a big deal."

"No big deal?" Tuesday let the badge drop down on the string it was attached to, tossing her hair back. "Are you kidding me? You were a wreck over this guy. You and Evan Monroe have enough baggage to fill a cargo plane and you just hopped into bed with him?"

"You made me go talk to him," she pointed out, feeling

defensive. So she'd slept with Evan? Who cared? Sex happened. Good sex was a rarity in her life these days. Actually, any sex was hard to come by. It had been a golden opportunity with someone she knew could please her so she had taken it, and she wasn't about to apologize for that.

"Talk to him, yes. Have sex with him, no. That was not in the instructions I gave you."

"Well, I did and it was good, so don't worry about it. It's no big deal."

Tuesday threw her hands up in the air. "Oh, my God, whenever you say it's no big deal, it *so* is a big deal. Look, you know I love you and I want you to be happy and as long as you're okay with the consequences you can sleep with whoever you want and I will never judge you. But you, my dear, do not do casual sex. My fear is that this will make you feel bad when he doesn't call you."

It already had. When she had walked out and he had let her. Damn it. Tuesday was right and she hated it. "Who says I want him to call me? I don't need any complications in my life. And thanks for assuming he won't call me. That makes me feel fabulous."

"Hey, Kendall!" Jim, her crew chief, called to her from where he was standing by the office door, his clipboard in his hand. "Got a sec?"

"Sure, just a minute." Kendall took a deep breath and inhaled the aroma of the garage—rubber and oil and the pizza some of the guys had ordered for lunch. It had a calming effect on her, oddly enough. "Okay, you're right," she told Tuesday. "I don't do casual sex, and it's going to bother me if he doesn't call me. And it will equally bother me if he pursues me, because the truth is, I can't handle any sort of relationship with him. So I screwed up by sleeping with him. But there's not a whole hell of a lot I can do about it now."

"Would you do it again? Was it good?"

Kendall tried not to sigh in contentment, but the sound escaped her mouth anyway. "It was better than good."

"So I was wrong. Apparently bad driver doesn't equal bad lover."

"Not at all. Though he's not a bad driver, just having a rough patch."

"Defending him already. Uh-oh. You're going to sleep with him again, aren't you?"

"No, of course not." Which was bullshit and she knew it. "Okay, fine. I'd be lying if I said I wasn't ever going to go there again. I have a hard time resisting temptation. Plus I like to win."

Tuesday laughed. "Oh, sweetheart, welcome to my world. So go forth and have sex. I admit I would do the same damn thing."

"Oh, I'm not going to." She wasn't crazy.

"You just said you would," Tuesday pointed out.

"I didn't mean it." Kendall threw her hand up. "Shit, okay, I did. But I can't! It would be a huge mistake." Super huge. Enormous. Mega mistake. "I think I just need to stay away from him. That's a good coping strategy, isn't it?"

"It's as good as any, I guess." Not that Tuesday looked remotely convinced.

"Kendall!"

"Damn, I need to go. What are you doing here, anyway?"

"Interviewing some of the guys on the restrictor plate issue since we're coming up on Talladega, where speed can get out of hand. This is for an article, not my blog."

"Okay, I'll talk to you later. While I'm avoiding Evan. I

can do this." She took a step and glanced back at her friend. "I can do this, right?"

"Of course you can." Tuesday nodded with a big, overly cheerful smile.

Great. Tuesday didn't think she could do it. Kendall had avoided Evan ten years ago. She could do it now.

But why was that actually the last thing she wanted to do?

Kendall ignored the sensation in the pit in her stomach that was not hunger and went to talk to Jim. About her career. The only thing that mattered.

A week later Evan was thinking it wasn't all good, and he was wishing like hell he hadn't let Kendall leave his bedroom so easily. He had figured he would bump into her all over the place. He certainly had when he'd been trying to avoid her. But now that he wanted to see her, she was proving to be as slippery as a greased pig.

Even in Dover at the race, he hadn't had a chance to see her. She had disappeared promptly after drivers' introductions, and likewise after the race, after finishing a respectable twentieth. He had actually had a decent race himself, finishing tenth, which these days was a victory all on its own.

But now he was antsy, and he had woken up every morning with a raging hard-on from night after night of erotic dreams involving Kendall and her breasts. Kendall and her tongue. Kendall and her sweet, wet, inner thighs . . .

Evan walked into a watercooler and almost knocked it off the stand. Whoops. He caught it and prevented a disastrous explosion outside his team owner's office.

"Klutz" was Eve's opinion.

He was a lot of things. Klutz wasn't the worst of them. "So why does Carl want to have this meeting? You promised me I wouldn't be fired."

"I didn't promise you anything. I told you it was highly unlikely you would be relieved of your car, but that securing another sponsor needed to happen quickly. Carl and I have been talking and we've come to an agreement."

Evan stopped walking. "Wait a minute? You know what he wants to discuss and you haven't told me?"

His sister stared at him impassively, her hands in the pockets of her suit jacket. "I wasn't at liberty to discuss the details with you. It wasn't a sure thing, and it's not my place to make you the offer, it's Carl's."

There were times when he hated the business aspect of racing, and this was one of them. "You work for me, Eve, not Carl. What the hell is going on?"

"Yes, I do. And as your employee, it's my responsibility to seize opportunities for you as they arise. But if said opportunity is not allowed to be discussed, I can't discuss it."

Working with family was hell, because at the moment he wanted to fire Eve's ass, but knew he couldn't. There was nothing he hated more than being kept in the dark. It was like people either assumed he couldn't handle the truth, or didn't think he was entitled to it.

"I think after this meeting we need to redefine our working relationship."

Carl's office door opened and Kendall stepped out.

"What is she doing here?" Evan asked Eve, shocked and, admittedly, instantly aroused.

Kendall was wearing a dress. Damn. When had he ever seen her in a dress? It was a stretchy red thing, worn with black tights and heels that made her calves look amazing.

Without waiting for his sister's answer, he said, "Kendall."

She looked up and ground to a halt, her hand coming up to her throat. "Evan! Oh, hi. Wow. Hi. How are you?"

Unnerved by how much she was unnerved, Evan shrugged. "I'm fine. You had a meeting with Carl?"

She nodded, darting a glance back at the door, chewing her bottom lip. "Great seeing you, talk to you later."

Then she tried to rush past him.

Evan reached out and grabbed her arm. "Wait."

The look on her face as she stared in horror at his fingers wrapped around her arm deflated any arousal and confidence he had. "What?"

Leaning in a little so Eve wouldn't hear, he said, "Wait for me. I'd like to talk to you. I won't be that long."

"Oh, I can't. I have . . . stuff to do."

"We need to talk."

She blinked up at him, her eyes wide. "About what?"

"The other night."

"I don't think that needs to be talked about." She shook her head rapidly. "Neither does what Carl is about to tell you."

Alarm bells went off in his brain. "What the hell does that mean?"

"Nothing." Kendall yanked her arm out of his hold. "See you later."

The door to the inner office opened and Carl popped his head out. "Evan, Eve, great to see you. Come on in." Then he called over top of them, "See you this afternoon, Kendall. Thanks."

Kendall gave a stiff smile and waved, then beat a fast retreat. Evan was suspicious and suddenly feeling really uneasy. But he put on a smile and stuck out his hand to Carl. "Hey, Carl, it's good to see you. How are things going?"

"Good, good. Come on in. We have some exciting news."

Shooting a glance at Eve, who looked impassive as she

greeted Carl, Evan followed them into the plush office and took a seat in a big overstuffed chair in front of the desk.

"Let's get right to the point." Carl glanced at his watch. "I have a meeting in ten minutes. But I wanted to make sure you understand that Hinder Motors supports you and your team. We believe that despite some minor setbacks, you're a stellar driver, Evan."

He felt a flicker of relief. Carl wouldn't fire his ass after a comment like that, would he? "Thank you. I appreciate everything you and the whole operation has done for me. We're working some kinks out, but I feel confident we'll be on an upswing."

"Good. Your new sponsor will be thrilled to hear it."

"I have a new sponsor?" Now he really was relieved. "That's fantastic."

"Your sister and I hatched a plan and the SL Smith Corporation went for it."

Eve was smiling as Evan tried to recall what products that company sold.

"You know that Kendall Holbrook has Untamed for Women deodorant sponsoring her. You are now the male counterpart to that—Untamed for Men. SL Smith is sponsoring both of you and wants to do a whole commercial and media campaign featuring both of you together. Isn't that fantastic?"

Evan grinned at Carl. "That is fantastic."

Not only did he get a cool black car with some electric blue accents like the deodorant label, he was going to get to spend lots and lots of time with Kendall. That made him feel a little untamed himself.

"Fans are going to love it," Eve said, gushing a little.

Or at least gushing for Eve. Anything other than a sour face was a triumph for her, in Evan's opinion.

"Do you know how much attention and coverage you'll get? You can't put a price tag on that," she said.

"I'm grateful for the opportunity," Evan said, feeling a whole lot better about his career—and his sex life. "I won't let you down."

Nor was he going to let Kendall walk out of his bedroom with a thumbs-up the next time he had her in it.

KENDALL forced a smile for the cameras flashing in front of her and wondered what the hell was going on with Evan. She had expected that he would be furious over having to essentially piggyback on her sponsorship, but he had shown up grinning from ear and ear. He'd shaken hands with the deodorant people and her. Now he had his arm slung casually over her shoulder as they posed for pictures wearing Untamed Deodorant ball caps and each holding up a stick of the product.

Maybe he was just grateful to have any sponsorship that wasn't adult diapers or erectile dysfunction pills.

He certainly didn't seem aware of the fact that she was monstrously uncomfortable with him being so close to her. Nor was she thrilled about the fact that the SL Smith Corporation seemed to be implying that she couldn't sell product on her own. That her fan base wasn't big enough. They needed the gimmick of his and her deodorants.

"Can you move just a little closer to Mr. Monroe?" the photographer asked, his hand waving her over.

Trying not to roll her eyes, Kendall scooted a few inches closer to Evan, well aware of his arm, his leg, his shoulder, his entire essence right next to her. She could feel the heat radiating off of him under the hot photography lights. She could *smell* him and it wasn't the scent of Untamed deodorant. It was him. Just warm and earthy and . . . sexy.

Kendall grimaced.

"Can you smile a little more?" the photographer asked, indicating the corners of his own mouth. "You don't look very natural."

"I don't feel very natural," she muttered under her breath, forcing her mouth open in a big smile.

"Just relax," Evan told her, his hand coming up to rub the knot in her shoulder.

How he knew she had a knot there was beyond her, but the last thing in the world that was going to make it disappear was his hands on her body. Even just him touching her shoulder made her want to jump out of her skin. And into bed.

"I'm trying to." The golf shirt they had her wearing was too tight and Kendall tugged at the collar. She felt like she was choking.

"Put your hand down, please."

That little twerp was starting to irritate her. Kendall knew he was just doing his job, but she was trying to do hers. She wasn't a model. She was a driver. And Evan breathing down her neck smelling of eau du sexy wasn't helping at all.

The lights made her want to blink. The clothes felt stiff and unnatural. Holding up the deodorant made her feel cheesy. She hadn't been sleeping well for the past week, worrying that having sex with Evan had been a huge mistake and stressing over her qualifying laps for Bristol. Her car had been running tight, and she'd much rather have been in the garage than here in this studio being posed like a Barbie doll.

Like a cranky, stiff, sexually frustrated Barbie doll.

That was going to read well in print.

The rep from SL Smith was standing next to the photographer and he was frowning, his mouth turned down as he held his jaw and chin with one hand. He was wearing an expensive suit and was an attractive man in his mid-fifties. The kind who got better looking with age and scored a new, younger wife every decade or so.

"I realize this is just a press announcement shot," he started. "But . . ."

Great.

"Untamed is marketed at the fourteen- to thirty-four-year-old crowd . . . it's a sexy, young, vibrant deodorant."

How the hell a deodorant could be vibrant was beyond Kendall, but she just nodded at Mr. Suit.

"These shots are too traditional. Too forty-year-old-on-the-golf-course. Ladies-at-the-salad-luncheon kind of bullshit. We need to sex it up a bit. Take a ten-minute break and let's see what we can do here."

Sex it up? Was he kidding? Kendall felt the remnants of her fake smile disintegrate altogether.

"I can definitely do that with you, Jay," Evan murmured.

She turned and glared at him. "Don't tell me you're going to agree to this. And stop calling me Jay. It's a ridiculous nickname."

"Relax. It's just a publicity shot. They're not going to do anything more than have us sitting on a car wearing jeans instead of these stupid khaki pants. And I'm looking forward to seeing you in jeans . . . you have a hot—"

Kendall cut him off. "Keep your voice down, God!" She felt heat rising in her face as she glanced around to see if anyone had overheard their exchange.

"Why? It's not like they can't see you have a great ass."

"Are you trying to wreck your career?" Kendall asked him, incredulous about his casual attitude.

There was no time for him to respond because the corporate executive came back into the room holding the smallest tank top Kendall had ever seen in her life.

That better not be for her.

"This is for you, Kendall." He held the scrap of black cotton out to her. "The golf shirt looks too unnatural on you . . . like you work at a Best Buy or something. This should help you feel looser."

Looser being the key word.

Kendall had opened her mouth to tell him "hell no," when Evan yanked the shirt out of the guy's hands and held it up. It looked even more offensive dangling in the air, a V cut out in the front for cleavage display.

"There is no way Kendall is wearing this," he said flatly. "I won't allow it."

Which ticked her off even more than the idea of wearing the Untamed boobie top. And that had her pretty hopping mad.

"Excuse me?" she said quietly, narrowing her eyes at him as all the blood in her body rushed way past the boiling point. "What did you just say?"

EVAN was well aware that maybe his choice of words hadn't been the best. But he had seen that trashy tank top and had seen red. They were going to take Kendall's very impressive cleavage and make it the center of the shots. He had told her not to play down her gender, but damn, throwing her chest out there would totally send the wrong message to fans.

Plus he'd seen the way that SL Smith executive had been leering at Kendall all afternoon. Evan wasn't about to let that old pervert have imagery to spank his monkey with later.

So instead of dealing with the storm gathering on Kendall's face, Evan just turned to the executive and said, "To have her in a tank top like this and me in a golf shirt is ridiculous. I'm not doing shots like that."

Kendall startled him by ripping the tank top back out of his hands and physically stepping between him and the guy. "I'll handle this, thank you, Mr. Monroe."

Mr. Monroe? What was he, his dad?

"I'll need to put in a phone call and check with my PR rep and the team owner, Carl, to see if this type of advertising is acceptable to them. I'm new to the cup series and I'd hate to misstep with my boss. I'm sure you can appreciate that."

The SL Smith guy met Kendall's gaze and then nodded sharply. "Why don't we schedule a meeting with my people and your people for next week? We can use some of the shots we already have for the press release."

"Excellent."

Evan felt his admiration for Kendall increase tremendously. It was clear she was furious, yet she'd handled it swiftly and professionally. "I'd like to be a part of the meeting as well," Evan said. "If you plan on continuing to link my image with Kendall's."

If anything, he figured he and Eve could be a backup for Kendall, helping her stand firm about not doing cleavage shots. But he didn't think Carl would go for it anyway. He wanted a clean image for his drivers.

"We definitely plan to have a joint publicity campaign this season for the two of you. So I'll make some calls and set it up. Thanks for your hard work here today." SL Smith Guy, whose name Evan couldn't remember, shook his hand. "Enjoy the rest of your afternoon."

"Thanks." Evan watched him turn and shake Kendall's hand, then exit the studio. The photographer was already shutting off his lights. Kendall disappeared to the dressing room and reemerged with her duffel bag.

Without a word, she stomped off towards the parking lot.

Evan grabbed his own bag and jogged to catch up with her. "Hey, hey, wait up."

She whirled to face him. "Just leave me alone. Please?"

There were tears in her eyes, shocking him into halting in the middle of the parking lot. "What the hell is wrong?"

Brushing at her eyes, she said tightly, "Don't worry about it. It's no big deal."

Yet Evan knew her well enough to know it was a big deal. It looked like she was crying out of anger, and about way more than some stupid tank top. "You're clearly angry. Just let it out. Use me as a punching bag. You'll feel better, I swear. Especially if it's me you're mad at."

"I'm not thrilled with you," she admitted.

"I didn't mean what I said to sound like you couldn't take care of yourself. It just really pissed me off that he wanted the shot to basically focus on your chest. I half expected him to suggest the stick of deodorant should go *in* your cleavage." Evan was only half-joking.

"I know. It made me angry, too. I'm angry that you feel paternal, I'm angry that I'll always be nothing more than just the token girl of stock car racing, and I'm angry that I don't know how to do this."

Evan wanted to touch her, to try to calm her down, but he valued his life too much. For such a tiny woman, she gave off a lot of rage. "First of all, my feelings for you are not paternal. In any way. Do I feel protective instincts? Yes, of course I do. All men do for women they care about. Does that mean I want to dominate you or think you can't take care of yourself? Hell, no. It just means, plain and simple, I care about you and don't want you hurt or taken advantage of."

She crossed her bare arms and shivered in the March breeze, gazing off across the parking lot. "What are we doing, Evan? We shouldn't have had sex. That was stupid. I can't handle my life as it is, I don't need this complication."

It's not like his life was simple either, given that his season was a total suckfest. But it seemed to him she was making it more complicated than it needed to be. "Nothing needs to be a complication, Kendall. We just had fun, that's all. We're old friends, with great sexual chemistry, and I don't regret one second of the other night. But I'm not sure that's what's really bothering you. What did you mean when you said you can't do this? Do what? Race?"

Sighing, she dropped her arms, letting her duffel bag fall to the blacktop of the parking lot. "This media stuff. This being famous stuff. Driving is my thing. It's what I do best, it's what I love. But the rest? I'm clueless."

"Every rookie feels that way. It's overwhelming. Ask Elec how he mangled his way through his first few interviews. And I accidentally made an ass out of myself last season when I broke Pete Briggs's track record."

"It's more than that. It's this feeling that people are coming at me all the time, do you know what I mean? Not the fans . . . they're awesome. I love meeting them at events. It's all this business stuff, these photo shoots and signing merchandise, and following a schedule so rigid that sometimes I feel like I can't breathe. Like I just want to run away . . ."

The tears were in her eyes again. "God, I sound like such an ingrate. Here I have everything I've ever wanted and I'm complaining."

She looked so vulnerable that Evan did reach out and touch her. He wiped off the stray tear that had escaped on her cheek, and dropped his hand to her shoulder and massaged it. It was tight with tension. "Hey. You're not an ingrate. It's a demanding job, and we all have things we like and don't like about it. If you're feeling overwhelmed by the media attention, you just need to make sure you have a quiet place to get away to. You have to build in downtime, even if it's just half an hour."

"Easier said than done . . . I have all this pressure. I mean, my car is running tight, and we have Bristol coming up and you know I'm not particularly confident on that track, and my motor home is being repaired so I have to stay in a hotel off-site. It's just . . ." She pressed her fingers to her temples. "A lot."

Evan put his free hand on her other shoulder and kneaded through her Untamed golf shirt. "Been there, done that. But worrying about everything and anything doesn't change the situation or make it any better. If you need a place to stay at the track this weekend, you can stay with me."

And if she were so inclined as to have sex with him Sunday night after the race, even better.

But she snorted. "Are you nuts? Do you know what people would say?"

"That we're friends?" he said, even as he knew that was naïve. The whole racing world would conclude they were sleeping together, which they sort of kind of were. Or at least they had last week.

"They'll say we're knocking boots."

"We did knock boots," he told her. "Three times in one night."

Her face contorted. "Ugh. Which was such a bad idea. I mean, I don't have time for sorting out relationship crap on top of everything else."

Evan didn't think she even realized how revealing that statement was, but he did. She hadn't said "sex," or anything about closure of their past . . . she had said "relationship" in the present tense. Which despite the negative tone that had accompanied it, made him feel pretty damn hopeful. "Alright," he told her easily. "But you need to find time for a massage. Your shoulders are so tight I'm surprised you don't squeak."

They weren't even relaxing under his touch as he rolled his thumbs from her neck to her arm in slow, even strokes.

"Where am I going to find a massage therapist at," she glanced down at her watch, "eight at night?"

"I'm sure your assistant can find you one. Or you can just let me offer up my very talented hands." Evan leaned just a little closer to Kendall as ran his hands lightly down her arms, then back up again to her shoulders, her neck, sliding up the base of her skull with rhythmic pressure. "We can grab a bottle of wine, go somewhere quiet . . . It would be my pleasure to help you relax."

"You're not talking about a massage," she accused, even as her shoulders relaxed, and her eyes darkened with desire.

"Of course I am. I'll massage every inch of your body until you're so relaxed you're about to fall asleep with a smile on your face." Evan brushed his mouth over her ear and whispered, "Then with you still on your stomach, I'll lick between your thighs until you come, a relaxed and lazy orgasm . . . you don't even have to move. Then when you're sighing into your pillow, I'll push my cock inside you and I'll move slow and easy, and all you have to do is enjoy it."

Her breathing had hitched while he was speaking, and for a brief exciting moment, Evan thought she would say yes. But then she shook her head. "I'm not in the mood. Plus it will just complicate things even more than they already are."

Smart enough to know when to retreat, he just nodded. "Okay. I understand. Now why don't you get yourself home? It's freezing out here and your goose bumps have goose bumps."

She smiled. "Thanks, I will."

Then suddenly she leaned forward and kissed his cheek, a soft, intimate caress. "Thanks, Evan. You really can be a good guy."

Which made him want to shuffle his feet sheepishly like a little kid who's been given a compliment from his adult crush. The only difference was Evan had a boner accompanying his sheepishness.

"And you're a cool chick," he told her, retreating behind flippant. She wasn't the only one who wanted to bury her feelings from time to time. "And if I don't see you tomorrow, I'll see you in Bristol."

Her forehead creased. "Don't remind me. Plus on Monday we have the Untamed commercial shoot in Los Angeles. That's going to be awful."

"Hey, hey. One day at a time. And remember, if you want a place to stay, my motor home is your motor home." He winked at her. "I won't even expect sexual favors."

He expected an eye roll or a bristling reaction. But Kendall just lifted her eyebrows. "Monroe, if I'm going to stay in your motor home and have everyone think I'm sleeping with you, I'm damn well going to be sleeping with you."

That erection he'd been fighting went one hundred percent solid and he nearly groaned out loud. "Is that a yes?"

"No."

Then she walked away.

Damn, she was getting good at that.

And Evan was really starting to feel like he didn't like it.

*   *   *

"HOW'S it looking, David? Do I have the room?" Kendall asked her spotter over the radio as she kept her eyes on the number 48 car in front of her. She was going to pass him on the rim, but with the sharp banking on the track at Bristol she wanted reassurance she had room if she started to lose grip on her tires and float towards the bottom.

"You got it. Go for it."

With fifteen laps to go of five hundred, it was now or never, so Kendall waited until the driver in front of her hit the turn and started to find his line lower. She kissed the wall, took the turn then shot past him on the straightaway before he could block.

"Good job, Kendall," Jim, her crew chief, said, his voice crisp and clear over the radio. "You're heading into some traffic ahead."

She could see at least three cars battling to get into sixth place, and she narrowed her eyes, concentrating. This could very well be her best finish this year, since she was set right now to make it into the top ten. Not bad for a rookie driver, and she wanted it desperately.

It was a balmy sixty-three degrees in Tennessee, and the track was running smooth, the overcast sky removing the sun as a factor in visibility on the turns, and she was feeling confident.

"A little bit of a battle going on ahead," David said. "Monroe brothers are jockeying for fifth place now and it's some damn aggressive driving."

"How aggressive?" Kendall asked as she went low and maneuvered past the number 23 car, which was spitting smoke and losing speed.

"Like sibling rivalry aggressive. Elec won't let Evan pass. He's holding him off with everything he has and Evan's pretty unhappy about it . . . riding up way too close on him."

Somehow that didn't surprise Kendall, but it didn't thrill her. If they knocked each other, they could take her and half a dozen cars out with them. "What are they saying?"

With the crew chiefs capable of hearing all the drivers, Kendall wanted to know how serious this could potentially be, especially with only ten laps to go.

"Uhh . . . Evan told Elec to move the hell out of his way. Elec told him not a chance, and it would be a cold day in hell before he ever let him pass. Then Evan said something that is definitely going to get him a fine for his language."

"Fabulous. Thanks for the update, and pray we don't have a caution." If they needed to drop down for a caution lap, she was going to have to pit for gas, which would more than likely drop her ranking by five spots or more. She was sitting in a damn good position right now at eighth and she didn't want to give it up.

"Go high, go high," David urged her. "Evan tapped Elec and they're sliding."

Shit. Kendall reacted, moving up the track with the car right behind her, as they tried to avoid getting pulled into a wreck. To her left, she saw the number 56 car spinning, but then smoke smothered her visibility briefly. Sweat trickled down her back as she held on, controlling her car with everything in her.

"You got it, you're clear. Caution lap, go to pit," Jim said.

Just what she hadn't wanted to do. Giving a grunt of frustration, she asked, "Monroe brothers okay?" Jim didn't sound like it had been serious, but she wanted to make sure.

"Fine. Both are going to pit, but neither looks like they have any real damage to their cars."

"Good." Though she had every intention of smacking Evan when she saw him later. What the hell was he thinking?

His brother was clearly wondering the same thing, because after the checkered flag, with microphones stuck in his face, Elec wasn't holding back on his feelings. "Even though Evan is older than me, that doesn't always translate to maturity. That was some damn foolish driving."

Hot and exhausted, Kendall winced as she heard the words, but thrilled at her own eleventh place finish. Her best yet in the cup series and not bad, though it would have been better if Evan and Elec hadn't created a caution lap. But that was racing. You had to be aggressive to win, and sometimes someone else's screwup made you a winner, and sometimes it took you right out of the field. There was a lot of skill involved, but also a lot of luck. Being in the right or wrong place.

A reporter popped up in front of her as she unzipped her racing suit and peeled the sleeves off, the cool air refreshing on her hot body, her microfiber shirt stuck to her skin with sweat. "Congratulations on your finish, Kendall."

"Thanks, it was a good race. My team did a great job and the Untamed Chevrolet was running really well today." Mention the team in a positive light. Mention the sponsor. Mention the car manufacturer. Golden rules for a driver.

"What do you think of the Monroe brothers' dustup out there?" The reporter was a perky brunette, and Kendall wondered, as she frequently did, why the reporters down on the infield and in Victory Lane tended to be attractive women, yet the broadcasters and analysts were men.

"I have no idea what happened out there without seeing a replay, but it's an aggressive sport. We're all trying to pass each other." She hoped that was sufficiently noncommittal.

After a few more questions, she managed to disengage

herself so that she could go have some pictures taken and hopefully get a meal before heading back to her hotel. Not that there was any hurry. Getting away from the track with all the post-race traffic was going to take a while since she wasn't staying in the motor home lot.

She passed Eve Monroe, who was biting her lip and looking like she wanted to hurl. "Hey, Eve."

"Oh, hi, Kendall." Eve was glancing back and forth between her brothers, who were both talking to reporters, both looking pissed off. "Total disaster. Total friggin' disaster. I swear to God I'm going to have a heart attack. Why do they do this to me?"

Kendall was pretty sure the disagreement had nothing to do with Eve personally, but she could certainly understand her distress. This was a big deal. They were airing their grievances in public.

"You get Elec and I'll get Evan, okay?" she told Eve.

"Really? You'd do that?"

"Sure. When he's not annoying me, I like Evan." Especially naked. Or when he was rubbing her shoulders and reassuring her, helping her calm down. She could certainly do the same for him.

The question was how did she interrupt without being rude?

It turned out she didn't even need to. Just walking over in front of where Evan was standing talking to reporters, and hovering there for a second, got him to spot her and excuse himself. "Can you believe this shit?" he said to her as a greeting.

"Keep your voice down," she urged him. "Let's go back to your place and get something to eat, take a deep breath and go over this."

"Really? Thanks, Kendall. Good finish, by the way." He raked his hands through his hair. "But I mean, what the hell? My brother is a dick."

"Evan, seriously. Zip it." Kendall tied the sleeves of her jacket around her waist and started walking towards the compound. "Come on."

Unfortunately, Elec was doing the same thing, and as they entered the gated area of the drivers' motor homes, the brothers came face-to-face with each other.

Kendall looked around for help. Eve was nowhere to be found, and she didn't see anyone who could be of assistance.

This looked to be good times. She braced herself for the confrontation, which came immediately.

"You're an asshole," Evan said heatedly to Elec.

"And you're a crybaby," Elec said in an easy voice.

Evan *hated* that. He really, really hated that. Why couldn't his brother ever yell or get pissed off or emotional? He was just even, calm, cutting. Looking unruffled and like he was damn sure he was right. That had infuriated Evan since they were kids, and it had the same effect now.

"Shut up, Elec the Eyeball. You know what you did was shitty."

"Oh, there's a good comeback. Telling me to shut up while using my stupid childhood nickname. How original."

Knowing he was going to punch his brother, Evan took a step forward. And smacked into Kendall, who had inserted herself between them. Evan grabbed her shoulders when he knocked her off balance. "Kendall, step aside, babe."

"Take this inside," she said in a firm voice.

When he tried to step around her anyway, she moved again, still blocking him. "Inside, Evan." She turned to Elec. "I think you two should *talk* inside, out of earshot."

"Your place or mine?" Elec asked with an enigmatic smile that made Evan immediately want to knock it off his face.

"My place. I don't want to scream obscenities at you with your stepkids around."

"They're back in Charlotte, but whatever." Elec rolled his eyes.

Evan fisted his fingers and said, "Seriously, Elec, why didn't you just let me pass?"

"Why the hell would I let you pass? I was going for the win, just like you were."

"Because you were risking losing control by all that maneuvering to keep me from passing. You were reckless." Evan glared at his brother over his shoulder as he stomped across the gravel to his motor home.

"You were being reckless driving up my ass."

"Because you should have let me pass!"

"Why?"

"I just told you why." Evan yanked open the door and gestured for Elec to go first. "And because you're my brother and you should know that I need all the points I can get right now. You're having a great season and I'm not. You could have given one damn spot to me."

"You would never expect me to do that for any other driver, so why should I do that for you? Why do you get special favors? Instead, you should just try driving better, crybaby."

Crybaby. God, why did such a childish taunt make Evan see red? Elec still sounded completely unflappable, and Evan waited until Kendall had followed Elec into the motor home, then he slammed the door shut and dove at his brother's back. Elec wasn't ready for the hit and he went crashing into the coffee table, then dropped down onto the floor hard.

"Get off me, you dickhead!" Elec said, struggling to roll onto his back.

Evan ground his brother's face into the carpet. "That's for being a selfish prick. And for ruining my science project by pissing on it when I was in the third grade."

Somewhere in the back of Evan's mind it registered that this was ridiculous and petty, but it still felt really, really damn good to have his brother down, even as he could hear Kendall yelling at them to knock it off.

Elec got a hand back and made contact with Evan's chin, hard. "What are you, twelve years old?" his brother asked, as Evan saw stars. "More brawn than brains, always have been that way."

Then it was on, like Donkey Kong.

They were rolling and landing punches, knocking into furniture, and swearing like drunken sailors. Or very pissed off brothers.

Evan saw with satisfaction that he had managed to split his brother's lip, though they had destroyed two dinette chairs in the process, when the door slammed.

"What in the Sam Hill is going on here?"

Uh-oh. That was his mother's voice.

He and Elec both went still, breathing hard on their sides, Elec's hands fisted into Evan's driving suit. Neither one of them spoke, waiting for the wrath to fall.

"Oh, hello, Kendall," his mother said in much gentler tone. "How are you, sweetheart? You're having quite a rookie season."

"Thank you, ma'am."

"But I'm sorry you had to witness such a shocking and childish display of bullshit. I hope you weren't injured in any way by their raging stupidity."

"No, ma'am. I was just letting them work it out."

Evan shook Elec off of him and sat up, wiping his nose. Blood. Fabulous. He looked warily over at his mother, who was standing with her arms folded, her purse over her shoulder.

Eve was behind her. "I hate both of you," his sister said. "You're determined to kill me."

"Oh, stop being so overdramatic," his mother told her. "No one is trying to kill you."

Then she rounded on him and Elec. "But you two . . . if you weren't grown men, I'd paint your back porches red. I didn't raise you like this. Trash talking each other, to the media of all people! Running off half-cocked instead of talking about it. Rolling around on the floor like a couple of twelve-year-olds!"

"See?" Elec, who had sat up as well, nudged Evan's leg with his foot. "Told ya you were acting twelve."

"Oh, shut up." Evan smacked his brother's foot away.

"Knock it off!" his mother roared. "I'm ashamed of both of you. You—" Her finger shot out and pointed at Elec. "You are a married man. A father to two small children! This is not how you act to set an example for those babies. And you were sadly lacking in sportsmanlike conduct today."

Evan felt a little smug when he saw the pained expression cross his brother's face. Damn straight.

"And you." The finger swiveled to point in his face. Uh-oh. "You know better than to expect special favors from anyone. It's every man for himself out there, and you needed to ease up. Your reckless determination to pass Elec could have seriously injured someone. And this foolishness is just that—the actions of a fool. You are never going to get a woman if this is how you behave."

Wonderful. Just what every man wants his mother to say

in front of the woman he's sort of sleeping with. A glance at Kendall showed she was fighting back a smile.

Furthermore, he knew his mother was right. He shouldn't expect Elec to make things easier for him just because he was having a rough season. Nor should he be driving that aggressively, especially based on emotion.

"Maybe I should head on out," Kendall said, undoing her jacket sleeves from her waist and pulling them back up onto her arms, making her chest do a lovely forward jut for a second.

"No, no, please don't go." Evan stood up and despite still feeling irritated, extended his hand to his brother to help him up. "We're finished. I'm sorry, Elec. That was uncalled for."

Elec took his hand and stood up. "I apologize, too. I was being stubborn on the track."

They clapped each other on the shoulder and that was it. If his brother thought he was going to grovel, he could kiss his ass.

But he knew he had to say the right thing to his mother. "You're always right, Mom. I'm sorry my behavior embarrassed you and Dad." He gave her a loud, smacking kiss on the top of her head, which he knew would cause her to melt a little. "What would we do without you?"

"Kill each other." Her shoulders relaxed, but she still gave him a stern look. "Y'all are going to have to make pretty in front of the cameras."

"I will. I say on Friday at qualifying me and Elec make a big show of joking around and hanging out. Then we'll do some interviews where he'll apologize for calling me immature."

Evan had to admit that was the one label that got under his skin and stuck there. Was he immature? He thought he was mostly just impulsive, emotional. Just because he tended to explode, because he felt things so deeply, and desperately avoided entanglements that might hurt him didn't make him immature. Did it?

"Right when you apologize for calling me a thick-headed mule."

They eyed each other warily. It almost sounded like Elec was itching to fight again.

"I really should go," Kendall said, gesturing towards the door and looking monstrously uncomfortable. "I have to get back to my hotel and get some sleep. I have a four A.M. flight to LA out of Knoxville."

"No, no, don't go." He almost added that everyone else was leaving, but his mother would have killed him for saying something so rude. He didn't need to tick her off any more today than he already had. "I was planning to fire up the grill and cook some steaks."

How desperate did he sound? He was offering to cook beef for the woman.

"Thanks, but I do need to go." Kendall started for the door. "Good to see you, Mrs. Monroe. Elec. Eve."

Evan followed her and stepped outside with her, shutting the door behind him. "Can I call you a cab or something? How are you getting to your hotel?"

"My driver is here. I'll text him and find him. Thanks for the offer . . . another time."

What did that mean exactly? The cab, dinner, sex . . . Evan had no clue. "I'll see you in LA tomorrow. I have the next flight after you. I'll be sliding in right when they need us at nine A.M."

"Shouldn't you go to bed then?"

"I need to eat. A lot. Then I'll go to bed. Alone, unfortunately." He gave her what he hoped was a charming smile. "Unless you change your mind?"

"Nice try."

Then Kendall shocked the hell out of him by leaning forward and giving him a kiss. Not one on the cheek, like she had the other day, but full on the mouth. It wasn't a lingering kiss, but it was no sisterly smooch either.

He barely had time to wrap his arms around her and kiss back when she was pulling away. Spinning on her heels, she called out, "See you tomorrow."

Then she was gone.

Evan was confused. And horny. Until the breakup, it had never been this complicated with Kendall back in the day. They had dug each other and that was that. Now it felt like they were playing a game he didn't know the rules to.

Which he didn't like one damn bit.

When he stepped back into his coach, all voices stopped mid-sentence.

"What?" he asked his family as they all stared at him, expressions guilty. "What were you saying about me?"

"Are you dating Kendall?" his mother asked.

"No." He shot Eve a glare. She had to have been the one to narc on him. "We've become friends again, that's all." They weren't dating. You couldn't call it that.

"After what happened before? Oh, Evan, she broke your heart."

Evan sighed. "Mom, that was a million years ago. Does anyone want a steak or what? Because I need to eat before I get really cranky."

"If you marry Kendall Holbrook you'll never give me grandchildren. She's just starting her career, she's not going to want to stop and have babies."

A throbbing started behind Evan's eyes. "Mom. I am not going to marry Kendall Holbrook."

He could barely keep Kendall in the same room with him.

He wasn't going to marry anyone. That's what he'd been saying for years and he meant it.

Because he hated to admit it, but if it wasn't going to be Kendall, he wasn't sure he wanted to do it.

CHAPTER
NINE

KENDALL cracked open her fourth Red Bull and took a sip.

"Are you sure you want to drink another one of those?" Kendall's personal assistant, Frankie Halliday, gave her a questioning look, eyebrows raised behind her cat-eye glasses.

Frankie was in her early fifties, was more stylish than Kendall could ever hope to be in six lifetimes, and had a steady stream of men through her life. She was efficient and breezy and had everything anyone could ever need in her expensive handbag, yet always produced a needed item with zero digging.

She was an excellent personal assistant, but at the moment, Kendall wanted Frankie, the cab, and the entire world to disappear around her. She desperately needed some sleep, but hadn't been able to get any in her hotel room because an amorous couple next door had still been going strong when her alarm went off at 2 A.M. Then on the plane to LA she had gotten the aisle seat next to a man who had snored violently the entire flight. If she had to guess, she'd say she had slept a grand total of an hour, coming off of a race day.

Hence the Red Bull.

"If I don't drink this, I'm going to take a facer in the middle of the commercial shoot. Or at the very least I'll be standing there staring vacantly at the camera, no clue what my lines are."

"Do you have your lines yet?"

"No. Again, the reason for the Red Bull." She held the can up in salute as the cab pulled up to the production studio. "They said they would be easy and that there would be a teleprompter. But I don't believe them."

Kendall also didn't believe that she was going to be able to make her feet stop jiggling up and down anytime soon.

"There is hair and makeup, I'm assuming?" Frankie reached into her bag and withdrew a lipstick, which she put on flawlessly without the use of a mirror.

"Why? Do I look that bad?"

"You don't look good."

If that was how the person she paid responded, Kendall shuddered to think what the average person would think of her appearance at the moment. "I've been awake for forty-eight hours. More than that. It's not my fault. And this is Untamed deodorant. Maybe this is the look they're going for."

"What look is that? The three-day bender?"

"No. Wild and free . . . sort of tousled and fresh out of bed. Untamed."

"Unclaimed is more like it." Frankie paid the driver and opened her cab door.

"Hey. That was just rude." Kendall put her hand to her chest. Her heart was racing a little faster than was strictly normal. "I don't look that bad."

Except when she walked in, the director introduced himself as Jonathan Anderson Catsgow and then turned and shouted, "Makeup!"

He smiled at Kendall. "We'll just freshen you up a bit."

"Thanks, I was driving yesterday—I came in eleventh place, by the way, which is pretty good—and then I had to fly here overnight and I didn't get any sleep at all, but I do respond well to concealer if you want to dab a little of that under my eyes—"

Jonathan cut her off. "We got it, hon. No worries."

A man with aggressively spiked hair and a lip ring stepped up and frowned at Kendall. "Oh, Lord. Okay, no problem, I can do this."

That was reassuring. Even a trained makeup artist was doubting he could make her look anything less than grotesque.

"Remember the look I want."

"Got it, got it. Kendall, right this way, please. I'm Trevor and I'm going to make you gorgeous."

"Good luck," Frankie said.

Kendall glared at her, but Frankie was playing on her phone and didn't notice.

Trevor plopped her down on a chair, ripped her purse out of her hand, and tossed it onto the counter. Hunching down, he scrutinized her for so long Kendall squirmed uncomfortably in her seat.

Clutching her Red Bull, she took another giant swallow, then said, "What? Is there a problem, Trevor?" Damned if she'd flown all night to have some hair-gelled twenty-two-year-old staring at her like she was gum on the bottom of his shoe.

"No, no. You're actually quite beautiful. Lovely cheekbones. Exotic eyes."

No one had ever called her eyes exotic before. "Trevor, you're my new best friend."

"And damn, what a rack." He eyed her chest. "How much did those run you?"

Or not her best friend. "They're natural!"

"I can back her up on that one," Evan said, strolling in looking well rested and generally pleased with the world. How he did that was beyond her. He'd had a lousy finish the day before, engaged in a public pissing match with his brother, then a private fistfight with Elec, and had probably gotten the same amount of sleep she had. Yet here he was, looking sexy and adorable and talking about her breasts with a roomful of hair and makeup professionals.

"Really?" Trevor asked Evan. "They totally have a roundness that you just don't see in nature."

"Trust me. They've been like that since before her eighteenth birthday. Totally hers."

"Do you mind not talking about my breasts?" Kendall went to take another sip of her Red Bull and hit her tooth with the rim. "Oww."

Evan leaned against the counter and studied her. "How many of those have you had, babe? You look a little jittery."

"Maybe it's because you're talking about my breasts like they're the weather forecast. And aside from being totally offensive, you're giving the impression we're in a relationship."

"I was just trying to prevent an implant rumor starting up, but alright, I apologize." Evan leaned over and kissed her on the forehead, his fingers lightly brushing her hair off her cheeks. "I wish you had stayed with me last night."

It must have been the lack of sleep, but Kendall thought he looked amazingly hot leaning over her in a T-shirt, a ball cap on his head, his breath smelling like coffee and cinnamon. The way he looked at her, like he wanted to just lick her from head to toe, made her heart race even faster than it did on Red Bull, and her insides went warm and squishy. "I wouldn't have gotten any sleep if I had stayed with you."

He grinned, a slow, lazy, arrogant smile that had her nipples hardening and her fingers twitching to touch him. His crotch was only inches from her hand and she desperately wanted to reach out and stroke the front of his jeans.

"But you would have had more fun if you'd stayed with me."

There was no doubt about that. She'd have been having an orgasm instead of listening to one.

But no need to swell his head. "Maybe."

Evan laughed. "I can prove it."

The loud clapping of hands startled Kendall.

"I hate to break up your early morning flirt, but I need to get to work here," Trevor said. "If you want to talk dirty to each other, send a text. You can sext and have your hair done at the same time."

Embarrassed, Kendall put her hand on Evan's chest and pushed him backwards. "No sexting, Monroe. We're doing this commercial and then I'm going to bed. In and out, we're done."

Evan laughed. Trevor's eyebrows shot up.

Her cheeks flushed. "I mean, the commercial! In and out, quickly, we'll be done. *Then* I'm going to the hotel and sleeping for eight hours before flying home. That's what I meant."

"Whatever, doll baby," Trevor said. "Doesn't matter to me as long as you let me at those eyebrows."

"What's wrong with my eyebrows?" Kendall had a very real fear of waxing. Ripping hair out of skin just seemed abusive. Self-mutilation. Unnecessary. And mostly, she imagined it just hurt a lot.

"Just a little trimming and shaping. Nothing major." Trevor shoved a fashion magazine in her hands. "Here, read this. Relax. And for the love of God, stop bouncing your leg up and down like that. Your whole body is vibrating."

Was she bouncing her leg? Kendall looked down. She was. She made it stop. But then she started tapping the arm of the chair with her fingers. And biting her lip. While turning her foot in circles. She ignored the magazine in her hands.

"I don't think Kendall knows how to relax," Evan told Trevor. "I would just slap some makeup on as fast as you can."

Kendall was about to open her mouth and deliver a scathing response when he added, "Besides, she doesn't need any makeup. She's gorgeous the way she is."

Well, that was sweet. Kendall stopped twitching her fingers quite so violently as she contemplated Evan's many good qualities. He was thoughtful and funny and loyal and so very, very sexy . . .

Trevor rolled his eyes. "Says the man who is playing hide the salami with her."

Trevor most definitely was not her best friend. In fact, she kind of didn't like him.

She was bordering on hating him twenty minutes later when she looked in the mirror and saw that somehow she'd entered into the Valley of the Dolls.

"Oh, my God."

"It's fab, isn't it?" Trevor asked, beaming behind her, hands still playing with her hair.

Her giant hair.

Her enormous, teased, massive, seven-foot-wing-span hair.

"I look like I fell into a seventies porno!" Kendall turned her head sideways, hoping that would help. It didn't. The bizarre thing was Trevor hadn't used a lot of hair spray, so it looked fairly natural. Just gigantic. "What am I supposed to be wearing?"

"Denim shorts, a tube top, and stilettos."

Not in this lifetime. Kendall shook her head so rapidly her vision blurred. "No. No, no, and no. No denim shorts. No shorts. No tube top. I'll wear the stilettos but that's it."

Evan came up beside her, a pastry in his hand, wearing sexy jeans and a black ribbed tank top. "You're wearing nothing but shoes? That will sell a lot of deodorant."

Kendall shoved Trevor's primping hands away from her hair and jumped up out of the chair. She couldn't sit still for another minute. "Very funny. I'll wear jeans. And a cute top, but not a tube top. Forget it."

"Why are you telling me? I'm not in charge of this gig. Nice hair, by the way. I think I had a poster on my bedroom wall of a chick with hair like that when I was thirteen."

Glaring at him, she yanked the pastry from his hands and took an oversized bite, closing her eyes as the icing melted on her tongue. Sugar made it better.

"I don't think you need any more sugar," Frankie said, strolling into the room looking very chic and modern and completely unslutty, unlike Kendall. "You're already hopped up on Red Bull."

"I am not. Frankie, tell the powers that be that I'm not wearing a tube top in this commercial."

"Of course you're not wearing a tube top." Frankie looked

at her like she was clinically insane. "Carl would birth a cow if you did that."

Kendall turned to Trevor. "Were you yanking my chain?"

"I was told tube top." He threw his hands up in the air. "Very *Dukes of Hazzard*."

"No tube top." Feeling a little weird and off-kilter, Kendall threw her arms back and forth and sang, "No tube top for me, you'll see."

Evan grinned. "You need a nap."

"What I need is another Red Bull." She snapped her fingers in the air in a diva imitation. "And another pastry, but I just want the icing this time."

She really felt strange, like she was having a bit of an out of body experience. It made her bolder than she probably would have been ordinarily, though maybe a touch less professional. "Trevor, you've got to tone down the hair. People are going to think they hired an actress to play me."

"No big hair?" Evan asked. "I kind of like it."

"Even more reason to get rid of it."

Evan waved another pastry in front of her. Where the hell was he getting those from? Kendall really wanted one. He held it right in front of her mouth, tipping it so that the icing touched her lip and clung there. Kendall licked it off, watching his eyes darken.

"Just as long as you don't get rid of me," he murmured. "I'll keep you in cherry pastries indefinitely."

Kendall couldn't think of a retort. Couldn't think to tell him how totally inappropriate he was being in a semi-public situation. Wasn't sure what he even meant. Was he talking sex or something more? Her Red Bull brain couldn't handle the puzzle.

All she could think as she sucked the remaining sugar off

her bottom lip was that the taste of Evan and a cherry pastry on her tongue would make for a very happy day.

EVAN knew he was taking advantage of Kendall's lack of sleep and overconsumption of caffeine. She was acting downright loopy, and he had to admit it was amusing to watch her. He had a feeling if he nailed one of her feet to the floor, she would just run in a circle. With her big hair. The hairstylist had tamed it a little, but it still had a volume Evan had never seen outside of beauty pageants on TV. In the late eighties.

"Okay, so what I need you to do is to lean on the car, ankles crossed, looking sexy," the director told Evan.

He could try to do that. He did feel a little self-conscious. Posing sexy wasn't natural. You just *did* sexy when you were attracted to someone. Which was why he was glad Kendall was in the studio with him. It made playing the part a lot easier when he had her to look at.

Leaning on the car—which was a generic Untamed deodorant car—Evan tried to relax and get in the mood the director wanted.

Kendall was bouncing up and down on the balls of her feet across the set, making popping sounds with her lips. They had compromised on her outfit. She was wearing jeans, heels, and a tank top, but she had a racing jacket on over it. It was full coverage everywhere, yet it was smoking hot. It was a lot of tight and a lot of tease.

"Now Kendall, you're just going to walk up to Evan and deliver your line. Okay?"

Kendall nodded, cracking all her knuckles loudly.

This was going to be interesting. Evan tried to stay loose, watching Kendall as she strolled across the set, which was supposed to be a parking lot. "Hey, there," she said, then stopped in front of him, her face scrunching up.

Oh, God, she was going to laugh. Evan bit his own lip and narrowed his eyes.

"I'm sorry." She turned to the director. "I just looked at Evan and I forgot the line."

"Cut."

They repeated the process, only this time Kendall tripped halfway. She burst out laughing, and Evan did, too.

The third time, she got all the way through her lines. "Hey, there," she said, her voice a low and sultry purr. "If you're going to be in The Chase, you need to be . . . Untamed."

At which point Evan laughed. He couldn't help it. The whole thing was so cheesy. Kendall was right. It was like a seventies porno. If this were an adult film, she would be going down on him on the hood of the car after delivering that lame line.

Of course, she had gone down on him on the hood of a car. But not for cameras, and not after that ridiculous line.

"Cut." The director sighed.

They tried it eight more times, until Evan's butt was numb from leaning on the car.

"Take five," the director said, running his hand across his shaved head. "God, this is not going well."

"I'm sorry," Kendall said.

"Don't apologize," Evan told her in a low voice. "This is stupid. We just need better lines. Like, 'Hey. Don't be a stinky chick. Wear Untamed.'"

Kendall tried to pat her big hair down flatter. "No kidding. Or something like 'Own it. Wear it.' You know, straight to the point."

"When it's hotter than a crotch outside, wear Untamed."

She nodded enthusiastically, her laughter ringing out in the studio. "When you're sweating like a whore in church, wear Untamed."

Evan grinned. "Good call."

Then he couldn't resist touching the edge of her racing jacket, tugging her a little closer, bringing her in between his legs. He liked her in his space, he liked the scent of her skin, and the heat of her body. "For life's hottest moments . . . Untamed."

Her gaze met his and her laughter died out. She licked her lips and bent down towards him, like she was going to kiss him.

Evan went instantly hard, his hand snaking around her waist.

Then she seemed to realize where she was and she snapped straight up. "Sorry."

"Don't be!" The director started clapping. "I'm going to roll that back, but people, I think we have a wrap."

What the shit? "What are you talking about?" Evan moved Kendall and her Texas-sized hair out of the way so he could see the guy's face. "We were just joking around."

"And we happened to still being taping, thank God. That was amazing! Perfect. The sexual tension between you two was fabuloso."

"But I just made that line up." Evan felt a little stunned. This wasn't good. That wasn't going to hang well with Carl. And everyone in America would see that there really was something between him and Kendall. Either that or assume that the two of them were willing to fake it for cash, which weirded him out. Actors faked romance for the camera. Stock car drivers did not.

The other guys would give him hell for this.

And Kendall would kill him. Cut his balls off.

Except when he looked at her, Kendall just looked relieved. "We're done? Hallelujah. Can I change?"

Her eyes looked a little glassy, and Evan suddenly wondered if she might actually faint. "Hey, you okay, babe?"

"I think I'm sleepwalking," she told him. "It's like my body is separate from my head. Or my face. Or something." Her arms waved around. "Parts aren't working right together."

"Alright. I'm taking you back to the hotel. Hang in there. We'll be there as soon as possible."

"Are you going to tuck me into bed?" She gave him a loopy grin.

"Yes." And under no circumstances was he going to take advantage of her weakened state to talk her into making love to him.

He didn't think.

CHAPTER
TEN

EVAN looked down at Kendall, completely passed out in his lap in the cab, and fought the urge to run his fingers through her enormous hair. She looked so young and sweet and vulnerable, her cheek on his thigh, her fingers clasped into praying hands on his knee. If anyone should be praying at the moment it was him.

Looking at her, seeing her eyelashes flutter in her sleep, her lips slightly open as she breathed deeply in and out, Evan was feeling emotions he shouldn't. She looked eighteen again. Back then, she had lain in his lap like this when they watched TV together and he had felt so strong, masculine, so protective of her. Kendall could take care of herself, then and now, but he liked the idea of being there for her. Of having her back.

Very, very dangerous feelings.

His hand reached out when he couldn't resist the impulse any longer.

"Don't touch her," Kendall's assistant said next to him.

Evan froze with his hand out, feeling like a kid caught reaching to swipe his finger through the icing on a cake. "Excuse me?"

"Seriously. Don't touch her. This day is disastrous enough."

Trained to consider where his words might end up, Evan glanced towards the cabdriver, but the driver was talking on his wireless headset in a foreign language. "How is my brushing her hair off her face disastrous?" And why was it any of this woman's business?

"Look. I know who you are, who your family is. I've been in this business a long time. I may be just a personal assistant but I've seen everything. I mean, everything." She pushed up her glasses and held out her hand. "Frankie Halliday. I used to work for Martin Fairfax before he retired."

"Evan Monroe. It's a pleasure to meet you." Evan shook her hand, impressed with the firm grip. "Fairfax was a legend."

"And a horn dog. I can't tell you how many indiscretions I had to cover up for him. But owners, fans, the media, they forgive a man . . . they're harder on a woman. It's just a fact. And Kendall is special. She's breaking the glass ceiling here. A whole generation of little girls will be watching her and dreaming of the day they can drive their own race car."

Elec's seven-year-old stepdaughter, Hunter, popped into Evan's head. There was a girl who was itching to grow up and drive. "I agree. Kendall is special."

"She's showing the industry you can be feminine and still kick ass on the track. And I'm not going to have her career compromised by rumors and a bunch of white noise bullshit."

Frankie was pretty damn smart, and more than a little scary. "I would never do anything to hurt Kendall."

"Which is why, if you want to spend time alone with her in her hotel room, you will not carry her up there yourself, or walk up there with her yourself. You will enter the hotel separately, wait an appropriate amount of time, then go to her room."

He liked the way Frankie thought. "She'll be asleep. She'll never hear me knocking."

"But I can give you a key."

His eyebrows shot up. "Are you serious? Why would you do that?"

"Because Kendall deserves to have a little fun." She opened her handbag and pulled out a condom.

Evan hadn't blushed since the sixth grade, but he came dangerously close to doing it with that foil packet thrust at him by this total stranger. "Kendall's on the pill," he told her. Then realized he shouldn't know that.

But Frankie still gave him the condom. "That I know. What I don't know is where your disco stick has been."

Now he was really embarrassed. "Nowhere."

"Uh-huh."

When feeling uncertain, turn it around and make the other person feel uncertain, too. That was his theory. "Aren't you worried you could get fired for this? I mean, what if Kendall really doesn't want me in her room?" Evan gave her a grin. "I know, it's hard to believe a woman wouldn't want me around, but Kendall can be stubborn."

"I know she does, because before she passed out she told me if she had a little more sleep she would jump your bones."

Speaking of bones. Evan's cock shot up at attention at those words. "Really? She mentioned me?"

"Not something she would normally have done, but she's at the end of her tether. So no, I'm not worried I'm going to get fired. Just don't suck in bed."

With that, she opened the door as they pulled up to the hotel. Patting Kendall on the leg, she said, "Come on, up and at 'em!"

"Huh?" Kendall's eyes opened and she shot up. "Oh, my God, where am I?"

"In the cab. We just got to the hotel," Evan told her. "Time for you to go in and take a real nap."

She rubbed her eyes in a way that was so freaking adorable Evan wanted to kiss her. Repeatedly. But Frankie reached out and took Kendall's hand.

"Come on," she said. "Bed is calling."

"I feel like ass" was Kendall's response as she shuffled out of the cab. She turned back to Evan. "See you later?"

Evan smiled, slow and easily. "Oh, yeah. Definitely."

And he couldn't wait.

KENDALL felt warm and relaxed as she dozed in and out sleep. She had no idea what time it was, nor was she really even aware of where she was. It just felt fabulous to float in semiconsciousness.

Part of her registered that something was off, but she ignored that niggling thought and snuggled deeper under the covers. When lips brushed over her shoulder, it seemed somehow normal, as if she were dreaming.

Rolling over, she started to move into the curve of the body next to hers.

Then her eyes flew open.

Wait a minute.

No one should be in bed with her.

Yet Evan was curled up next to her, looking like he belonged there. "I'm sorry, did the TV wake you up? I can turn it off."

Kendall frowned, glancing around the room. It was dark outside, or at least the drapes were snuggly shut. She wasn't sure which. The glow of the TV bounced light around the dim room. She didn't even remember getting into bed. Patting herself under the covers, she was reassured that she was wearing a T-shirt and panties at least. Then again, she didn't remember changing.

"Did I overdose on Red Bull?" she asked him, aware of a sticky sweet taste lingering in her mouth.

"I don't think that's possible. But you did crash. Hard. You fell asleep in the cab."

She vaguely remembered waking up briefly in the elevator, but honestly, that was it. Scary. "Maybe I haven't been getting enough sleep."

"You think?" He rolled his eyes at her.

Evan wasn't under the covers with her. He was sitting on them in his jeans and T-shirt, barefoot, propped against the headboard.

"Why are you in my room?" If she was dressed, mostly, and he was dressed, entirely, then she doubted somehow they had had sex while she was half-asleep. Besides, she was damn certain that no matter how tired she was, she would remember if that man's penis had penetrated her.

The thought of which made her grow a little warm under the heavy blanket.

"You were so out of it, it actually worried me a little. I'm just checking on you."

"How did you get in here?" Kendall felt like she was

missing a whole vat of information. Like why Evan had appointed himself her keeper.

"Frankie gave me a key."

Kendall stopped mid-yawn, outraged at her staff member. "She can't do that!"

"Don't blame her. I bullied her into doing it. And don't worry. No one saw me come in here, so there won't be any gossip."

That hadn't even occurred to her. Now that he'd brought it up, though, she suddenly felt worried. Along with irritated over Frankie betraying her. Frustrated with her inability to process sugar without blacking out. And stressed over the fact that she was clearly running on empty these days.

Not to mention the little question of what the hell she was doing with Evan Monroe. She had flirted with him at the commercial shoot.

"Hey. Stop worrying. Everything is cool."

"How do you know I'm worrying?"

"Your pretty little face is squinching up."

"Squinching?"

"Yeah. Like this." Evan made a face, his mouth and nose lifting, eyebrows drifting together. It wasn't a good look.

Kendall laughed. "Shut up. I don't look like that."

"Yes, you do."

"What time is it?"

"It's eight."

"P.M.?" Kendall looked to her wrist, like a watch was suddenly going to materialize there. "Are you serious? Oh, my God, I slept for . . ."

"Over eight hours."

"Wow." Kendall stretched a little, feeling very lazy and

content under the covers. "Of course now I probably won't be able to sleep the rest of the night."

Then she realized immediately the opening she had just given him. She put her hand out in front of his already opening mouth. "Don't even say it. I'm not sleeping with you. In fact, you should probably go. I'm clearly fine."

Evan eyeballed her. "You are most definitely *fine*."

"Be quiet." It was a knee-jerk reaction, but the truth was, she appreciated the naked desire on his face.

"Do you really want me to leave for real?" Evan sat up on the bed, his expression very sincere. "I will if you do."

Kendall hedged. There was something nice about having his body heat and goofy grin next to her. Not only was she burning the candle at both ends, she was spending the vast majority of her time with paid employees. Other than an occasional chat with Tuesday, she was work, work, work. Except for the night she'd spent with Evan, she hadn't been having a whole lot of fun.

"You don't have to."

"That's just a begrudging concession to politeness." Swinging his legs around, Evan stood up.

Kendall thought about trying to fall back asleep alone. Thought about watching TV alone. Thought about showering alone.

And she blurted out, "Stay. Please. For the night."

Evan stopped cold. He turned around, and when she thought he would have teased her, he simply said, "Okay."

As he settled back onto the bed, she asked, "Don't you need your bags?"

"Nah." Evan actually pulled the covers back and slipped under them. "I can sleep in my boxers. I can strip my jeans off in a bit."

Or he could strip naked. Kendall was very aware of the fact that she wasn't wearing any pants as Evan settled into bed next to her, and she found herself craving a cuddle.

God, she was seriously stressed out if she needed arms around her to stave off the loneliness.

"Do you want some room service?" he asked, reaching over for the book on the nightstand. "You must be starving."

She was. For all manner of things. Lying on her side, Kendall wondered if she had the guts to go after him a second time. She had initiated sex the week before. Well, he had kissed her. But it was her who had jumped him on her car at the track. Then she had turned him down both times he had suggested sex after that.

At the moment, he didn't look like he was going to offer a third time. He looked perfectly content staying clothed, watching the Discovery Channel, and eating a burger and fries with her.

But she wanted more than that. Crazy or not, stupid or not, she knew what she wanted, and it was Evan.

Again.

"Sure, I could eat." Kendall shifted closer to him, leaning against his side and his chest on the pretense of looking at the menu in his hands.

Evan cleared his throat. "What are you in the mood for?"

"Something hot."

Evan paused at Kendall's words. She could mean soup. Or she could mean sex. He seriously hoped it was not that she was having a hankering for lentil soup. "I can see what kind of soup they have," he said, trying to sound casual.

He wasn't feeling it, though. Ever since he had come into Kendall's room and seen her sleeping, her face somehow worried even in her sleep, he had been feeling an odd assortment of emotions. Tenderness. Compassion.

And good old-fashioned lust.

He could admit he'd lifted those covers earlier and discovered Kendall was only wearing a T-shirt and panties.

"Mm," she said in a noncommittal voice, propping her head up with her hand. "How long does it take for room service to arrive?"

"Usually thirty minutes."

Her foot slid along his leg, her thigh making contact with his. "Just order me a cheeseburger and some chocolate cake if they have it."

"Okay. Do you want a drink, too?"

"Just water is fine."

"Probably a good idea for you, Miss Red Bull."

He expected her to stick out her tongue at him. Roll her eyes at the very least. Or make a smart remark. But instead she just made a contented sound in the back of her throat, a sexy, sleepy sigh that was like fingers sliding down his cock. Kendall looked beautiful lying in bed, her hair still fuller than normal, an endorsement for the hair spray Trevor had used given that it had held through a marathon sleep session. There were still smudges of eyeliner above and under her lids, giving her a smoldering tousled bedroom look.

She looked so lazy and content it did seem as if she had just spent the afternoon being made love to.

"That was the best nap I've ever had in my entire life," she said, sighing again.

God, it was seriously like she was talking about sex. Everything about her was screaming sex, and Evan remembered what Frankie had told him. Kendall wanted to jump his bones. Just because she wasn't actually making a move didn't make that any less true. Kendall had made the move last time. It was his turn.

Okay, and so technically he had asked her twice after that to have sex with him and she'd shot him down, but what was a little rejection? Given the state of his career, by all accounts he should have no ego left whatsoever, but he did. He could handle it if Kendall said no. In fact, he totally expected her to say no, but hey, you never got anything if you didn't ask for it.

Evan picked up the phone and tossed the room service book onto the nightstand. "Is there anything else you want? On or off the menu?"

Her eyes widened, but it was a mock innocence. "What do you mean?"

"We have thirty minutes until the food gets here."

The room service operator picked up. Evan said hello and placed an order for a turkey club sandwich and fries for himself, using his free thumb to reach over and stroke across Kendall's bottom lip. Now her wide-eyed stare was genuine. Trailing down her jaw, to her shoulder and beyond, Evan found her nipple through the cotton of her T-shirt.

"Yes, and a cheeseburger with fries please." Listening to the operator, he made circles over her nipple as Kendall's eyes darkened. "What kind of cheese, Jay? American okay?"

She nodded. "Sure." Her voice was breathy.

"American, yes, thanks. And a slice of chocolate cake for dessert." Evan pinched Kendall's nipple hard, enjoying the gasp she gave. He loved her breasts, their fullness, perfect shape, very responsive nipples.

"Just a water and a Coke please." Evan was running on empty himself, and unlike Kendall he hadn't napped, knowing he would then be up all night. A beer would just put him straight to sleep, and it was a few hours before he wanted to crash. There were some things he intended to do before he passed out.

Trailing his thumb down from her nipple over her abdomen, Evan slid it across the silkiness of her panties, up and down over her mound, lightly, teasingly, enjoying the hitch in her breath, and the way she seemed to be holding her whole body very still, like she was afraid he'd stop if she moved.

Which was what he did as soon as he thanked the room service person and hung up the phone. Lazily pulling his finger back, he told her, "Yep. Thirty minutes."

She didn't say anything, just stared at him with hooded eyes for a second.

Then she said what he'd been hoping to hear. "We can each have an orgasm in that time."

Evan sat up and stripped off his shirt. "I'll save mine for after dinner. Which means you get two now."

It was clear Kendall was still sleepy, because instead of him smart-ass response, she just said, "Oh. Okay."

Her eyes were enormous, her hair equally so, her cheeks flushed pink from sleep, and Evan had never seen a woman look so gorgeous. Ever.

"Roll on your stomach. I'll massage you."

She made a sigh of pleasure as she started to roll. Then she stopped abruptly. "If you rub my back, I'll probably fall asleep again."

The naïveté. "No, you won't. I promise."

Evan helped her finish her roll by taking her hips and forcing the turn. Her face fell into the pillow with a soft thump, hair a fluffy cloud around her. She turned her head so she was looking to the right, crossing her arms up above.

"Mmm. This feels good already."

It did. As he ran his hands up either side of her spine, giving a slow, deep rub to the muscles, Evan appreciated the softness of her skin under his callused fingers. On his knees, he stroked up under her shirt, over her shoulders, and down her arms as far as he could reach, before getting entangled in her sleeves. He wanted to take her T-shirt off, but room service was on its way, and truthfully there was something very sexy about touching her under her shirt . . . like he was being granted access to somewhere private.

She had beautiful skin, paler than it had been in their younger years. It was clear she wasn't lying out in the sun the way she did then, which had probably helped preserve the softness he felt beneath his fingers. Kendall gave soft moans of encouragement as he dug in and rubbed with a fair amount of pressure. She stiffened slightly when he crossed over her panty line and cupped her backside, but once he started to massage her rounded cheeks, she relaxed again.

"I should be weirded out by that, but it feels too good to object."

"Why would it be weird? It's just another muscle, and I've touched it before. Many times." Evan ran his hands over her panties, kneading very lightly. "Remember those skirts you used to wear? The little short denim ones? I loved those. It was so easy to just sneak my hand under there and touch your ass. And then I got cocky and started fingering you every chance I got . . . in the car, at the park, in the movies."

He was getting hard just remembering it. He had gotten off on getting Kendall off.

"That's why I wore them all the time," she said, her

voice slumberous yet sexy. "After the first time you got me off that way, I ran out and spent my whole savings buying four more of them."

Evan paused. "Are you serious?" That was seriously, seriously hot, and he suddenly had a full-fledged erection to prove it.

"I'm totally serious. I was a horny little thing." She twisted her head a little to look back at him. "I never thought to question why you were always so willing to do that for me when I never gave it back. That really wasn't fair of me."

Running his hands inside her panties, he drifted to the center and low with his index finger, turned on by the idea of turning her on the way he used to. "I enjoyed it. And I was a horny thing, too. I think it was still always a little shocking to me that you were willing to let me have sex with you. I would have done anything to express gratitude."

"Gratitude, huh? I think there was plenty of mutual pleasure going around. It always amazed me that you could barely touch me and I was going crazy."

He liked the sound of that. Slipping his finger between her cheeks, he rounded the curve and teased at her entrance, not touching her so much as hinting that he might. Her hips rose slightly off the bed in invitation.

But instead of giving her what she wanted, Evan pulled back and removed her panties, taking them all the way down her legs, bending over so his mouth was close to her flesh, but not touching. He drank in the scent of her skin, still warm from her nap, free of lotions and other mysterious products. She just smelled like . . . Kendall.

She sighed again.

And again her hips lifted slightly off the bed.

Evan ignored the invitation. He returned to her back,

massaging right above her pert backside, wanting to touch her, but wanting to tease more. Her shoulders had tensed and her teeth were worrying her bottom lip. Evan moved farther away from her ass, up to those clenched muscles. She didn't relax one bit, so he skipped right over her midsection and went down to her feet. Starting at the heel, he pushed his thumb up to her toes, repeating the action until she did manage to release her lip and relax her head back down.

But when he moved to her other foot, he lifted it in a way that pulled her legs a little apart, and Kendall drew in a sharp breath. But Evan ignored her reaction and repeated his movements on the second foot, shifting his knee in between her legs, forcing her leg up against his erection as he massaged. Then he leaned forward and sucked her toe, the cute one next to her big toe.

Kendall jumped. "What the hell are you doing?"

"Just playing." He pulled it in his mouth again, getting it nice and slick. He'd never really done that before, but it had been right in front of him and it had seemed like yet another way to tease, to stroke up and down, get her wet, while her legs were spread and her clit was pressing into the bed, her inner thighs aching.

She didn't resist, which he took as a good sign. Pulling back, he trailed his tongue down the back of her calf, up and down, leaving a damp path that he used to follow with his finger, going up and down to the back of her knee until she shivered. When her hips wiggled a little, Evan gave in to her silent request and moved his thumbs to inner thighs. But instead of pushing inside her, he just massaged up and down, up and down, on either side of her glistening opening. The sight of her damp desire had his mouth thick and salivating, but he was intent on making this last all night, long after room service showed up. Way into the dark, quiet hours of the night, when Kendall was so hot and ready and turned on, she was insensible. Crazy with want.

That's what he wanted. To take her to a place where she would agree to anything, a place she would never forget, with him, the man who had been her first, and should have been her last.

"Evan," she said, her voice a warning.

"What?"

"You're being cruel."

But her breathless excitement told him she didn't really mind.

"Don't always be in such a hurry. Just enjoy it."

"I like speed. So do you."

"On the track." Evan slipped the tip of his index finger inside her and hooked it, just giving a small back-and-forth tickle inside her. "But not in bed. Not with you."

"There's slow, and then there's just torture. This is in the torture category."

When she used her elbows to leverage herself and raise her hips to try and drive his finger deeper inside her, Evan took his palm and pushed her ass flat onto the bed and held her in place. "I don't think so."

She was growing wetter by the second, even as she let out a sound of frustration, and Evan was rock hard watching her, feeling her, enticing her. He wanted out of his jeans but he wasn't about to stop and take the time for that. This was about her.

Finally giving her what they both wanted, he moved his finger fully inside her and stroked. While he still held her down, it made for a tight, hot passage, and Evan added a second finger to the first, enjoying the reaction she gave him. Her hands snaked up to the headboard and she gripped it tightly. Her shirt was bunched up at her shoulders, her hair covering her upper back and sliding across her cheek. Her eyes were closed, teeth on her lip again, and she was still trying to move, still trying to buck her hips and force a faster rhythm between them, but he held her firm. She was sexy and amazing and so damn dripping wet.

Backing out, he trailed her own moisture all over her inner thighs and her perfect little tight ass.

"Oh, my God, you're just a horrible man . . ."

Any further protests she was about to give were lost in a moan when he lifted her hips and buried his face between her thighs, flicking his tongue across her slowly and with a great deal of exploration.

"You taste delicious," he told her.

"Oh, damn" was her response, before she buried her face in the pillow.

Evan tugged her clit into his mouth and pulled it, enjoying the way she jerked, her thighs squeezing around him. Then he went back in with his tongue, licking and tasting and pleasing both of them with every long stroke.

"I'm going to come," she told him, panting heavily.

He pulled back. "No, baby, not yet."

"Yes. Now."

She was wiggling in front of him so enticingly that Evan almost gave in, but the knock on the door stopped him.

"Room service." He ran his hand across her ass, then pushed her back down onto the bed. He yanked the covers out from under her and pulled them over her up to her shoulders.

As he climbed off the bed, adjusting his erection to somewhat hide it, Kendall smacked the pillow in frustration. "Just send them away. Who cares about the food?"

He didn't really care about it either at the moment, but

they might regret it later. "It's already here. Just lie there and look cute. I'll get it."

Her answer was to flip him her middle finger. Evan laughed as he wiped her sweetness off his lips. "Charming."

By handing him a twenty, Evan managed to convince the waiter to just pass the cart over to him instead of coming into the room. "I got it, thanks."

There was a moment's hesitation in which the older man glanced into the room, but then he seemed to figure out the score. "Sure, no problem. Enjoy." The took the cash, winked at Evan, and left.

"Are you hungry?" He maneuvered the rolling cart into the room and pulled the top off of a tray. "Looks good." Picking up a fry he was about to pop into his mouth, he glanced up.

And promptly forgot all about the fry. Kendall had kicked off the covers and turned onto her back. Which gave him a perfect view of her legs apart and her fingers between them, stroking herself, a finger deep inside her wetness.

"Holy shit."

"You'd better get over here," she told her, her back arching, making the display even more erotic. "Or I'll come without you."

"You are so fucking hot." Evan tossed down the French fry and strode to the bed, undoing his jeans as he went.

She had totally turned the tables on him, and damn, he had to respect and appreciate that.

"Let me help you with that." Putting a knee on either side of her thighs, Evan slipped his finger in alongside her own.

"Oh, damn." Her eyes rolled back.

He knew the feeling. Having her finger alongside his, in all that tight slickness, had him gritting his teeth. He followed her rhythm. When she sped up, her breath getting more and more frantic, he sped up with her. When she got too excited and slowed it down, he followed.

And when she used her other hand to push on the swollen button above, Evan did the same, so that when she came, hard, her body exploding, they were both in her and on her, sharing the hot, hurtling outcome.

"You're a dirty bastard for doing that to me," she said, her eyes glassy, her words breathy and soft.

Evan grinned. "A dirty bastard for making you come? That seems a little paradoxical."

"Five-dollar word. Impressive. I have no brain left." Kendall closed her eyes, her chest rising and falling with her breathing, her breasts half-covered with her bunched shirt.

"Just enough to still be a smart-ass." Evan stroked over her clitoris again. "And you have big hair. Can't expect to have brains, too."

She slapped at his hand. "Now who's being charming? Get off me, you'll kill me."

"Killed with kindness. Here lies Kendall Holbrook."

"Speaking of ass."

"Were we speaking of ass?" Evan debated bending over and sucking one of her nipples, just to see her reaction. Besides, they were firm and clearly begging for his attention.

"Show me yours. Take off your jeans."

"I'll take off my jeans, but I'm not some boy toy. Just so you know."

Her eyes popped open, her mouth pulling up at the corner. "For tonight, you'll be whatever I say you are."

What he wanted to be was her boyfriend, which was so lame and stupid and high school that he almost threw up in his own mouth at his schmaltziness. There was no way in hell he was sharing that little sentiment with her.

"Use me and abuse me, baby."

"Oh, I intend to."

Which totally one hundred percent turned him on.

Evan reached for his zipper.

CHAPTER
ELEVEN

KENDALL was going to claim later that it was the after-effects of sleep deprivation that had her impatiently reaching out and ripping Evan's jeans down his thighs as she embraced her inner dominatrix. It was like the walls that surrounded her self-control had been shattered by Red Bull and a lack of REM sleep, because she was shocking even herself. Yet in a really, really good way.

She was so aroused it was unbelievable. It was like Evan had turned her fierce with all that teasing massaging, because she wasn't normally like this. Given the look on his face, though, and the way his erection sprung out of his boxers, it was damn clear he appreciated her determination.

"Don't you want to eat your dinner?" he asked.

"I'm looking at it." And she flicked her tongue across his cock, amazed that she had actually said that out loud.

"Oh, fuck, Kendall."

That was the plan. She covered him with her mouth, riding up and down his shaft with her slick saliva, loving the way he suddenly gripped her shoulders and helped her create a sharp, pumping rhythm. It seemed her fierceness was driving his.

He had played slow. She wanted fast. So gripping her left hand under his testicles, she cupped them, earning a nice low moan. Then with her right hand, she squeezed at the base of his shaft, her mouth taking him nice and deep before pulling back over and over.

It was a serious turn-on to be on her knees, inner thighs still wet and aching from his stroking and sucking her, and to have him losing control as she stroked and sucked him. She was never quite this wild, quite this into it, and she had never let a man finish in her mouth, but here, in this dark hotel room a million miles from Charlotte, with the first man she'd given her heart to, she wanted all of it. She wanted it fast and furious, slow and sensual, to be at his mercy and to have him at hers. To lose control together again. After he lost it right now.

"Kendall. Oh, damn, slow down. You need to stop."

As if.

She didn't break rhythm at all, and Evan tried to pull back, but she just followed him, keeping her mouth solidly on his erection.

"I'm going to . . ."

Then he did, his hands grabbing wildly on to her head as he exploded in her mouth. Kendall closed her eyes and enjoyed the satisfaction of knowing she had done that to him, and that quickly. Swallowing, she slowly stopped stroking as he shuddered. When she pulled all the way back, she glanced up at him and smiled. "Mmm."

"Oh. My. God."

"Yeah? I hope you liked it." Kendall lay back down, lounging across the bed, relaxed and feeling like the proverbial cat who ate the cream.

Evan was still on his knees in front of her, jeans flopping open, chest heaving up and down, looking a little stunned as he ran his fingers through his hair. It was a good look for him, or at least one she enjoyed.

"I don't even have words to describe how much I liked that. You are crazy sexy."

Crazy sexy. She liked that.

Kendall tugged her T-shirt down since it was lumping under her back, and looked up at Evan. Her feelings for him were confused, jumbled. Sometimes she looked at him and didn't know who she was seeing—the boy she had loved, the man she had hated, or the man who was that boy grown up.

Their new relationship had no real parameters, no guidelines. They knew each other, yet didn't. They had a past, but never talked about a future.

But at the moment, it didn't matter to Kendall. What mattered was just enjoying herself, relaxing and having fantastic sex with the man who could make her laugh.

"Why, thank you." She crawled up onto all fours and moved to the end of the bed. "And I think I'm going to actually eat my burger."

Evan blinked, but he still didn't move. "Good call."

Amused, Kendall grabbed a French fry and moved it to his lips. "Hungry?"

He bit it so hard and unexpectedly that she screeched and jumped backwards. Snapped out of his haze, Evan grinned as he chewed. "Very hungry."

"You're a punk."

"Thank you."

"Where are my panties?" Kendall glanced around. "I can't eat without underwear."

"That's the weirdest statement you've ever made, and you've said some weird-ass things in the past."

"What?" She spotted them on the floor and leaned over, trying to snatch them up without falling off the bed. "It's just strange to me to be eating without underwear. It's like peeing standing up. Just something I never do."

He startled her again by smacking her backside, which she realized was probably a stone's throw from his face.

"Whatever works for you, Jay."

"Stop calling me that stupid nickname." Though she had to say, she was already used to it. There was something about an endearment from Evan, crass and sexist though it might be, that made her melt just a teeny-weeny bit.

It was a little bit pathetic.

As was the way she enjoyed curling up on the bed with him, as they chowed down on their dinners and watched Shark Week episodes on the Discovery Channel. As she trailed her fries through a thick pile of ketchup, she watched great white sharks trolling for seal pups.

"You've got to admire their speed," Evan said as he pulled the bacon out of his sandwich and ate it solo. "Its like that poor seal is just hanging out there looking for fish and then bam! He gets shot up five feet in the air when that shark nails him at full blast."

Unlike her, who had put her clothes back on to eat, Evan had actually stripped his jeans off, and was half-sitting, half-lying in nothing but his boxers, his club sandwich hovering in front of his mouth.

This was so ordinary. So something two people in a relationship would do. Sit around their hotel room watching TV.

"It's definitely a good strategy on the shark's part. They come so fast, the seal can't react."

"They need spotters on the radio like we have." Evan smiled and leaned over and stole one of her fries.

"Why are you taking my fries? You have your own."

"Yours taste better."

She let an eye roll go. "You're ridiculous." And cute.

Damn it, why was he so cute? Why did he have those luscious brown eyes and sexy little dimples? It wasn't fair. It made her want things she couldn't have.

Especially when he leaned over and gave her a kiss on her forehead. A sweet, smacking kiss that was not sexual and yet totally made her toes curl from the sincerity of it. They really were blurring the lines here between just sex and something else entirely.

"Do you ever wonder what it would have been like if we hadn't broken up?" Evan asked her.

Apparently his thoughts had been going in the exact same direction.

"No," she lied.

"Liar."

Damn it. "Fine, I'm lying. Of course I wondered about it after we broke up. I missed you, stupid."

"You should really hold back on complimenting me so much. I might get a big head." Evan glanced down at his boxers. "Well, a second big head."

"See, this is what happens when we try to have a serious conversation. I insult you and you turn it sexual. We have a pattern, you know."

She thought he would answer with a joke, but Evan set his sandwich down on his plate and leaned towards her. His expression was serious, eyes searching.

"I don't think we have a pattern so much as a fear of showing our real emotions."

Oh, God, he was serious. And he was right.

"Maybe the problem is, I don't know what my real emotions are."

"Fair enough. I guess I don't really know mine either. But I did then. Ten years ago." Evan gave her a fleeting smile. "I was going to ask you to marry me, you know."

The fry she'd been holding up to her mouth fell out of her fingers as she stared at him in shock. "What?"

"Yep. I had a ring bought and everything. I was going to ask you on your nineteenth birthday."

Kendall sucked air in and out, desperate to fight the tears that were crowding her eyelids and threatening to spring out. Evan had been planning to propose to her? He'd bought a ring? She tried to comprehend what that meant in the grand scheme of things . . . It meant he had really, truly loved her. Had intended to spend his life with her. Or at least he had with the optimism of nineteen. Who knows what really would have happened?

But he had loved her. No question of that.

"I don't know what to say . . . I had no idea."

"Say that you would have said yes."

She nodded, without hesitation. "Yes. I would have said yes. No doubt about it."

They stared into each other's eyes for a minute, the emotion in Evan's dark and lusty and raw.

Then suddenly they were grabbing for each other, falling over plates of food as they fought to get their lips on each other. Their kiss was a collision, chests together, arms grappling, mouths angling for a deeper, all-consuming touch.

Kendall wouldn't have thought it was possible to be

so hot for him again so soon, but she was even more so. Now it was physical and emotional, an explosive cocktail of desire, her tongue desperately sweeping across his. The thought that this man had wanted to marry her, spend his life with her, was possibly the hottest thing she'd ever heard.

His tongue mated with hers, and then he bit her lip, tugging it with just enough force to send a jolt of ecstasy to her inner thighs. Her nipples were tight and aching beneath her T-shirt, and she had managed to maneuver her legs on either side of his and now shamelessly rubbed against him.

Evan yanked her head back with her hair, breathing frantically, and kissed her neck, his desperate desire driving her own. Before she could even really react, he had tossed her back onto the bed, the French fries flying in all directions as a plate tumbled to the floor.

Neither of them paused, the mess wasn't acknowledged in any way, and they were back at it instantly, making out with all the fervor of teens on curfew, with the added kick of being full-fledged adults with hands that knew exactly how to move on each other. Kendall had hers in Evan's boxers, stroking him with the stickiness of his obvious arousal. He had his hands in her panties, moving inside her with a similar intensity.

"Roll on top of me," he panted. "I want to feel you move on me."

When they rolled, still connected by mouth, Kendall kicked the remaining plate, but it didn't slow her down. Once on Evan's body, she spread her legs and mimicked sex, their mouths tangling and teasing and pressing. It was old school—the clothes still somewhat on, the hands in each other's hair, their bodies moving together but stopping short of that ultimate connection—but that's what made it even hotter. This was about the kiss, the wanting of each other, not just their bodies.

It should have scared her, but there was no thought in her head other than that she wanted him. Always had. Probably always would. Even when she had convinced herself she hated him, she had still wanted him.

He had loved her.

She had loved him.

And they, mostly her, had destroyed that.

Now she wanted to dig her fingers into his flesh, take him into her body, hold on to him in the only way she could, for right now, here, in this room, this night.

He flipped her onto her back, and then she was shoving his boxers down, he was tugging her panties past her thighs. Evan grabbed her leg and put her ankle on his shoulder. Then he was inside her with a hard thrust that pushed the air right out of her lungs.

"Oh, God." She grabbed his arms and held on as he went deep inside her, again and again.

Her fingers dug blindly into his bicep muscles, and her head jerked upward with each desperate plunge inside her hot, moist body. It was acute pleasure, almost painful in its overwhelming intensity, his teeth gritted, eyes locked with hers. Her ankle bounced on his shoulder, their bodies connecting as deeply and tightly as was possible at their most intimate and sensitive spot.

"Kendall."

It almost sounded like a question, like he wanted to say something to her. "Yes?" she asked, struggling to focus, her back arching, her nipples taut against her T-shirt as it moved with her body. She bit her bottom lip, losing focus on his as she careened into ecstasy, her orgasm hitting her with the force of a tsunami.

"Come for me, baby," he urged, his words followed by a deep, throaty groan.

"I am, I am." She was—a wild, clawing, surreal explosion of pleasure on Evan, under him, with him.

He came, too, their moans blending together as easily as their bodies, a crashing erotic burst of pleasure, bodies, voices, and hearts.

She clung to him, stunned, blinking and forcing herself to breathe as her inner muscles vibrated with tiny aftershocks of pleasure.

That was . . . she didn't even know.

Something she had never experienced, free and elemental and totally in her body, yet somehow totally out of it.

"I . . ."

She hadn't even intended to speak, so she wasn't sure what she was trying to say. Evan had the same stunned look on his face she imagined she was sporting.

"That was insanely good," he said, pulling her ankle off his shoulder and moving her leg back down onto the bed.

Which was good because Kendall realized it was trembling a little from the position. She sat in a race car for four hours straight yet couldn't handle five minutes with her leg in the air? Also suddenly aware of a pinching sensation on her back, Kendall shifted slightly. "Something's stabbing me."

"It's a fork."

"Well that explains that." Kendall grinned up at him.

"Why did they even give us silverware? We had a burger and a sandwich."

"They come rolled in the napkins."

"Are you okay?" He turned her onto her side and massaged her back.

Kendall felt more than okay. She felt punch drunk. "I'm

fantastic." She felt boneless and satisfied and goofy, inflated with emotions she had no intention of examining. She was just going to enjoy the high.

When he let her go, she flopped back, unable to hold herself up.

Evan laughed. "You look loopy and adorable." He leaned down and kissed her, a quick, hard smack.

"You have ketchup on your arm," she told him, seeing a long red streak from his elbow to his wrist.

"Damn." He glanced down at it. "I sure do. And the bed is wrecked."

It was. They both peeled themselves up off the mattress and into a sitting position. Kendall realized she actually had a pickle slice stuck to her thigh. She flung it onto the tray. There were French fries everywhere, and her burger had tumbled to the floor, leaving a trail of ketchup and mustard behind it. Evan had ketchup on his stomach as well as his arm, which struck her as hilarious.

"We're going to have to tip the maid really well," he said, using a napkin to swipe at his gut.

Kendall just laughed. Plucking a fry off the bed, she dipped it in the ketchup on Evan's arm and stuck it up to his mouth as a joke. But he actually ate it, pulling the whole thing into his mouth.

He made a face. "Cold."

Which made her laugh even harder. Pulling her T-shirt down as far as it would go, attempting to cover her bare butt, Kendall started gathering the fries and sandwich guts, brushing them off the bed and onto the tray.

"Worry about that later," he told her. "Let's go wash the stickiness off in the shower."

While the thought of him wet and soapy held a great deal of appeal, Kendall was also very logical. "If we finish the job now we won't get sticky all over again." She held up a smushed tomato slice to prove it. "Dang, what happened to your sandwich? It's all over the place."

"I think I stuck my knee in it." Evan held up his leg and sure enough, there was a slimey sheen on it.

They both laughed, and Kendall felt something inflating inside her—pure happiness. When Evan reached for her and wrapped her in his arms for a tender kiss, it felt normal and right and sweet.

"Come to the shower. This mess is as cleaned up as it's going to be."

When Kendall smiled and gave in to him, taking his hand and pulling him towards the bathroom, Evan refused to label the feelings that were rattling around inside him. Or maybe more like they were crawling up his throat, threatening to burst out of his mouth.

He hadn't intended to tell Kendall about buying a ring, meaning to propose to her all those years ago, but it had just popped out, and the look on her face . . . well, he was glad he had. He'd seen her eyes melt, seen a glimmer of that love she had worn so blatantly for him when they were young. It had been intensely satisfying, and arousing.

Which is why they'd wound up having killer sex on top of their dinner five seconds later.

When they got in the bathroom and he saw the soaking tub, Evan changed his mind. "Hey, let's take a bath. I'm sure they have bubble crap and stuff. We can just relax and soak."

Kendall looked sleepy and satisfied. She actually made a low sigh of approval, like she thought the idea was delicious. "Sounds good." Turning to the counter, she added, "And yes, they have bubble crap here. Though I think they're called bath beads."

"Whatever." Evan leaned over and started up the water, holding his fingers under it until the temperature was just right. "Hand me some."

"Here." She gave him the bottle of beads, then said, "And then you need to step out for a second."

"Why?"

"I have to go to the bathroom."

"You can take a leak in front of me."

"Actually, I can't."

Evan dumped half the bottle of beads into the large tub and pondered the mysteries of women. He was fairly certain he'd piss in front of anyone. But he wasn't going to argue. "Alright. Don't let the water overflow."

"How long do you think it's going to take me?"

"I don't know! First you use the toilet, then you wash your hands, then you decide to brush your teeth, then tweeze your eyebrows, then inspect your face because you're sure you have a zit starting, then put lotion on your feet . . . and the next thing you know there's water on the floor and I've died of boredom in the other room."

"It sounds like this has happened to you before."

Maybe once or twice. "I know women."

Kendall put her hand on his chest. "Out of the bathroom. And don't you dare fall asleep and leave me alone in this warm tub with nothing to do."

That sounded intriguing. "I'm sure you could find something to do."

"Playing with a friend is always better." As she spoke, her tongue came out and slid from one corner of her lip to the other.

Evan felt a jolt of lust. "Good call. Hurry."

Then he let the bathroom and paced back and forth with an erection. Deciding that wasn't helping the situation, he grabbed his phone off the desk and checked it. Three missed calls from Eve, plus two texts saying he needed to call her immediately.

Not.

Reality could wait just a few more hours. Right now, he was enjoying all this time with Kendall. It wasn't likely he'd get to do this again anytime soon. If ever.

Which really sucked when he thought about it.

"You can come in," she called, the door popping open.

Thank God. She was saving him from getting morose.

When he strolled—okay, maybe rushed—into the bathroom, Kendall was already in the tub, bubbles up to her chin. He was a little disappointed he couldn't see a single part of her body. Even her hands on the sides of the tub were loaded with suds.

"I think you might have been a little heavy-handed with the bath beads," she told him.

Considering that when she shifted, she had a bubble beard, he had to agree with her. "There weren't directions."

"Actually, there were. You just didn't read them. It said to add three beads. How many did you use?"

Evan stuck his foot into the tub, hoping he wasn't going to step on Kendall. "I didn't count." But probably more like twenty.

She smiled. "Just barrel in and hope it works out. That's you."

"It's worked for me so far. For the most part." Evan sat down and reached for her. "Lean against me. I don't want to be on this end and you're on that end."

After a bit of readjusting and water sloshing and bubble spreading, Evan settled back in the tub, Kendall between his legs, leaning on his chest. "Perfect."

It was. He closed his eyes and let the warm water seep

over his tired muscles. Kendall fit perfectly against him, and he wrapped his arms around her middle, wanting to touch her bare skin, feel her everywhere he could. Being naked with her in a way that wasn't sexual was intimate, soothing.

"So what did the ring look like?" she asked, the curve of her bottom brushing his leg when she shifted.

"Hmm?" He wished he had a bottle of beer in his hand, but other than that, this was fantastic.

"The ring you got to propose with. My engagement ring. What did it look like?"

Interesting that she would ask that. Evan rubbed his thumbs over her stomach. "I don't know. It was a diamond. A square diamond."

She made a sound of disgust. "That's not a description. What was the band? Gold? Platinum?"

"Well." Evan nibbled at her ear to buy himself time. He wasn't about to confess that he didn't exactly remember what it looked like. He had shoved it into a box in a drawer ten years ago and hadn't looked at it since. "It was silver. Is that platinum?"

He did remember that much.

"Not always."

"I don't know, Kendall. I was a kid. I took Eve with me and she helped me pick it out."

"Your sister knew you were going to propose?"

"Yep." Her ear really did taste good. Evan was starting to get turned on, his hands roaming just a little higher to cover her slick breasts.

"Huh. What did you tell her when we broke up?"

"I didn't. Guys don't talk about that kind of stuff. It was just obvious."

"I wonder what she thinks of me."

"Who cares? And I doubt she gives it much thought."
Though truth be told, Evan had no clue what his sister
thought about. She was wound tight, and he didn't really
understand her most of the time. He just knew that if he
needed a sparring partner, Eve was always ready to go a
round.

"But I don't want to talk about my sister. I want to talk
about your perfect nipples."

Evan tweaked them both at the same time, appreciating
the gasp Kendall gave.

"What about them?"

"About how much I adore them and how badly I want to
suck them right now."

"I'm facing the wrong way and I'm covered in bubbles."

"Always so damn logical." Slipping his hand down between her legs, he teased at her clitoris. He loved when he
got her so hot she forgot to make sense.

"I don't think I can come again . . . I've already achieved
some kind of record."

"Who says you have to come? We're just playing. Half
the fun is getting there, you know." Evan dipped his tongue
into her ear at the same time he moved his finger inside her.

She sighed. "Okay. I guess I can handle that."

"You can handle a lot of things." His erection bumping
into her backside, Evan suddenly wanted more. All. Everything Kendall had to give. If this was it, he wanted to milk
every moment of pleasure that he possibly could. "Up." He
patted her bottom.

"What do you mean?"

"On all fours."

"No. I'm relaxed."

Evan pulled his fingers back, his mouth thick with desire,

the heat of the water steaming up the room, turning Kendall's skin pink and dewy.

"Why did you stop?"

"Because I want you on all fours."

"Oh, for crying out loud." She made lots of grumbling sounds that Evan knew were pure bullshit.

She wanted to mess around just as much as he did, which was evidenced by the way she stroked his erection in the process of changing positions.

When she was up on her knees, her perfect little ass facing him, covered with bubbles, her back arched, damp tendrils of hair trailing down her back, she asked, "What am I doing like this, exactly?"

As if she needed to ask.

Evan got on his knees also and pushed his erection inside her, finding her tight and welcoming. She gasped.

"Give a girl some warning."

"You knew what I was going to do." She knew it and she loved it. Just like he did. Evan held her hips and thrust into her, glancing over and discovering that while he couldn't see their bodies because the mirror was too high, he could see Kendall's face reflected in it.

Her eyes were closed and her mouth was open in pleasure. Her hair was clumped to her forehead, finally losing some of its height and volume as it wilted in the heat, and her cheeks were pink. Everything about her seemed to glisten and glow and she looked absolutely beautiful to Evan. More than beautiful. A word beyond beautiful that he couldn't think of, but knew had to exist.

Kendall started to move her hips, so that when he thrust, they collided together hard. "Oh, damn," he told her. "You're so sexy."

The heat of the room, the sloshing of the water, the slap of their skin, and the increasing volume of Kendall's cries rose around him, but all he could think about was how amazing it felt to be with her, to be inside her, to give, to take, to share their pleasure.

When he felt her orgasm, those inner muscles contracting and clinging to him, he gritted his teeth and let himself explode along with her.

It was intimate and almost profound, the scent of the bath beads clogging his nostrils, and the taste of her still on his tongue, the need for her, an ache ten years long, still in his heart.

CHAPTER
TWELVE

KENDALL really thought it was possible she wasn't going to be able to hold herself up as she climbed out of the tub. She felt exhausted, in a good way, but drained nonetheless. Evan was holding her hand, which was probably the only thing keeping her from puddling to the ground in a post-orgasmic blob.

She hadn't been kidding when she'd told him that this was a record for the highest number of orgasms in one day. One night, really. And yet he was still giving her lecherous looks as he handed her a towel.

He swiped a stray bubble off her shoulder before leaning in and kissing her mouth, then her nose, which just made her want to rub it. It was such a strange feeling, this sort of intimacy swirling around them. They had done something here tonight, changed the rules of the game, and she wasn't sure what that meant exactly.

Just that she couldn't stroll away with an awkward thumbs-up this time.

"Let me dry you off." Evan opened the towel and rubbed it down her arms with just the right amount of pressure, not wimpy, but not vibrating her whole body as he peeled a layer of her skin off either. It was like his massage technique—just perfect.

"I can dry myself off."

"But this is more fun."

"This is going to lead to more sex, which is going to lead to me being crippled and unable to walk tomorrow."

Evan grinned. "Yeah? Because I have such a big dick, right?"

She could have bet twenty bucks he'd say that and won easily. "I'm not even going to respond to that. Wait. Yes, I am. Thanks for the sympathy. You'll be bouncing around tomorrow and I'll be carrying a doughnut pillow to sit on when we're on the plane."

"You're exaggerating."

"Not by much."

"Okay, I'll leave you alone, Jay. But I'm going to cuddle with you whether you like it or not."

He dried her legs, and managed to lick her inner thighs only once. Kendall was amazed she felt anything at all. She would have thought she'd be numb there by now. Or that all her girl bits might have fallen off from overuse.

But they were still there and still capable of feeling a pang of arousal. Certain that she would die if they tried to have sex again, Kendall backed away from him. "I'm a kick-ass cuddler."

"You're kick-ass all the way around."

"Why thank you." She took the towel from him and wrapped it around herself. "Umm. I'm so relaxed. I don't think I've been this relaxed in a year."

Evan didn't bother to put a towel on, he just strolled out

into the room still naked. "Sleep and an orgasm. Best things I can think of to relax and re-energize."

"What time is your flight tomorrow?"

"Seven A.M."

"We're on the same flight then, I imagine. Damn, that's early."

Evan lifted the duvet cover and shook it, forcing the remaining salt and a stray fry off of it. "Guess we really should go to sleep."

They crawled into bed together, both smelling like bubbles, with the underlying scent of sex on them. "Can you set the alarm on your phone?"

"Yep."

He reached for his phone and pushed some buttons while Kendall yawned and shucked the towel she was wearing, dropping it to the floor. She didn't normally sleep naked, but she felt so warm and delicious and satisfied, it seemed appropriate for her mood.

Then he was pulling her into his chest, and Kendall breathed deeply, wrapping her leg over his.

"So, I hate to ruin the mood, but I have to ask, Kendall."

She stiffened a little. "Ask what?" she said suspiciously as she looked up at him.

"What happens when we get home? Is it like last time, where I don't see you for days?"

It was a conversation they had to have, but dang, she didn't want to ruin the mood. Nor did she want insecurities to come flooding to the surface, yet they already were. She didn't know what he wanted, if anything, and she did not want to be the first one to admit out loud that she would like to be together, in whatever way they figured out how to do that. She didn't want to not see him. That much she knew.

"It's complicated."

But Evan shook his head. "Not really. You either want to spend time with me or you don't."

When put like that . . . "I want to spend time with you."

"Good. Because I want to spend time with you. Hell, I want to date you. But we can call it whatever you want. I just want to know that when I wake up in the morning, I have the right to expect to see you that day, and when I go to bed, it's you I say good night to. I just want to get to know you again."

Put like that, it sounded so simple. So easy. "I'd like that, Evan. I really would."

"Good." He tilted her chin up to him. "So now kiss me good night."

"Bossy," she muttered, but annoyance was not what she felt as she raised her lips to his and softly kissed him.

What she felt was pure happiness.

EVAN blinked in the bright sunlight as he and Kendall stepped out of the hotel lobby to catch their ride to the airport. Frankie had arranged a private car for them. "Oh, my God, it's bright," he said, lifting his arm to shield his retinas.

Kendall was turned, gawking behind her. "There's like six famous people in this hotel lobby right now. I'm counting three actresses, one actor, one lead singer of a rock band, and I think that's a basketball player, given his height."

Evan tried not to wince when the flash of cameras went off in front of him. "That explains the paparazzi. And smile, because guess what? You're famous, too."

He needed coffee and he was pretty sure he looked like shit given he was running on about five hours of sleep. Not that anything was going to spoil his mood, since Kendall had pretty much agreed to date him. But he hadn't been thinking about paparazzi. Unlike Hollywood types, drivers weren't always as easily recognizable. But these were clearly pros who took shots of everyone who looked like anyone. They'd figure out what to do with them later.

Which would hopefully be nothing.

"Smile for who?" Kendall turned and stopped walking.

"Just smile. No big deal." Evan raised his hand in a wave at the cameramen snapping their picture. "How are you all doing this morning?"

They were probably used to scowling and being punched, so he got some friendly waves and hellos.

"What are you in LA for?" the one asked.

"Commercial shoot. Heading back to Charlotte now. Have a good one."

"Thanks, you, too. Can we get a pic of the two of you? Kendall Holbrook, right?"

"Yeah, that's right." Kendall's smile didn't look particularly natural, but she did manage one.

And she didn't pull away when Evan put his arm around her as they posed.

Evan pulled away and gave another wave, before opening the door to the car waiting for them. He handed their bags to the driver then tipped him. Frankie was frowning at both of them as they climbed into the car. She was like an older version of his sister, which was frightening.

"That was weird," Kendall said as she clicked her seat belt in place. "They wanted to take my picture."

"Why is that freaking you out? People want your picture all the time in Charlotte."

"But that's Charlotte. This is *LA*."

He didn't get what the difference was, but he was used to it. His phone rang and he knew from the ringtone that it was Eve. "I'm sorry, I'd better answer this. Eve has called me like seven hundred times since yesterday."

"Sure." Kendall looked back behind them as they pulled out, like she still couldn't believe that anyone had wanted to take her picture.

"Hello?"

"Where the *hell* have you been?"

"I'm good, thanks for asking. How about yourself?" Evan leaned back against the seat and wished coffee would magically materialize in his hand.

"Don't be cute with me. Carl wants to have a meeting with you this afternoon in his office. You know it's going to be about Sunday and that little pissing match you had with Elec."

Evan winced. That probably hadn't been the most brilliant thing he'd ever done, getting into it with Elec both on the track and off. But tempers flared between drivers sometimes, brothers or not, everyone knew that. "What time?"

"As soon as your ass touches down in Charlotte. Drive straight to the office. Let me know when you land and I'll meet you there."

Evan reached over and took Kendall's hand in his own. He squeezed her soft fingers and tried not to sigh. Reality was back. Big-time.

"Alright. Talk to you later."

As he hung up his phone, he leaned forward and said to the driver, "Can you swing through a drive-thru for a coffee? I'll give you an extra ten bucks."

"Sure, buddy, no problem."

"What's up?" Kendall asked Evan.

"Carl has requested a meeting with me today. Eve says it isn't good."

"That's interesting," Frankie said, glancing up from her BlackBerry. "Carl wants to have a meeting with Kendall as well."

"Maybe he just wants to tell us how cool we are." Evan tried to smile, but he suddenly felt a little nervous. "What time is Kendall's meeting?"

"Tomorrow morning at nine A.M."

Kendall gave him a worried look that he was certain reflected his. "When's yours?"

"I believe the phrasing was 'as soon as your ass touches down in Charlotte.'"

Her eyebrows shot up, but she covered her look of horror quickly. "I'm sure it's no big deal. Your sister is overdramatic, your mother even says so. Don't worry." She leaned over and kissed him. "And I'm here if you need to talk . . . or anything."

Which made the potential end of his career suddenly seem not very important at all.

WHEN Kendall turned her phone back on after landing in Charlotte, it immediately buzzed with a text message from Tuesday.

U & Evan???? Call me.

Kendall frowned at the screen on her phone. What did that mean?

"I need to take a cab straight to the office," Evan told her. "Did you drive here or take a cab?"

"I drove. Are you sure you don't want me to give you a ride?"

"No, it's out of your way, and something tells me it would raise eyebrows if you dropped me off."

Kendall shifted her carry-on bag on her shoulder. "We're not keeping this relationship a secret, are we? I don't want to take out a billboard ad or anything, but I'd kind of like to be able to go out in public from time to time."

"Of course it's not a secret." He winked. "I just may take out a billboard ad. 'Kendall is Hot.' That's what it will say."

"Very romantic."

"I thought so." Evan leaned in and gave her a kiss. "See? Public display of affection. Trust me, if you're cool with it, I will tell anyone and everyone that we're an item."

Which kind of made her heart swell in an embarrassingly girly fashion. "That's not necessary. Let's just be normal."

"Normal. Got it. Now I'm off to face the chair. Be careful going home and call me later, okay?"

"Okay. Good luck. Let me know what happens."

He gave her a cheerful wave as he stepped into the taxi queue, and Kendall kept walking to the parking garage. Sometimes she wished she could be more relaxed, like Evan was. He took so much more in stride than she did. She was worried sick over this meeting in the morning.

Yet not worried enough to suck all the glow off her sex-filled night. She and Evan were dating. How insane was that? Yet she was so freaking giddy, goofy, shout-it-out-loud happy.

Feeling the need to share it, she called Tuesday.

"Thank God you called, I totally need to talk to you."

"I need to talk to you, too. I slept with Evan again and it's so—"

Tuesday cut her off mid-gush. "I know. You know I'm

•

on the gossip sites every day, hell, every hour practically, for news to write my blog. Well, there are pics of you and Evan coming out of the hotel in LA together."

Kendall frowned at her surroundings, the parking garage huge and dark. Where the hell had she parked? "So? We saw the paparazzi. They were camped out waiting for real celebs and they caught us."

"Yeah, but they seem to have the impression that the two of you are dating. A couple."

"We are." And she couldn't help but grin in the sea of parked cars as she said those words out loud.

"You are? I thought you just had sex. Big difference, sister."

"I know that! I'm not sixteen. We've talked, and we want to try this . . . being together, that is."

Though they hadn't really defined exactly what that meant. But Kendall didn't care at the moment.

"Oh. Really? Are you sure about this?"

"Yes," she said in annoyance. "Don't be a killjoy. Just be happy for me. And I'd rather the press think Evan and I are dating than randomly shagging."

"But you've done both."

"So? No one needs to know my business, but if they're going to know my business, I'd rather it be that we're dating than just hooking up." Starting down a row she thought looked vaguely familiar Kendall felt her pleasant mood slipping away. "Why does it feel like you're not on board with the idea of me with Evan?"

"I don't know you and Evan as a couple. I'll reserve my opinion until I see the two of you together."

"Or you could just trust that I'm not a total moron and can make decisions on who to date all by myself, and they might actually be good choices. Imagine that."

"Don't be upset. I'm sorry. I don't mean to sound bitchy, it's just I worry about you. You guys have a history and, well, a very complicated working relationship. I just don't want to see you hurt."

"I'm fine. And this has nothing to do with our careers. It will all be fine."

But even as she spoke the words, she wondered if she was deluding herself just a tiny bit.

EVAN stared at Carl, equal parts outraged and appalled. "Excuse me?"

"I am strongly advising you against dating Kendall Holbrook."

It took Evan a second to swallow his anger, then he said carefully, "I don't believe it's anyone's business but my own who I'm dating."

He wanted to glance over at Eve and see how his sister was digesting this bullshit, but he didn't want to break eye contact with Carl. He understood the game, realized that everyone's money was on the line every week, but this was ridiculous. They owned his car, not him.

"If you were dating a cute blonde waitressing down at the sushi joint or a lawyer or a teacher, I'd agree with you. But another driver? Think about it."

"I don't see what difference it makes."

"Which shows me your judgment is already compromised." Carl leaned forward on his desk. "Just take your dick or your heart or whatever body part is involved out of it and see it from my perspective. You offended a whole set of fans last year by accidentally taking a potshot at a dead driver. You're having your worst season in the cup series ever. You did better as a rookie, for Christ's sake. We lost a major sponsor. Just this past Sunday you got into it with your own brother, and you came off sounding like a spoiled brat."

Evan shifted uncomfortably in his seat. When put that way . . . "I'm trying to win again, Carl. That's why I got into it with Elec."

"I doubt you'd have gunned that hard for him if he hadn't been your brother. Which proves my point about dating Kendall. So let's say the two of you have a fight. You're going to take that out onto the track."

"I'd never go after Kendall on the track."

"No? But what about the distraction? You're upset, you can't concentrate. Or you've just spent all night doing the horizontal shuffle and you're both a wreck waiting to happen out there."

"I think that everyone runs that risk, regardless of who they're dating or who they're married to. Everyone out there has sex, I would assume, and everybody's had a fight with a loved one if they're human. And I think I've proven that my personal life has no bearing on what happens on the track." Frankly, he was offended that Carl thought otherwise.

"Yeah, but I hear that Kendall was the only woman who's ever really got under your skin. I heard about the rough breakup when you dated before."

Now he was just pissed. "That was ten years ago. We were kids. And again, nobody's business but my own."

"You're skating on thin ice, Evan. I'm just again advising you to think long and hard about dating Kendall and the impact that might have on your career."

Evan finally glanced at Eve. She was just sitting there, her lips pursed together, hands gripping the arms of the chair.

"I thank you for your concern. I'll take everything you've said into consideration."

Then completely disregard it.

"By the way, how did you even know we were in any way involved with each other?"

Carl shrugged. "It didn't take a genius to figure it out. It's not like it's been a secret."

Evan knew exactly who wouldn't have kept it a secret—Eve.

"I see." He saw exactly what he needed to do.

"*I* look like crap in this picture." Kendall stared at the shot on her computer screen, of her and Evan exiting the hotel in LA.

Tuesday was over at Kendall's and she had showed her the picture on a popular gossip site. "You don't look like crap. You're not even facing the camera in this shot."

Tapping her finger on the computer screen, Tuesday indicated the picture that had Kendall turned almost entirely around, craning her neck to see back into the hotel lobby. Evan looked hot, smiling and lifting his hand in greeting to the paparazzi.

"I do so look like crap. My hair is practically still wet from my shower and I have no makeup on."

"When do you ever really wear makeup?" Tuesday asked, perching on the corner of the desk, wearing makeup.

Her friend had a point. "I know, but still. If I had known I was having my picture taken, I would have calmed down the hair frizz and slapped on some mascara. And this other shot is even worse. It looks like Evan is posing with a middle school–aged fan. I look twelve!"

"You're exaggerating. You look at least eighteen. It's the big boobs."

"Thanks."

Tuesday grinned. "Come on, don't worry about it. These are not bad shots. I've seen really awful shots. Cellulite butt hanging out, panty-less crotch flashes, breasts popping out, nose picking, the walk of shame shots, wedgie digging . . . it's all out there. Though for some weird reason my personal favorites are the spray tan screwup pictures. You know where some celebrity has either a horrid orange tan or it looks great everywhere but then you see their armpits are lily white, or they have streaks on their fingers. For some reason, those make me laugh."

Kendall just stared at her friend. She had no interest in giggling over a woman's spray tan gone bad. "You're right. That is weird."

Her phone started ringing and she glanced at the screen. "Oh, this is Evan. I need to answer this and see what happened with his meeting."

Tuesday made kissy-kissy sounds, which actually made Kendall laugh. "Very mature."

"Don't take forever. We have Chinese food arriving any minute now and I don't want to eat it alone."

"I won't be long." She hit answer on her phone. "Hello?"

"Hey, gorgeous. How's it going?"

"Fine. What happened with Carl?"

"Well . . ." There was rustling, like Evan was readjusting his phone next to his ear. "Carl suggested that you and I becoming involved with each other was a particularly bad idea."

"What?" Kendall popped up off the computer chair and started pacing. "How would he even know about us?"

"I think Eve might have said something. Or maybe he saw the pictures online. I don't know. But the bottom line is, he told me not to date you."

She needed a second to pick her jaw up off the floor. "What did you say to him?"

"I told him to go fuck himself, though much more politely. It's none of his business who I'm seeing in my personal life. And his arguments were all ridiculous."

"Great. This is just great." She was going to have a heart attack. Why was nothing ever easy?

"Don't worry about it. Just nod and agree with him and then we'll just ignore his so-called advice."

"Evan . . ." That didn't seem like a good idea. None of it seemed like a good idea.

"Come on, it's no big deal. Can I see you tomorrow night? I want to see your beautiful face and touch your amazing body."

Even as she bit her fingernail in worry and indecision, she was nodding. "Okay. Sure, of course. I'd like that."

She had just found Evan again.

She really didn't want to lose him before she really had him.

"WHAT?" Eve shouted at Evan.

"You're fired."

God, that look on her face was priceless, worth every bit of hell he was going to catch for this one.

"You can't fire me," she sputtered, feet on her coffee table.

Evan figured he deserved points for being considerate enough to come to her apartment to fire her, instead of making her drive to him. "Yes, I can. And considering that you have been going behind my back feeding information to Carl I don't see how you expect me not to fire you."

"I've been working in your best interest."

"You kept the sponsorship deal a secret from me. And running off and telling him I'm dating Kendall Holbrook was not in my best interest. All you did was contribute to the shit storm. He's going to be watching both of us like a hawk."

She folded her arms over her chest belligerently. "I do what I consider is best for you and your career. Dating Kendall isn't best for you."

"That's not for you to decide!" Evan stared at his sister in disbelief. "Look, you're my sister. I love you, most of the time. But I'm going to kill you if I have to keep working with you."

"Dad will freak out when he finds out."

"I can handle it. I'm not doing this anymore." Evan pulled his keys out of his pocket. "You're fired. That's final. And I think you need to evaluate your true motives."

"What the hell does that mean?"

"You reek of bitterness and I get it. It's not my fault that I was born a boy and you were born a girl. It's not my fault I get to drive and you don't. Nor should it be a strike against Kendall that she beat the odds and made it to the series as a woman. Those are your issues, not ours."

His sister picked up a throw pillow and threw it at him. "Fuck you. I'm grateful I wasn't born a man. I just wish I didn't have to be surrounded by them all the time. And you just saved me seventy-five percent of my stress by getting out of my life."

He dodged the paltry missile. "Glad I could be of help."

"I just bet you are. Now get out of my apartment and good luck running your career without me. You'll be up shit creek in a week." Eve smirked. "Oh, wait. You already are."

Evan's first response to Eve was always to give as good as he got. But for some reason, today he felt her palpable unhappiness, and it made his anger deflate. "Being with Kendall makes me happy. I hope someday you can be happy, too."

If he was hoping for a Hallmark moment, she didn't give it to him.

"Thanks, I'll put that on my calendar. Be happy on Thursday."

Holy shit.

Stunned, Evan realized that his sister sounded exactly like he had for the last ten years.

And a way he never wanted to sound again.

CHAPTER THIRTEEN

"I thought we were going to lunch," Evan said as he sat down in the Adirondack chair next to Kendall on her patio.

Kendall was trying to relax, trying to enjoy the sweep of early spring they were getting in North Carolina, but she stared out across the green space behind her condo development and fretted. "I can't stop thinking about what Carl said to me this morning."

"It's not a big deal." Evan seemed to have no problem relaxing, stretching his legs out in front of him, kicking away a pile of leaves that had clung to the furniture legs all winter. "God, it's gorgeous outside. It must be eighty degrees."

Kendall didn't get his total nonchalance. "Carl is pissed, Evan. He said the commercial shoot was 'not the direction he intended for us to take' and that we should be aiming for funny, for a sense of camaraderie between teammates, not a sex fest campaign."

"We didn't write that commercial. It's not our fault." Evan sat forward and peeled his T-shirt off, before leaning back in the chair and closing his eyes, the midday sun caressing him.

He was gorgeous without his shirt on, all hard muscle and tapered waist, and Kendall felt a physical reaction to him at the same time she wanted to grab his shirt out of his hands and jam it back over his head so she wouldn't be distracted from the real issue at hand. "I don't think you're understanding the severity of this situation."

One eye popped open. "Apparently I'm not."

"He told me that you and I dating is bad for my career. That to come out of the gate with the image of sex symbol will be establishing a pattern and reputation that will follow me for the whole of my career. I don't want that."

"How does dating me establish you as a sex symbol?"

"The commercial, the paparazzi shots . . . the fact that we give off pheromones whenever we're around each other." She didn't understand what he wasn't understanding about this.

Evan grinned. "That's true. We do look like we're about to tear each other's clothes off most of the time. So, okay, what are we supposed to do about it? I can cut down on PDA, not that we've really done any of that so far. We haven't even had a chance to go out on a real date, let alone make out in public."

Kendall bit her lip. He wasn't going to like this. She didn't like this. But given his conversation with the team owner, and hers, it was in both of their best interests to proceed with caution. "I think we should either stop seeing each other for now or do it very, very discreetly."

"What?" Evan sat straight up. "Hell no. We just started seeing each other, I'm not about to pull the plug already."

Part of her wondered if she had thrown that out there as a test, to see how he would react. Because even as she was saying that they shouldn't see each other, Kendall knew she was falling harder and harder for Evan. It was old feelings blending with new and taking her out at the knees.

She wanted to be with him desperately.

But she wanted her career, too.

And she trusted that if she gave it her all, her career would last.

With Evan, she wasn't so sure. It hadn't lasted the first time around.

"I just think it's dangerous . . . me in my rookie season, you in a transitional phase . . . we need to be careful."

"Transitional phase. That's a nice way to put that I suck." Evan winked at her. "But okay, I get what you're saying. I respect it. But come on, Kendall, we can't sacrifice spending time together, having fun with each other, on the whim of a team owner."

Frustrated, Kendall stood up and leaned over the wrought iron fence that contained her patio. "It's not a whim. These are our *careers*. The rest of our lives if you want to get overly dramatic."

"Apparently you're going to get dramatic enough for both of us."

That was enough to send her opening the gate and strolling out across the grass, leaving him on her patio asking in surprise, "Where the hell are you going?"

"On a walk." To figure out why nothing could ever be easy, and why when she was given some kind of happiness, it had to be taken away.

Was she destined to be a career woman only? Sacrificing love for the sake of getting ahead? Was that the irony of the glass ceiling for women? You shattered it, but then you sat at the top alone?

That didn't seem fair. She wanted to drive, she wanted to

be the best in her field, she wanted to win The Chase some-day. But she also wanted love. Marriage. Maybe even kids.

"Slow down, Kendall, wait for me." Evan caught up to her, his shirt in his hand. "Hey, talk to me."

She sighed. "Is there anything to talk about?"

"Uh, yeah. Like the fact that we just agreed we're going to spend time together and yet you're running away from me."

"I'm not running away from you. I'm thinking. Thinking that this is a sucky position to be in." Kendall paused in her striding across the field to look at him. "I feel like I'm being forced to make a choice and I don't like it."

"You don't have to make a choice." Evan reached out and rubbed her forearms up and down gently, his brown eyes serious and compassionate. "We can do this on the down low. We can still see each other but not make a big deal out of it. We'll redo the stupid commercial. It will all be fine."

"This feels complicated, not fine."

"It's only as complicated as you make it."

Was he right? She didn't know. Feeling torn and dissatis-fied, Kendall glanced over at the old barn tenaciously cling-ing to existence at the back of the field. "I wonder what it looks like in that barn."

"Dirty."

"Let's check it out." Kendall started walking towards it.

Evan pulled his shirt on. "We used to go drink beer in-side it when we were in high school. What's really cool is there's a little tiny lake hiding behind it."

"Yeah? It must be really hidden."

"It is. The perfect place to make out."

He tried to take her hand, but Kendall evaded his touch. She was too keyed up, too worried. Besides, holding hands felt like it belonged to a different Kendall and Evan, much younger ones.

"What, I'm not even allowed to touch you now?" Evan sounded completely put out. "We're in a field and no one is anywhere around us."

"I'm just wound tight today. Just let me worry for a while, alright?" Was that really so much to ask for? Sometimes she just needed to fret and worry things over until she came to some kind of peace with them. It was a process, and she wasn't someone who could be teased or hand-held out of a fear or concern.

She expected him to tell her that was ridiculous, or crack a joke, or give her some kind of pep talk.

But Evan just walked in stride with her and said easily, "Alright, let you worry. I can do that. I can do whatever you need me to do, baby."

That he could agree so easily, so nonchalantly, to give her whatever she needed, put the squeeze on Kendall's heart. God, she didn't want to lose this man, not again. Nor did she want to be stupid enough to shove him away.

Maybe she needed to embrace a little of his attitude and just enjoy yourself. Enjoy the success of her career, and the growing feelings between them.

Not to mention the absolutely amazing sex.

"Thank you."

"My pleasure. I mean that most sincerely. I want to be with you, Kendall. In whatever way you're offering."

The simple words took her breath away. Kendall followed Evan into the dark interior of the barn, a little stunned at the intensity of the emotions coursing through her.

"See? Dirty. But a good place to hide from the world."

"And make out."

Evan's eyebrows shot up. "Are you offering?"

She was. She wanted to feel him on her, feel that chemistry that sparked so quickly and burned so hotly between them, let his tongue sweep away her tension and make her appreciative, grateful, for all that she had.

"I'm not offering. I'm telling you. Kiss me now."

The streak of sun from a hole in the roof was hitting the dirt between them, and Evan didn't hesitate to step into it, closing the distance between them. "Offering, telling—either way, I'm taking it."

"I don't want to hide," she told him as he wrapped his arms around her. "I just want us to be smart."

"I know. It's all good, sweetheart. We'll work it out. One way or another, we'll work it out."

She didn't know how or why, but looking deep into his eyes and seeing something there so familiar, so warm, so honest, she absolutely believed him.

"Okay."

"I have something to tell you."

There was something about the way he said that, the way he held her, that made her heart beat a little bit faster. "Yes?"

"I fired Eve."

That wasn't what she'd expected him to say at all. She wasn't sure what she had expected, but something more romantic than that. "What?"

"I fired my sister. I felt like we were working at cross purposes."

"Is that going to be a problem?" She didn't imagine his family was going to be very happy with him.

But Evan just shrugged. "Everyone will just have to get over it."

That was the confidence and blasé attitude she was totally missing. As Evan tugged her back outside by the hand

and they strolled by the little lake, a few ducks splashing around in the sunshine, Kendall let his hand rest in hers. It felt good, right.

"Okay, that really wasn't what I meant to tell you."

"No?" She stopped when he did and glanced over at him. What she saw in his eyes didn't make her heart beat faster—it just about stopped it. "What?" she whispered.

"I love you. I loved you ten years ago, and I love you now. Kendall, you just make me happy, plain and simple."

His hand squeezed tighter in hers and Kendall swallowed hard, emotions welling up and threatening to overwhelm her. "God, I love you, too. And you make me happy."

Plain and simple.

Just like that.

"Shhh," he said, as he leaned down and brushed her lips across her temple. "Don't tell anyone. It's a secret."

"Cross my heart," she told him, her fingers mimicking his, before their lips met and she gave herself into the kiss.

CHAPTER
FOURTEEN

TO the average working American, having a housewarming party in the middle of the afternoon on a Wednesday might seem like a strange choice, but in the world of stock car racing, weekends were off limits for the most part, and it made more sense to pick a weekday. Which was why Kendall was stepping into Ryder and Suzanne Jefferson's new house with a plate of brownies in her hand.

She had thought about sending her regrets instead of attending and having to be around Evan but not be with Evan, but she didn't want to be rude. If any of the other drivers or their wives were willing to let Kendall into their social circle she wanted that opportunity. So often she felt like the outsider.

"Brownies, bless your heart." Suzanne took the plate from Kendall and eyed the dessert squares with naked longing. "God, I love being pregnant. I can eat whatever I want and blame it on cravings."

"Every girl needs her chocolate."

"Well, not every girl." Suzanne made a face at Kendall before looking behind her and calling a greeting. "Hi, Nikki, Jonas, glad y'all could come."

Kendall turned and saw Jonas Strickland and his wife. They'd only been married a few months if she remembered correctly. Tuesday knew the gossip better than she did. But what Kendall did know for certain was that Nikki was, by far, one of the skinniest women she'd ever seen in her entire life.

"Hey, Suzanne! I brought a salad." She thrust a bowl at Suzanne, who juggled it with the brownies.

"Well, thanks, Nikki. But sweetie, this is just a bowl of lettuce." Suzanne peered closer. "With birdseed scattered on top."

"Flaxseed. Protein and fiber, all you need!" Nikki went sailing past her into the house.

"Some of us need a little more than that." To prove her point, Suzanne reached under the cellophane and took out a brownie.

Jonas nodded. "I hear ya." He made sure his wife was really gone before he reached under his sweatshirt and pulled out a bag of Doritos.

Kendall and Suzanne laughed. "Here," Kendall said, taking the bag from him. "I'll carry it to the kitchen so you don't get busted." She opened the bag and offered it to him. "But grab a handful for the road."

"Thanks." He held his hand out, she shook a few chips into it, and he popped them all in his mouth. "God, that tastes good. I'm starving. Nikki has me on a diet."

Jonas wandered off, and Kendall followed Suzanne to the large kitchen with its granite-covered center island. "The house is beautiful, Suzanne."

It was very clean and decorated simply, with strong lines

and warm, neutral colors. There was a lot of black-and-white photography on the walls, and fuzzy blankets in dark baskets next to chairs and the sofa. The kitchen had a few guests in it, including Evan, but most people were in the backyard.

Kendall couldn't help the jump her heart gave at the sight of Evan, a beer bottle in his hand, leaning against the counter by the refrigerator. He was talking to Jonas and hadn't seen her yet.

"Thanks. We figured with the rugrat on the way, we needed a fenced-in yard and a kid-friendly house and neighborhood. We're five minutes from Tammy and Elec and thirty minutes from Ryder's folks, so it's nice."

It was nice.

And something Kendall wondered if she would ever have.

She had been raised to feel like she had to choose between racing and a family life like this, in a house in the suburbs.

Her priority had always been racing, her choice a career. But now she wondered if that was the right one, because with Suzanne and her adorable pregnant belly in front of her, in her gorgeous new home, with Evan five feet away from Kendall, she had a longing she'd never had before, for a home and family of her own.

Which wasn't good to dwell on.

This wasn't an option for her. Not right now, anyway. She and Evan couldn't even acknowledge their relationship in public, let alone set up house and start having kids. It was going to be five years before she could even consider kids, once she was established and could take a season off.

Suddenly feeling very depressed, she grabbed a brownie off the plate Suzanne had set on the island and bit into it. "Congratulations, by the way. When are you due?"

Suzanne opened her mouth to answer, but then clearly spotted something behind Kendall, her eyes going wide. "What the hell are you guys doing?"

Kendall swiveled around and saw that Ryder's crew chief and two guys who drove for Carl in the truck series were sitting in the front of the computer. Which had an image of a very large, very naked penis on it.

The crew chief turned. "Hey, sorry, Suz. It was an accident. I was trying to show the guys the new fishing rod I got and I typed in dicks dot com, which apparently does not take you to the sporting goods store."

"Oh, for crying out loud. Just close it then. I don't want some porn site virus on my computer," Suzanne said.

"Holy shit . . ." One of the drivers, Jake Wesson, who was in his early twenties and didn't look like he needed a razor yet, stared in raw fascination. "That's unnatural. That's the biggest dick I've ever seen in my life."

"How many dicks have you seen, exactly?" Suzanne asked him, which was a legitimate question. "Now turn that shit off, this is a grown-up house now. We're not going to talk about big dicks."

Kendall found herself liking Suzanne more and more, as she didn't seem to realize the irony of swearing while saying it was a grown-up house.

"Wait, just let me print one of these out." The other driver, Marlin Jasper, turned and grinned. "Figured I'd give it to Kendall. She needs a dick if she wants to win a race."

Kendall wasn't so amused anymore. He meant it to be funny, sure, but he also meant to get in a legitimate dig. Marlin had been none too happy when Kendall had hit the cup series. "So that's what it takes? Interesting. Since I've won more races than you, I'm a little curious as to what that means you have in your pants."

And with that, she turned and headed for the backyard, swiping another brownie on her way by the island.

EVAN had been aware of Kendall from the very minute she crossed the threshold of Ryder and Suzanne's new house. He had been standing in the kitchen, getting a beer out of the fridge and talking to Ty McCordle when he had heard Kendall's voice, exchanging words with Suzanne in the foyer. He had watched out of the corner of his eye as she came into the kitchen with an opened bag of Doritos and set it on the counter.

He had desperately wanted to speak to her, but she wasn't looking his way, and Jonas had joined him and Ty, his lips slightly orange.

"Dude, you should be able to eat whatever you want," Ty was telling Jonas. "Seriously, man up and tell her no."

"I can't!" Jonas said. "Nikki gets really upset. She says that I think her ideas are stupid if I say I don't want to do it, and Nikki really hates being called stupid."

Evan found that rather entertaining since Nikki had the IQ of a chickpea. And weighed about as much.

"I'm just saying that she'll beat you down if you let her. It should be an equal partnership between a man and a woman."

"Ty?" His fiancée, Imogen, called to him from over the fruit platter, where she was piling grapes on her plate. "Remember not to drink too much tonight. It has a negative effect on your already compromised ability to get up in the morning, and we have that appointment with the florist for the wedding at nine."

"I won't." Ty set his beer down on the counter and made a face.

"Man up, huh?" Evan told him with a grin.

"Screw you. I guess while Strickland here is bingeing in secret on chips, I'll be chugging my beer in the bathroom."

Evan saw that Kendall was coming back through the kitchen on her way outside, her face stormy as she grabbed a brownie and brought it to her lips. He had seen her at the computer with some of the guys, and clearly something had irritated her.

He wanted to touch her. He wanted to put his hand on the small of her back and lean in and kiss the top of her head. He wanted to hold her hand like a teenager and let everyone know that this amazing woman loved him.

It wasn't planned or intentional, but he couldn't stop himself. He blurted out, "Hey Kendall, want to be my partner in a game of cornhole?"

She stopped walking, startled, and turned towards them, brushing crumbs off her lips. "No."

Then she went through the door to the back patio.

"Guess she told you," Ty said.

Except that Evan had seen what Kendall was hiding by keeping her head down—there had been tears in her eyes.

His phone vibrated in his pocket. He had a text from Kendall.

Sorry, guys are giving me shit. Kinda wish you could give me a hug.

Evan was both touched that she had confided in him and wanted comfort from him, and seriously pissed that anyone was giving her a hard time. He sent her a reply.

There's a hug with your name on it.

But she didn't answer, and Evan found himself eating chip and dip and worrying.

This secret relationship crap was not a good time, and he didn't like it one freaking bit.

EVAN was definitely feeling the cold sting of rejection all the way around.

Kendall had avoided him at the Jeffersons' housewarming party completely despite her text, always leaving a room when he entered it and only staying an hour and a half before she just up and left.

He had wanted to point out to her that acting like he was contagious was just as noteworthy and obvious as a public make-out session would have been. But he hadn't been able to tell her anything because she'd taken off like the hounds of hell were at her feet.

Now sitting on the patio at his brother Elec's four days later, he was being ignored by his entire family except for his sister-in-law, Tamara.

The news of his firing Eve hadn't gone over well.

So while he had still been invited to Easter brunch, no one was throwing any warm fuzzies his way.

Which was bad enough, but the burden of seeing Kendall in secret was also wearing on him. After a week of pretending they weren't together, weren't completely crazy about each other, he was wondering how in the hell he was supposed to pull this off long-term. It wasn't natural to have to play it cool when you were in love. Not that he wanted to recite poetry to her or jump on a couch about it, but he wanted to not have to pretend that she was just a casual acquaintance.

Like here it was Easter and all he really wanted to do was spend the day with her, showing her off to his family.

He wanted to claim her, around the people who mattered the most to him, and in public. Like a normal couple.

But Kendall hadn't even answered the text he had sent her an hour earlier, and the other people who mattered the most to him, his family, were acting like he was the devil in a navy blazer anyway. Nothing felt easy or normal, and he was aggravated with the whole thing.

When his phone vibrated in his pocket, he eagerly pulled it out, only to have his hopes dashed when it saw it was Sara, Nikki's friend he had slept with that one night on the guys' camping trip. She had texted him a couple of times over the last few months and he had politely deflected her interest. It was kind of weird she was contacting him on Easter, but he didn't even bother to read the message.

It wasn't Kendall, that's all he cared about.

Tugging his tie off, he wondered why the hell he had even bothered to dress up. His mother demanded it, but then she'd said all of two words to him all day.

Elec, wearing his own monkey suit, plopped down on the chaise chair next to him, holding his hand up against the sun. "Damn, it's bright out here."

Evan just grunted and took a sip of his beer. Elec's stepkids were in the yard playing on their swing set, and Evan figured they had about three minutes before their mother realized and came to holler at them about ruining their Easter clothes.

Women were difficult. No two ways about it.

"You're being a douche bag, you do know that, right?" his brother asked.

Evan glared at him. "Me? I'm the one getting treated like an infectious disease."

"You fired Eve, man, that's heavy-duty shit. And you didn't even bother to talk to anyone about it."

"It was overdue. She and I don't work well together, and I don't know on whose behalf she's strategizing, but it sure in the hell wasn't mine. She basically handed me over on a platter to Carl."

"I can appreciate that she's difficult to work with, trust me. But Eve's intentions are always to sell you and me to the team owners and to the public."

"Look, I don't really want to talk about this." The truth was, he knew Eve wanted to advance his career. But she was also calculating and underhanded. There was no reason to argue over it. "What's done is done and I bet we'll all be happier once everybody gets the hell over it."

Evan could hear the women chatting in the kitchen behind him and he watched the kids romping around. He wanted this for himself someday, this domestic simplicity, a family of his own.

The pathetic thing was that he'd always wanted it with Kendall. When he'd lost her, he'd given up on that dream. Now he wanted it again, full force, with an ache that sat in him like a serious case of indigestion.

He knew he couldn't have it. Not anytime soon, anyways. And that sucked.

"Uncle Evan, look at me!"

Elec's stepdaughter Hunter, who Evan thought was seven or eight by now, was dangling upside down off of a trapeze swing on the play set, her pink poofy dress falling over her face, exposing her tights.

"Hey, that's awesome," Evan called back to her. "You're like a little monkey. Without a head."

Her laughter rang forth even from beneath all that fabric. "Headless monkey! Headless monkey!" she shrieked.

The kid made Evan laugh. She was random and full of adventure.

"Be careful getting down!" Elec called as Hunter started to flip her legs all the way over for a dismount.

She landed safely. On her knees.

"I saw that one coming," Elec said, wincing as Hunter stood up, covered in mud from hip to ankles. "Tamara is going to kill me."

"It's an ugly dress," Evan told him. "It looks like she's a giant cupcake. No loss. And how is that your fault anyway? She's the one who fell."

"Tell that to her mother."

"We can tell Tamara I pushed Hunter."

Elec looked at him and they both started laughing.

"I just might do that."

"Everyone else is already pissed at me. Might as well make it the whole family."

"No one is pissed at you. Well, okay, Eve is. But the problem is, you don't talk to anybody. You just do stuff, and then no one knows how to react. No one even knows what you really want, man."

Evan scoffed. "Are you for real? I'm supposed to run around talking about my feelings? When did that ever become something a dude does?"

Besides, who would listen?

"I'm not talking like deep dark secrets. Hell, I don't want to know those. But tell us what's going on in your personal life. Explain what you want from your career, out of life."

Draining the remains of his beer, Evan watched Hunter following her brother down the slide, not the least bit deterred by her mucked-up dress.

"What do I want? What do I really want? Damn, I don't know, Elec. Sometimes I don't even know why I drive."

"I don't always know why you drive either. Sometimes

it seems to me like you do it because this career was put in front of you."

"It was. Maybe I do." Their summer weather had retreated and a biting breeze cut over him. "It's what a Monroe does—we drive."

"Only if you want to. Is there anything else you could see yourself doing?"

Evan pondered that for a second. "Hell, I don't know. I've never thought about it. I wouldn't mind being an owner someday. But I'm too young to do anything but drive, aren't I?" The very idea of not being the one behind the wheel was strange in the extreme. But not all that unpleasant, actually. It would be nice to have a different challenge for a change.

"Not necessarily. I guess I question if you drive for the win, or because you love to drive."

"Aren't they one and the same?"

"No." Elec shook his head and stood up. "They're not. Not at all. And I'm going to let you think about that while I make my daughter go change out of this dress."

"You want me to do a fucking Sudoku while you're at it? I'm not big on puzzles."

"Then don't make life one."

Evan shook his head at his brother. "Thanks, Mr. Miyagi." God, his brother got married and started raising kids and thought he was full of wisdom. If Elec tried to get him to wax his car, he was leaving.

"Hunter Jean Briggs!" Tamara's horrified voice came hurtling out of the back door.

Oops. Evan tried to look innocent, shrugging his shoulders at his sister-in-law.

Elec was already walking across the grass. "I'm on it, babe. Don't worry about it."

Tamara slid the patio door shut behind her and shook her

head. "That girl attracts trouble like roadkill does vultures. And she has Elec wrapped around her finger."

"I think you have him wrapped around your finger as well, Mrs. Monroe."

She grinned at him. "Yeah, maybe. But it goes both ways."

"So the marriage thing is working out for you?" He knew it was, he just wanted to hear it said out loud, have validation that someone was happy.

"Splendidly. You should try it sometime."

"I wouldn't mind doing that."

Her mouth dropped open. "Wow. I didn't expect you to actually say that."

"I never said I was anti-marriage." Well, he might have, but that was just his sour grapes talking.

"Well, well, well . . . it seems Kendall Holbrook is quite a woman if she has you admitting that marriage doesn't totally suck."

But Evan shook his head. "Don't go hanging paper bells for Kendall and me. That's not going to happen."

"Why not? Did you honestly think I would be marrying your brother? Did you think that Suzanne and Ryder would get back together and be having a baby? That Ty and Imogen, total opposites, would be planning their fall wedding?" She crossed her arms and rubbed them against the cool air. "You and Kendall make way more sense as a couple than any of us do."

"It's complicated," he told her. It was.

And hell if he really knew why.

He just knew that nightly phone calls and a stolen kiss here and there weren't cutting it for him.

* * *

"YOU'RE so good with the kids," Kendall's mom said, beaming at her as she bounced her niece on her knee. "You really should have one of your own."

Her mother was subtle as usual.

"Kind of hard to race Daytona with a pregnant belly, Mom."

Giving a long-suffering sigh, her mother passed the platter of ham past Kendall. "It's just not natural."

She couldn't help herself; she rolled her eyes at her mom. "Thanks."

"Oh, leave her alone," her sister Kaylynn said from across the table. "I think it's awesome that Kendall is doing what she loves and she's hugely successful. More women should have the guts to go for their dreams."

"Didn't you go for your dreams?" her mother asked. "You have everything you every wanted—a career as a nurse and a lovely family. Kendall doesn't have any of that."

"I'm still sitting here, Mom. If you're going to insult me, maybe it would be nice if you went into the kitchen to do it."

Her mother gave a contrite look. "Well, I'm sorry."

She wasn't, not really, and most days Kendall let it roll off her. But she'd been feeling out of sorts for the last week. Hiding her relationship with Evan was challenging, and sucked some of the joy out of it. It was nerve-wracking thinking she might get caught and have to deal with the career consequences of that.

It was just so frustrating that someone who made her so damn happy was the very man she wasn't supposed to be with according to the boss. They loved each other. They'd even said it out loud. Once you did that, you were supposed to get to walk around making everyone else sick with the gushy looks on your faces and by the way you spent every living breathing minute together.

You weren't supposed to be apart on a day meant for family.

Now sitting here alone and listening to her mother describe all the things she was missing in life was the last thing on earth she needed. Doubts were plaguing her from every direction and she didn't like the feeling at all.

"But you're denying yourself so much, sweetheart. I mean, you haven't even had a boyfriend in several years. Think of all you're missing."

Wanting to bring a halt to the conversation, Kendall hit on a perfect way to appall her mother, especially since every adult family member was seated around the table. "Don't worry, I'm still having sex. I don't need a boyfriend to do that."

Her brother-in-law guffawed. Her father set his fork down with a clank. Her sisters both looked amused.

And her mother looked like horns had shot out of Kendall's head. "Kendall! Good Lord, I can't believe you said that in front of the baby."

Little Jocelyn was six months old and didn't even know where her nose was. Kendall doubted she was being potentially scarred or morally compromised.

"Well, I wouldn't have to if you would just give it a rest." For some reason, Kendall actually felt her lip starting to tremble. Dear Lord, she was going to *cry*. She hadn't cried since she didn't know when. Maybe since she and Evan had broken up ten years ago. "Can't you just respect my choices? Can't you be happy that I'm happy? Can't you just be proud of me instead of disappointed and embarrassed?"

There was a lengthy pause as everyone stared at her in shock.

Kendall swallowed hard, fighting emotion.

Her father frowned. "No one is embarrassed of you. Of

course we're proud of you. We just never expected you'd be successful as a driver."

Carefully handing her niece to her sister, Kendall tossed her napkin on the table. "I don't know what's worse—the fact that Mom has always thought I was a gender-challenged nut job, or that you encouraged me to race cars, and then when I got serious and thought I could do it, you acted like I was insane. You gave me this dream, and then you took it away."

"What the hell are you talking about?" Her father just stared at her, his ruddy complexion growing redder as anger started to mingle with his confusion. "I always encouraged you to drive, even when I thought it was a dead end. And I have to say you're sounding pretty damn ungrateful, young lady. We worked hard to have the money for you to indulge your obsession with cars when you were a kid."

For which in return Kendall had grown up, made a living out of that obsession, and paid off her parents' mortgage and bought her father a sixty-thousand-dollar car.

Feeling slapped, she stood up. "Never mind. I apologize for ruining dinner."

"Where are you going?" her mother asked as she walked away from the table.

Kendall picked her purse up off the credenza, resisting the urge to shake it at her mother as proof of her femininity.

"I'm going to see my boyfriend. He digs me just the way I am."

"I'M not mad at you, you know," Eve told Evan begrudgingly as they poured coffee into mugs at the breakfast bar after dinner.

Evan paused mid-pour. "Are you serious?"

"Nah. I get it. And the truth is, you and I don't work well together."

He couldn't have been more shocked at her reasonable tone. "Who are you and where is my sister?"

Eve laughed, dumping a boatload of creamer into her coffee. "Shut up. But hey, it's true. We butt heads too much to be productive and of use to each other. I hope you can find someone who you see eye to eye with."

"I'm dreaming, aren't I?" Evan just held his coffee and stared at his sister for a second, totally caught off guard. But in a good way. "Thanks, I appreciate that."

"You were right, you know. I do resent the fact that I didn't have the guts to go for it, be a driver myself."

What did he say to that? It wasn't fair that Eve hadn't been given the same support and encouragement as he and Elec had. "You still could, you know."

But Eve just shrugged. "I'm too old now. It is what it is."

Now he really felt like shit for firing her. "Look, I'm sorry for springing that on you the way I did. I should have been more tactful and discussed the fact that we were having problems with you sooner."

"When have you and I ever discussed anything? We'd have just ended up screaming at each other."

He laughed. "True. But I'm glad we're cool. We have to be relatives forever."

"Exactly. Someday our kids are going to play with each other, right?"

Never had he heard Eve mention the desire to have children. Apparently it was a hell of a day for revelations. "Yeah, in about twenty years."

"That's the bitch about it . . . you really can wait twenty years since there's no expiration date on sperm. My eggs will be dried up by then if I wait."

Evan could only handle so much revelation and contemplation in one day. "Jesus, I don't want to talk about your eggs." He felt his phone vibrate in his pocket. He pulled it out and saw it was a text from Kendall asking where he was.

That connection, that simple contact from her, immediately made him happy. God, he wanted to see her, be with her. All the time.

He quickly answered that he was at Elec and Tamara's, hoping she was going to suggest they meet up later.

When he looked back up at his sister, she was grinning at him. "I know who that was from. It's amazing, it's like your whole face just sorts of melts in ecstasy."

Evan frowned. She made him sound like a marshmallow. "I'm just squinting to read the screen in the sunlight."

"Uh, the sun has set already. Please. Just try and deny it was from Kendall."

His phone vibrated in his hand. He shouldn't read it, not with Eve watching him, gloating. But he couldn't resist. He wanted to know what Kendall had to say.

Can I come over there? Or can you meet me somewhere?

Evan got over letting Eve gloat. "Hey, do you think anyone would care if Kendall stopped over?" The thought of spending any time with her worked for him, even if he had to share her with his family. Hell, he wanted to show his family how great she was, how happy she made him.

Eve pursed her lips, like she was trying to prevent a laugh from spilling out. But then she just shook her head. "No, I don't think anyone will mind at all, but you should run it by Tamara just to be courteous."

"Good call."

"And I want to say that while I don't think it's all that smart to be dating another driver, especially one who shares a sponsor, even I can't argue with the shit-eating grin she puts on your face."

Approval from Eve was no small feat, and Evan, despite their differences, did respect her intelligence and savvy. So he gave her a light punch on the arm and said, "Thanks, I appreciate it."

Then he abandoned his coffee and went to his sister-in-law, who was loading dirty dishes into the dishwasher. "Hey, Tammy, would you mind if Kendall stopped by for a half an hour or so?"

She smiled at him. "We'd love to have her. We're just about to cut dessert."

Impulsively, he leaned over and kissed her on the forehead. "Thank you."

"Are you kissing my wife?" Elec asked, strolling into the room with Hunter on his back. "Hey, Pete Junior, hands out of the sugar bowl."

Their oldest child stopped, caught eating a heaping teaspoon of pure sugar straight out of the bowl.

Evan laughed and went to text Kendall in private.

FIFTEEN

"WHAT'S with him?" Elec asked his wife, watching his brother head outside onto the patio to fiddle with his phone. "It's not like him to be that affectionate. To anyone."

"I think your brother is contemplating marriage." Tamara removed the sugar bowl from her son's hands and put it in the cupboard.

"Marriage?" Elec stared at her, dumbfounded, grabbing Hunter's legs when she started to slide down his back. "To who?"

"Kendall, of course."

"Marriage?" he asked again. His brother never had serious relationships. Never mentioned marriage or kids. Hell, his brother didn't even seem to be dating Kendall in any real sort of way from what he could tell. Where the hell did Tamara get marriage from that? "Why would he marry Kendall?"

"Is she pregnant?" Hunter asked over his shoulder.

Elec fought a grin, knowing that would not be well received by his wife. But damn, the kid was funny.

Tamara's mouth dropped open. "Good Lord! I swear, Elec, I don't know what I'm doing wrong with this child. The things she says."

"What? Suzanne's pregnant," Hunter pointed out. "And she and Ryder just got married."

"That is true," Tamara conceded. "But most people aren't pregnant when they get married."

"Seems like the best reason to get married to me" was Hunter's opinion on the subject.

"Love is the best and, really, the only reason to get married," Tamara said firmly to her daughter. Then she glanced out the window at Evan. "I suspect Evan is very much in love with Kendall. She's coming over here in a bit."

"Really? In love?" Huh. That might explain the brooding Evan had been doing lately. He wasn't much of a deep thinker or a melancholy guy, but lately he'd been moody. Elec had chalked it up to losing his sponsor.

"What were they like as a couple when they were together before?"

Elec shrugged, bouncing Hunter a little in the process. "I was like sixteen at the time. I didn't pay attention. There was a lot of moony looks at each other, kissing, hours on the phone." As Hunter continued to wiggle, Elec bent over and set her down. "You're getting heavy, girl."

"Then you should work out more" was her response before she scampered off into the dining room.

Elec looked at his wife. "You're right. The things she says sometimes are appalling."

Tamara grinned. "Told you. Well, I definitely think there's

some unfinished business there with Evan. You can see it on his face."

Not entirely convinced, Elec watched his brother tuck his phone in his pocket, a hint of a smile on Evan's lips. Elec thought back to the conversation they'd just had an hour ago on the patio where Evan had gone sarcastic on him as usual when Elec tried to talk about his career.

If that was love, he wasn't sure it looked a whole lot different on Evan than not being in love did.

"I just think he's had a few too many beers."

Tamara snapped his stomach with the kitchen hand towel. "You'll see. Trust my woman's intuition on this."

"I'd rather touch your woman's intuition than trust it."

"Don't be dirty." But she was already smiling and sidling up to him.

Elec kissed his wife. "Mmm. I love you."

"I love you, too."

If his brother found something half as wonderful as what he had, Evan would be one lucky guy.

KENDALL made it over to Tamara and Elec's house in record time. She wasn't sure what the urgency was, but she just needed to see Evan. She needed to see his smile and casual confidence. The comfortable way he reached for her.

Sitting at dinner with her family had made her realize that while they loved her and she loved them, she was the odd man out. They didn't understand her dreams, her desire, her passion. They didn't understand her.

Kendall was used to straddling two worlds, being forced to decide at parties like Suzanne and Ryder's if she should align herself with the women, who were wives and mothers, or with the men, who were her coworkers. But she was tired of it. She wanted to belong somewhere, and her gut, her heart, kept telling her that place was with Evan.

Evan came out the front door and down the porch steps, smiling at her as she beeped her car locked. He was wearing khakis and a blue blazer and looking really damn sexy.

"Hey, I'm glad you texted me." Evan leaned down and gave her a kiss that was so sweet, so perfect, it was like coming home.

Kendall suddenly realized what it was she wanted. What she had always wanted. "Evan."

"Yeah?" He cocked his head a little. "Are you okay? You look beautiful, by the way."

Instead of responding to any of his questions, Kendall just held his hands and looked into his eyes and blurted out what was swirling around in her head and heart. "Will you marry me?"

His eyes got huge. "What? Are you actually serious?"

"Yes, yes, I'm serious." She had never been impulsive, and she spent all her time worrying and stressing and over-thinking. She didn't want to worry about her relationship anymore, she just wanted to enjoy it. Besides, she didn't think this was really all that impulsive. Evan had been the man she'd wanted to marry ten years ago. Knowing that he had always supported her made her wish she'd been smart enough to let him put a ring on her finger all those years ago. "I love you. I don't want to pretend I don't. Remember that first night, at the bar, when we started talking? And I said if we hadn't both been chicken, we would probably have never broken up? I don't want to be a chicken this time around . . . I want to be with you."

A grin split his face. "I want to be with you, too. I would

absolutely love to marry you. I love you, too, Kendall. God, so much."

"So we're getting married?" She was strangely shocked he had agreed that easily. She had expected questions, concern, distrust at her out-of-the-blue decision. But that would have been her reaction, not his. Evan just went with his feelings, and she was grateful that he loved her enough to just take that leap with her.

"You asked. I said yes. So I'd say we're getting married!" He picked her up and spun her around, making her laugh breathlessly. "Holy shit, I just wish I'd asked you first."

All the stress she'd been feeling, the worry, the doubt, disappeared when he held her like that, solid and purposeful. She felt giddy, relieved. "This week was hard, you know? Wanting to be together and not being together. I thought about you all day, about how you understand me, how you love me, how I hate having to pretend we're not dating and I just thought . . ."

Suddenly she really was crying. The tears that had threatened earlier came spewing out, and Kendall bit her lips, horrified. She wasn't even sure why she was crying.

"Hey, hey, it's okay." Evan put his hand under her chin. "Love doesn't have to be complicated. Life is, but not our love. I just want to be with you."

"Carl is going to flip, isn't he?" It had only been a couple of minutes, and she could already feel doubt creeping in. She wanted to smash it instantly. Evan was right. They were making it complicated, when it didn't need to be.

He just grinned. "He said he didn't want us dating. He didn't say anything about getting married. I figure his whole problem is with presenting a sexual image, which being married tempers. It's acceptable and romantic for a married couple to kiss or gaze hotly at each other."

"True. And I'm looking forward to that." The next party she went to, she was walking in with Evan at her side.

"And he was worried about us dating a few months, then having a tiff and breaking up." Evan gave her a look so hot, yet so tender, Kendall literally forgot to breathe. "We're not breaking up."

"No," she said in a breathy little voice she never would have recognized as her own. "We're not."

"Would you like to invite Kendall in," a voice called from the front porch, "or are you just going to keep her in the driveway all night?"

Elec was standing on the front porch and Kendall fought a blush. Crying and blushing in one day. She clearly was in love. "Hi, Elec, how are you? Thanks for letting me stop by."

"We're glad to have you, if my brother will ever let you inside."

"We're getting married," Evan told Elec, squeezing Kendall's hand.

She hadn't expected him to blurt it out like that, and when Elec's eyes widened in surprise, the blush she'd beaten back emerged victorious. Here it came, the first of many people who would tell them they were nuts. She steeled her back for it.

But Elec just nodded. "Well, congratulations then. I wish you both much happiness."

He sounded so calm, so matter-of-fact, that Kendall didn't even know how to react. That was not what any of her family would have said. There would have been all sorts of opinions about rushing into something so impulsively, and truthfully they weren't going to support her marriage to another driver, long engagement or not, because it would keep her firmly entrenched in a career they didn't approve of.

Which made her phenomenally sad, but she refused to feel that right now.

Now there was just joy, that life had taken her full circle back to Evan.

"Thank you."

Evan kept her hand snuggly in his and started up the steps of the front porch. Then he stopped suddenly. "Hey, let's get married tonight."

"Tonight? How would that be possible?" Kendall laughed, knowing it wouldn't work, but a part of her was giddy and inflated with the intoxicating thought that she could be married by tomorrow.

"We'll go to a chapel. I'm wearing this jacket already, and hell, you have on a white dress. It doesn't get any more convenient than that."

"But we'd need a license and it's Easter."

Elec paused with his hand on the doorknob. "Being a local celebrity has its benefits. I went to high school with a woman who works as a clerk at the courthouse and she's a huge racing fan. If you're serious."

Kendall looked up at Evan, her heart suddenly kicking into overdrive. "Are we serious?"

"Oh, we're serious. I already have a ring, remember?"

Which made her burst into tears.

Which sent Elec into the house faster than a cat after tuna.

"I'm sorry." She sobbed and clung to Evan's chest, not really sure why she was crying.

He rubbed her back, her hair, her arms. "It's okay, baby, I get it. This has been a long time coming, huh?"

She nodded, peeling herself off of him, and contritely brushing at the tearstains she'd made on his white shirt. "A very long time."

"Are you done?" he asked her with a grin.

"Shut up," she said reflexively. "But, yes, I'm done."

"Good, because I don't want to go into the house and announce we're getting married with you looking like someone just died."

Kendall sniffled. The truth was, Evan always knew exactly how to make her feel better. He knew when to tease and when to be serious. He knew when to grin and when to take her into his arms. He just . . . knew.

Feeling like she might start bawling in earnest, Kendall took a deep breath and rubbed her hands down the front of her black-and-white wrap dress. "Is your family going to freak?"

"Yeah, but in a good way."

Freaking out and good didn't go together in Kendall's book, but when they went into the house, hand in hand, she absolutely trusted him.

"Hey, everyone," he said by way of greeting as they walked into a cozy yellow family room, the gas fireplace lit. "Kendall and I are getting married!"

There was a pause while all heads swiveled towards them, then the congrats started pouring in.

"Of course you are," Tamara said, with a knowing smile and a kiss for each of them.

Evan's mother wrapped Kendall in a big hug. "That's wonderful, dear." Then she murmured in her ear, "He's been waiting a long time for you to come back around, you know."

She hadn't known that a month ago. But she did now. Maybe she had since that first night Tuesday had forced them to talk to each other in the wine bar. "I know. I guess I needed to be sure, and I wasn't at eighteen."

"There's nothing wrong with caution."

"So we have a wedding to plan?" Eve looked surprisingly gleeful at the prospect.

"No wedding. We're getting married tonight," Evan told her.

It was the second time in ten minutes they had brought his family to complete and total silence.

"Tonight?" his mother asked, her hand fingering the pearls around her neck, her expression bewildered. "Can you do that?"

Elec, who Kendall hadn't even realized was missing, came into the room with his cell phone at his ear. "We can go pick up the license in half an hour. Kendall, we just need your birth certificate and a few other details like that. I found a chapel right here in Mooresville that will do a wedding at midnight for you."

Tamara looked at her husband with naked adoration. "You're a good, good man, do you know that?"

At the moment, Kendall wasn't going to argue that point one bit. Elec had just made it possible for them to get married in five hours. At midnight. That seemed wildly romantic to her.

Elec just shrugged, then held up his finger and started talking into his phone. "That's right. Evan Roscoe Monroe. R-o-s-c-o-e."

"Your middle name is Roscoe?" Kendall grinned at Evan. "You never told me that. Geez, you think you know a guy . . ."

"It's a family name." He leaned in and kissed her. "No making fun," he murmured. "And I don't know your middle name either."

"Carolina." Which she had to admit was appalling in its own right, given she was born and raised in the Carolinas. But it still wasn't Roscoe.

"Kendall Carolina Holbrook Monroe. Now that's a good name."

It was a good name. Kendall felt that feeling again, that weird inflating in her chest, like she was inhaling helium. Everyone else in the room receded and it was just her and Evan, her first and last love.

Until Tamara's daughter Hunter squeezed in between them. "Does this make you my aunt Kendall?"

She blinked down at the little girl, who was wearing a jacked-up ponytail and an Elec Monroe T-shirt. "Yes, it does. I'm looking forward to spending time with you, Hunter."

"Cool. Us girl drivers have to stick together."

"Hunter's got her heart set on the cup series," Evan told her.

"I see. Yep, we definitely need to stick together." Kendall reached down and did a fist bump with Hunter. "Right now I'm a little lonely in the girl's clubhouse."

"That sucks. I cheer you on, as long as you're not ahead of Elec. Or Ty. Or Ryder. Or Evan."

She grinned at the little girl. "So far I haven't been, so no worries. And I appreciate you cheering me on."

"You're welcome." Then Hunter seemed to lose interest in the conversation and went to retrieve the grape soda she was drinking.

Tamara said, "Thank God she didn't ask you anything inappropriate. I was waiting for it. That was borderline rude, but I expected worse."

"I'll ask something inappropriate," Eve said. "Are you pregnant?"

"Eve, come on," Evan said. "Mind your own business."

Kendall felt her stomach drop to the floor at the very thought of being pregnant. And she wasn't sure if that was a good feeling or a bad feeling sending her gut plummeting. It didn't occur to her to be offended at the personal nature of the question. She just shook her head. "No, I don't think so."

Evan's eyes went from his sister to her. "What do you mean? You think you might be?"

Oh, Lord. Her cheeks were feeling a little warm again. "No, no, of course not. I'm definitely not." Well, she supposed she didn't know that one hundred percent, but she was on the pill, so what were the odds? It was too frightening to even contemplate, really. She'd just impulsively asked Evan to marry her, but the thought of starting a family made her brain freeze. It was one thing to fantasize about the picket fence and babies, another altogether to actually take that gigantic step.

"Oh, okay."

Damned if he didn't look a little disappointed. A warning bell went off in the back of Kendall's mind, that maybe they should discuss what they wanted in terms of the future, but she didn't want to ruin the mood. This was a moment to celebrate, to be certain.

She had broken the pattern of worrying herself into inaction and she needed to stick by her decision. She wanted to marry Evan. There was no doubt.

Looking up at him, at the tender expression on his handsome face, she realized she wanted that more than anything else.

And there was no time like the present to make it a reality.

EVAN stood at the front of the chapel fidgeting with some nerves, but mostly excitement. The venue wasn't the stuff bridal dreams were made of, but Kendall hadn't seemed to mind the indoor arbor and the plastic flowers. He certainly didn't care. They could have been married in that dirty old barn and he would have been happy.

"Do you have the ring?" he asked Elec for the third time.

His brother patted his pocket. "I have it. Relax."

In the interest of not offending anyone in Kendall's family or any of their friends, they had kept it simple. The only people with them were Elec and Tamara, who were acting as witnesses. Other than that, it was just the minister, or whatever he was, and a female staff member taking pictures for them. It was some kind of package deal that Elec had figured out and paid for.

Evan had to say he owed his brother big-time, because he wasn't sure he could even read words on paper at the moment, he was so agitated. But in a good way.

"I can't relax. I'm getting married."

"Just take a deep breath. You're going to end up screeching at the girl if you don't calm down."

"I'm not going to screech. When have I ever screeched?" Evan was about to tell his brother how stupid that was, when he saw Kendall appear at the back of the chapel, under the fake arbor with fake flowers.

He'd seen her not ten minutes ago, and for hours earlier, wearing the same simple black-and-white dress she'd had on for Easter. He'd driven her over here himself after securing their marriage license. Yet somehow, seeing her standing there, as a bride, his bride, overwhelmed him. God, she was beautiful, her blond hair pinned straight and falling over her shoulders. She was wearing a little bit of makeup, something she didn't normally do, and her cheeks were flushed, eyes bright with excitement and love.

That she wanted to marry him, now, humbled him and

thrilled him. Evan didn't necessarily think he'd done amazing things with his life, in fact, outside of his career, he had to say he hadn't done much worthy of praise. He hadn't done anything wrong, he just hadn't done as much as he could have. But being secure in a relationship with Kendall, knowing he had someone to come home to at the end of the day, it just made him want to strive to be a better man. He had influence and he wanted to use it. He wanted to be worthy of this scrappy woman who had fought so hard for all of her success.

"You okay?" Elec murmured to him.

Evan shook his head. "Yeah. More than okay." He couldn't take his eyes off his bride as she slowly walked down the aisle, looking a little shy. "She's beautiful, isn't she?"

"Definitely."

"I'm pretty damn lucky." He went still, all his excited jitters gone. His mind, body, heart, and soul all went quiet with the certainty of what he was doing. He loved Kendall, always had, always would. Now he was going to make her his wife.

When she got to the front, she paused, like she wasn't sure where she was supposed to go, but she was smiling at him, a big, wide open grin.

He moved in alongside her. "You're supposed to stand next to me, you know. Like you like me."

"Shush," she told him, elbowing him with another smile.

Evan took her hand in his and squeezed it. He knew that wasn't standard wedding protocol, but hell, they were already doing everything their way, what difference did a little hand holding make? He just wanted to feel her grip in his.

"Dearly beloved, we are gathered here"—the overweight

and bearded minister glanced at his watch—"this evening to join Evan Roscoe Monroe and Kendall Carolina Holbrook in marriage."

Those words hit Evan with the impact of a head-on crash at Talladega. Only while both things were equally as intense, the result was totally different. Happiness swelled in him, and the subsequent words the minister spoke were lost as he just savored this pure moment of love and joy.

"Do you, Evan, take Kendall to be your lawfully wedded wife?"

"I do." Evan only hesitated for a second before he said, "Can I say something here?"

The minister nodded. "Of course."

He turned to Kendall, who was staring at him blankly, like she wasn't sure what was going to come out of his mouth. Hell, he wasn't entirely sure himself, but he knew a simple "I do" just wasn't enough to express how he felt. "Kendall, you know me, and I've always thought writing your own vows was well, kind of corny. And obviously I didn't write any ahead of time since we just decided to get married tonight, but I want to say something to you."

She smiled and took both of his hands in hers. "Okay."

"I just want you to know that in a lot of ways I've been lost the last ten years. You and me, back in the day, maybe we were too young, but we were always meant to be together, and when I didn't have that direction, when I didn't have you, I spent a lot of time wandering around trying to figure out what I was supposed to do with my personal life. A life without you didn't make sense. When Tuesday asked me at that wine bar what it was about you that I'd fallen in love with, I told her it was your smile, your laughter. That was an answer that barely skims the surface.

I don't have enough time to describe all the wonderful things about you, but I love that you don't do anything half-way . . . when you do something you do it one hundred and ten percent. With your driving, with your friendships, with me." Evan took a deep breath, aware that he was never going to be able to say everything he wanted to. "I don't have the pretty words, the right words, to describe how I'm feeling, but just know that I'll always love you. For better or for worse, through failed sponsorships and lousy finishes, through endless miles on the road and champagne celebrations, I'll love you."

Kendall was glad her earlier tears seemed to have vanished, because if ever there was a moment to cry, this was it. Evan was standing in front of her, looking absolutely gorgeous in his blue blazer and white shirt, his brown eyes filled with love and certainty, as he spoke words of total commitment. She couldn't believe how lucky she was. She had screwed up bad when they were young, and yet he'd essentially given her a second chance without hesitation or mistrust.

"And I just want to say thank you," she told him. "For understanding that I was young and stupid and maybe needier than I ever realized. Thank you for leaping back into this relationship with me, and for agreeing to marry me."

He grinned at her pronouncement. "No need to thank me."

But Kendall held his hands tighter. "I'm serious. I tend to shut people out, and when I offer to let them back in, most people don't want to be, with good reason. You never hesitated, and if I didn't already love you, I would love you for that alone. I love your sense of humor, your easygoing personality, your unconditional affection and love. You have a good heart. A good soul." She grinned. "Not to mention your biceps are pretty amazing."

"Sexist," he murmured. "I could never get away with naming body parts in our wedding ceremony."

"We ladies need to take double standards that work in our favor whenever we can." Kendall stroked his hands with her thumbs. "But seriously, I am just so in love with you, and I can't wait to spend the rest of our lives together."

She turned to the minister. "I guess I should officially say 'I do.'"

He nodded.

So she said, "I do."

Then even before they were instructed, they were both leaning in for a kiss. It curled Kendall's toes, seared her heart, and shattered her ability to think.

"You need to put the rings on," the minister told them.

"Oh. Right." Kendall broke away from Evan, but stayed close to him, eyes still locked on his, not wanting to put any space between them. "Remember I will get you a better one than this," she said as she took the silver band they'd bought at Walmart on the way over from Elec's. She slid it on his finger.

"It doesn't matter," he said. "It's what it stands for, not the ring itself."

Then he pulled a ring out of the box Elec was holding and put it on her finger. Kendall looked down at it, amazed that it was ten years old, surprised at how pretty and delicate it was. She had braced herself for something gaudy, given Evan's age at the time. But it was lovely, a silver band with a princess-cut diamond. Simple, sweet, stunning.

He slid it on her finger and they were married.

Kendall was aware that around her Tamara and Elec and the minister were offering congratulations, but she couldn't do anything more than grin and nod, her focus on Evan.

They were married.

How crazy was that?

CHAPTER
SIXTEEN

KENDALL let out a startled yelp when Evan lifted her legs out from under her at the door to their hotel room. "What the hell are you doing?" she asked him.

He didn't think it took a genius to figure it out, and Kendall was pretty damn smart. She was just fussing, which he had noted over the last ten years, she liked to do. "I'm carrying you over the threshold."

Evan looked down at his grinning wife. His wife. Even as her ass started to sink and he bounced her to get a better position, he couldn't help but just stare at her as she smiled up at him. They were married.

"I thought you were supposed to do that at home, not a hotel."

"There are rules on it?" Evan wasn't big on rules. Pulling the key card out of his pocket, he realized he should have opened the door first, then picked her up. This romantic crap was complicated.

But this was their wedding night and he intended to persevere.

"Wait, where are we going to live?" Kendall's eyes went wide. "We have two condos and two motor homes. Which ones are we keeping?"

Evan shrugged, more concerned with holding her one-armed while he crammed the key into the slot then with whose house they were going to live in. "Whatever you want, sweetheart."

"One should be yours and one should be mine. To be fair." She was biting her lip. "Do we have to let go one of our motor home drivers? I'd hate to do that. I don't have a lot of furniture in my condo, so maybe we should move into yours."

Had he mentioned he didn't care? He just wanted to enjoy the moment.

"What do you think?" she insisted.

"I think that sounds fine." Evan shoved the door open and walked quickly to get her inside before it slammed shut on them. The overnight bags they had packed he left hastily in the hallway, hoping she wouldn't notice.

"You left the bags in the hallway."

Damn. "I know."

"Someone is going to steal them."

Evan set her down on the bed. "Kendall."

"What?" She looked past him to the door, clearly worried about the bags.

"Do you hear that?" he asked her.

She cocked her head. "Hear what?"

"Nothing. Absolutely nothing. It's just you and me in the hotel room tonight, our wedding night. There are no condos, no worries, no nothing. Just you and me."

Her eyes softened. "You're right."

Then, because he knew her and loved her, he went for the bags, dumping them at the foot of the bed.

The corner of her mouth turned up and she smiled shyly. "Thank you."

"You're welcome. Now forget all that other stuff and let me make love to you the way a man does his wife." Evan yanked on his tie, loosening it.

Her breath caught. "Oh? And how is that?"

"All night long." Evan balled up his tie and tossed it on top of the bags she'd been so concerned about.

He loved the way she looked, resting on her elbows, ankles crossed as her legs dangled off the bed. Her dress flowed over her thighs, her hair down over her shoulders. Evan could count on one hand the number of times he had seen Kendall in a dress, and he had to admit, he liked it. It brought to the forefront all those soft and feminine curves she had. Of course, he thought she was just as hot in a racing suit, but here, right now, on their wedding night, he appreciated the dress.

"You look beautiful," he told her, kicking off his shoes. "The most beautiful bride ever."

She smiled, her eyes sparkling. "I don't even look like a bride, but thank you."

"You look like a bride to me." Evan reached down and pulled her shoes off her tiny feet and set them carefully by the suitcases. "But are you sorry we didn't have a traditional wedding?"

"Of course not. I proposed, remember? And you know, I'm not exactly a traditional kind of girl."

Evan climbed onto the bed with her, sliding his hand up the smooth skin of her calf. "I noticed. Just one of the many things I love about you."

She leaned closer to him, a grin on her face. "Do you love me?"

Evan paused, his throat suddenly tight. There was no way to express what he felt. "I love you beyond measure."

"I love you, too."

No words had ever sounded sweeter to him. Evan moved his hand farther up her leg, caressing the inside of her thigh. "So no regrets? I could propose to you now if you want, just so we're even." He did worry about that. Didn't every woman want some crazy-ass romantic marriage proposal?

She laughed, reaching out and undoing the top button on his shirt. "Nah, I'm good. But maybe someday you can serenade me."

"Serenade you?" Evan brushed his thumb over the fabric of her panties, finally having made his way all the way up her leg. With her own fingers teasing over his second button, he had to admit, he was losing the thread of their conversation. "What does that mean?"

Kendall kissed the inside of his neck. "You know, like sing to me. In public. Where other people can hear you."

Shifting under the satin of her panties, Evan teased through her soft curls into the moisture waiting for him. He loved the sound of her breath hitching. "So you want me to make an ass out of myself for you?"

"No. It's romantic. A public display of affection." Kendall undid his second shirt button and moved on to the third.

"A kiss is a display of affection. Off-key singing is not."

"You asked what I wanted."

She had him there. "Okay. Duly noted. But what do you want right now?"

"What do I want right now? Hmm. I think you can figure it out." Kendall's eyes were drifting closed, her fingers slowing on his shirt button.

Evan kissed her soft, pert mouth. His wife. She was his wife, and it made every touch, every kiss that much more exciting. "This? Is this what you want?"

She sighed. "Yes. That. Among other things."

"Like this?" Evan moved down her chin to her neck and kissed the soft skin there.

"Hmm."

"No?" God, he really was in love. Every inch of her body, every sound she made, gave him intense, deep satisfaction. She smelled like the crisp spring air and the light floral perfume she always wore. She smelled like his.

"That's nice. Not quite what I had in mind though." Kendall guided his head down to her chest.

Evan grinned at her take charge approach. Yet another thing he loved about her. "What am I supposed to do here?" he teased her.

"Shut up and suck me. Please."

"Since you asked so nicely." Evan reached behind her and undid the zipper on her dress. When he slid the fabric off her shoulders and down over her bare breasts, it was a happy discovery to find she wasn't wearing a bra.

They were amazing breasts, as Trevor the makeup guy had agreed. Evan leaned over and drew one tight pink nipple into his mouth, laving his tongue across her flesh.

Kendall buried her fingers in her husband's hair and let her head fall back as he sucked on first one nipple and then the other. Her husband. It had such an amazing sound to it.

As he teased one finger between her thighs and flicked his tongue over her breasts, Kendall felt her heart rate jump at both his touch and the emotional overload of knowing she and Evan were married.

Suddenly, she wanted to have sex with her husband. She wanted him inside her, no teasing, no lengthy foreplay, just him in her body, joined with her. Lying back, she pulled him down on top of her and reached for the zipper on his pants.

When he started to go down between her legs, his intention to lick her clear, Kendall grabbed his head and pulled him up. "I want you inside me," she said, staring up at him, losing herself in his eyes as they went dark with desire and tenderness.

She expected him to argue or comment or tease her, but Evan just shucked his pants with lightning speed, his eyes never leaving hers. Her throat tightened, her body arched towards him, and goose bumps rose all over her flesh.

Evan shoved the bottom of her dress out of the way, and then he was inside her, his face a mixture of awe, ecstasy, determination. Kendall dug her fingers into his back and held on, her body singing with pleasure, her heart open and vulnerable. This connection, this trust, amazed her. She hadn't experienced love and pleasure all swirled together like this since she'd been eighteen and she had discovered her sexuality with Evan.

Now he was her husband and now she was going to have an orgasm.

Forcing herself to keep her eyes open so she could continue to see him, so he could see her, Kendall flexed her inner muscles on him. When she was certain he was going to come, a moan escaping his mouth, Kendall let herself fall over the edge.

They came together, eyes locked, and bodies entwined.

As husband and wife.

No orgasm had ever felt quite so satisfying.

* * *

"SO," Kendall said to Evan as he sat up sleepily in bed, after giving her a good morning kiss. "I guess I need to call my folks."

He ran his hand over his head. "That would be a good idea, Jay. It wouldn't be cool if they found out from some-one else."

"I don't want to." She knew her parents were going to be hurt. But they had hurt her, and she wasn't particularly good at discussing those kinds of feelings with anyone, especially not with her parents. It seemed the more she cared, the less she was able to express her emotions.

"Babe." Evan reached over and drew his finger across her lip. "They love you. They want you happy. You can't just shut out the people you love when something bad gets tossed your way."

She made a face. "You're right, you're totally right."

"You know, we both have 'patterns.'" Evan gave air quotes and rolled his eyes to indicate what he thought of the term. "I tend to just react to life and the people around me. I don't initiate anything. So maybe this is a good time for both of us to set those patterns behind us and move forward in life, you know?"

Kendall thought her husband was both cute and smart. "I think you make a lot of sense, Monroe. Okay, I'll call my parents."

He leaned over and kissed her again. "You do that. I'll jump in the shower."

"Can I watch?"

"After your phone call." Evan ambled into the bathroom, his bare butt dragging a sigh from Kendall.

She was satiated and sore, but damned if she didn't want another piece of that. Forcing her mind out of the gutter, she called her mother, lying on her back in bed still.

"Kendall? Why on earth are you calling so early? Is everything okay?"

"Everything's great. I eloped last night. Evan Monroe and I are married."

There was a pause that stretched out so long, Kendall counted five blinks of the red light on the ceiling smoke detector. "Mom?"

"I'm sorry, I think I went into shock. You're married? To Evan? Where? How?"

"Last night at the courthouse at midnight. Just me and him." She crossed her fingers behind her back. That was almost the truth. "I'm really happy, Mom. I hope you'll be happy for me."

"Well, of course I'm happy. Marriage is a good thing for you, it will help settle you down."

She would not let her mother spoil her mood at all. "I'll call you later, Mom, but I wanted to let you know before the news picks up on it. I love you and Dad. Talk to you soon."

After she hung up, she wondered if giving her mom the bum's rush qualified as shutting her out. Kendall didn't think so.

She dialed a second, more desirable number.

"What the effing time is it?" Tuesday asked, her voice cranky and gravelly.

"I have an exclusive for you," Kendall told Tuesday. "And it's a good one. You'll be glad I woke you up at seven A.M."

"Oh, yeah? Is someone changing teams?" Tuesday's sleepy voice perked up. "Coffee. I need coffee."

"No, no one switched teams. But rookie driver Kendall Holbrook and teammate Evan Monroe got married last night right here in Mooresville." Kendall lounged on the bed in her sleep shirt, the sound of Evan's shower soothing to her ears.

There was stunned silence, then Tuesday said, "I don't need the coffee anymore. Are you kidding me?"

She grinned in the empty room. "Not kidding. I'm married, can you believe it?"

"No, I can't . . . my God. Wow. Congratulations! How did this happen?"

"I asked him. He said yes. We did it."

"Just like that? Girl, I didn't think you had it in you." Tuesday's voice was admiring. "And you asked him? Wow."

"You said that already." Kendall held up her left hand and admired her ring in the morning light. "I give you permission to post this information as soon as you'd like. I would do it before someone tattles. Only the courthouse clerk, the minister, and the photographer know about it, but someone always tells a friend, who tells a friend."

"I'm on it. I'll have it out there within the hour. Your phone will be ringing off the hook."

"We talked about it. We're planning to do a press conference and photo shoot tomorrow. Today is just for relaxing."

"Yeah, I bet that's what you're doing."

She laughed. Tuesday definitely had the right of it. Kendall was planning on making the most of their limited remaining time. "This is my honeymoon, after all."

"Where are you?"

"The Hilton."

"That's your honeymoon? Make that man take you to Bora Bora."

"Sure, in about six months. Until then, we have to work."

"This is when I'm glad I'm me, and you're you. I can't be that disciplined. I'm too impulsive."

"I'm more impulsive than I thought."

"Apparently." Tuesday's voice softened. "You know I'm really happy for you. I know you must really love him."

"I do." Kendall sighed, feeling very content.

"So give me details. Who was there, anyone?"

"Just Elec and Tamara Monroe. The ceremony took place at midnight. And if you're really nice to me, I'll send you one of the pictures."

"I'm not going to say no to that. But you know you could sell those shots."

"Who wants to pay for our wedding pictures?"

"Ask your PR person. Plenty of media outlets. You could donate the money to charity."

That held a certain appeal. But it also was another responsibility she didn't want to think about at the moment. The shower cut off. "Alright, I'll talk to my people. But go ahead with your story."

"Awesome, thanks, babe. Maybe we can grab a cocktail in a day or two and you can gush about your new husband to me for an hour."

She laughed. "Sounds fabulous."

They said their good-byes and Kendall hung up right as Evan strolled back into the room, hair wet and chest still damp from his shower, the towel around his middle nice and low on his hips. "Who were you talking to? Didn't sound like your parents."

"Tuesday."

"Yeah? What did she have to say?"

"I don't care." Kendall sat up in bed and reached for his towel. "At the moment all I care about is you."

He dropped his towel. "Do you care if I'm naked?"

"Even better."

CHAPTER
SEVENTEEN

BREAKING NEWS
from Tuesday Talladega

.

Exclusive sources inform me that Kendall Holbrook, the female rookie driver burning up the cup series this season has just up and MARRIED Evan Monroe. You heard me, people. Married. A secret ceremony at midnight last night right here in Mooresville. Hell has frozen over and pigs have flown because the driver who swore he would never "put a ring on it" has done just that, achieving a first in stock car racing. Two cup competitors are married to each other. Eat your heart out, ladies, because for the number 42 car hottie his personal chase is over . . .

Let's hope a little home lovin' fixes whatever has been ailing him on the track. Screw the honeymoon. Give the fans a win at Phoenix on Sunday and we'll forgive the both of you for having the nerve to fall in love behind our backs . . .

KENDALL still felt sleepy and rumpled and the most sexually satisfied she'd ever been in her life, and the last thing in the world she felt like doing was greeting the first day of her marriage by having a meeting with Carl, but it was necessary.

Smoothing her hair down again, she cleared her throat and steeled her back. Knocking on his door, she didn't wait for a response before walking in.

"Kendall, good morning. What can I do for you? I was surprised to hear from you so early today."

Ignoring the feeling in the pit of her stomach, Kendall said, "I just wanted to let you know, before you found out from someone else, that Evan and I got married last night."

The team owner's eyebrows shot straight up to his hairline and his smile disappeared. "Excuse me?"

"I realize this is a bit unexpected, but we're very happy and would appreciate your support."

Her heart was thumping hard, but she stood her ground.

Carl stared at her, the pause growing uncomfortable, but Kendall refused to pander.

"I told Evan this could have disastrous consequences for his career," he said finally. "I'm not concerned about you, but him? That's another story. He's risking a lot."

She had been afraid that's what Carl would say, and the last thing in the universe she wanted was for her proposal of marriage to damage Evan's career. He was her husband and she wanted to support him, not hinder him. He didn't even know she was at the office. He had gone home to pack some bags and handle some business and had been intending to just give Carl a call.

"Marriage is enough of a risk, Carl, don't put added pressure on him. What Evan is doing on the track has nothing to do with our relationship."

"Look, I'm not some old codger down on love."

She wanted to ask how old Carl actually was. She was thinking he was really only in his mid-forties, but she wasn't sure given the silver in his hair.

"But racing is big money, you know that. I can't afford to lose and neither can your husband."

"Then don't make it harder for him by giving him threats instead of congratulations." She was well aware she was treading on thin ice here, but it was the right thing to do for her husband, her marriage.

Kendall braced herself for a reprimand but Carl just grinned. "I'll see what I can do, Mrs. Monroe. Congrats. And bust some ass on that track, you hear me?"

She let her shoulders relax. Smiling back, she was tempted to salute him, but restrained herself. "Thanks. You can count on it."

Feeling much lighter, she said good-bye and left, wondering if she could talk her brand-new husband into a nooner.

"WHAT'S married life like?" a reporter asked Evan on Sunday as he strolled from pit road to the platform for drivers' introductions.

Evan grinned. "So far, so good. Best six days of my life."

The reporter, a guy named Ed, who had been around stock car racing for the majority of Evan's career, grinned. "Never thought we'd see the day. You guys are all falling like dominoes."

"I guess we're smart enough to know a good thing when we see it."

"Can I get a quick interview with you and your wife?"

"If you can find her." Evan glanced around and didn't see

Kendall. She liked to be alone before a race, and the last he'd seen her, she was in a quiet corner in the garage. It wasn't his style, but he respected hers.

It had been a hell of a week. A fantastic, bliss-filled whirlwind. The press conference had gone well. Carl had chewed him out privately, but had smiled publicly, and Untamed Deodorant was going gaga, in a good way, over the news.

As Tuesday had blogged on Monday, it was a stock car racing first. Husband and wife both driving in the cup series. Never been done before.

Evan didn't care about being first, he just cared that he'd won the ultimate race of all—the one for love. It was corny and sappy and had him eating all the words he'd ever spoken in disdain to his buddies, but he'd gladly swallow them down if it meant feeling like this.

"Hey, here she is." Evan couldn't stop the grin from spreading across his face when his wife came into view. Wife. It felt even better than he ever could have imagined.

"Kendall, congratulations," Ed told her.

"Thanks." She smiled at the reporter then raised her eyebrows at Evan. "Are you talking trash, Monroe?"

"I'm just telling Ed you're the best thing that's ever happened to me."

"Smooth." Ed nodded in approval.

A female reporter had noticed the two of them and joined in. "Can I see your ring, Kendall?"

"It's locked up. Didn't think it was smart to wear it driving. But trust me, it's beautiful."

"Practically vintage," Evan told her.

"Practically? How is a ring 'practically' vintage?"

"He bought it for me ten years ago," Kendall said, surprising Evan. He hadn't thought she'd be willing to share that. "Only we broke up before he could offer it to me."

"Sometimes you're in the chase longer than you expected," Evan said, knowing he sounded like a complete dork. He kissed Kendall on the top of her head in a move he was sure would embarrass her, but he didn't care. "But the win is worth the wait."

The female reporter actually put her hand over her heart. "Oh, my God, that was so sweet."

Ed rolled his eyes. "You're ruining it for us, man. First McCordle pops the question on live TV, then Jefferson re-marries his ex-wife, and now you've gone all Air Supply lyrics on us? Bachelors everywhere are weeping."

"Don't let him fool you. He's a real jerk at home." Kendall smiled and leaned over and kissed his cheek. "See you in five. Love you."

Evan grinned as he watched her walk away. "She's hot and funny. Damn, I'm a lucky man."

He hadn't turned his cell phone off yet and it buzzed in his pocket. Pulling it out, he saw it was another text from Sara. Frowning, he wondered if she'd seen the news about his marriage yet. Surely that would dissuade the girl.

I really, really need to talk to u. Now.

Was she nuts? He had a race starting in an hour. And what the hell was there to talk about?

Can't, race is going to start soon. Look, I'm sorry, but I just got married. Don't think we should talk.

He had barely hit send before he got another text from her.

I'm pregnant. Ur the father.

Evan stopped walking. All the blood rushed out of his head and he felt like he'd had the wind punched out of him. Like he might pass out. Like the entire world around him had started to tilt and spin.

Oh. My. God.

It couldn't be true. There was no way. It had been months and months since he had stupidly slept with Sara, and if she were pregnant, wouldn't she have said something sooner?

"Jesus," he whispered, his face burning, mouth pooling with nervous saliva, stomach churning like a whirlpool of acid.

He deleted the noxious message, unable to even look at it.

How far along?

Maybe if she was lying, that would trip her up.
But her response was immediate.

Nineteen weeks. It's a girl.

Evan thought back to the camping trip he'd taken with the guys, when the women had crashed. That had been before Thanksgiving, early, maybe mid-November. He wasn't exactly sure. But it was almost the middle of April, which meant five months, which meant about twenty weeks . . . "Oh, my God."

For a horrible second, he thought he was going to hurl, but he drew a few deep breaths and managed to control it.

"Hey, you okay?" Ed asked him, clapping him on the shoulder. "You look a little green."

"My breakfast isn't sitting right," he said, forcing the words. "I'm okay though, thanks."

"I think they're about to call your name."

Evan looked at the stage, feeling a little frantic. Damn, he had to pull it together. If Sara was pregnant, it was possible he wasn't the father. They had only spent one night together, and hell, that had really only been about thirty minutes, not a *night*. Maybe she wasn't even pregnant. Maybe it was just a ploy to get his attention since he had politely turned down her advances in the months since.

Or maybe she was pregnant and he was the father.

A baby.

With a woman who wasn't his wife. His brand-new, only-been-hitched-for-six-days wife.

Oh. My. God.

"I don't know, Kendall, I think you're a bad luck bride," Jim teased her over the radio. "Your new hubby is awfully distracted out there today."

"What's he doing?" Kendall frowned as she took turn two on lap fifty-seven, wishing she had an additional blocking strip on her visor, since the sun was brutal on the track in Phoenix. Evan had seemed fine before the race. Downright relaxed.

"He's all over the place. Skittish. But don't you worry about him, you've got your own problems given how tight you're running."

"Then quit teasing me about my husband," she told him, still getting a thrill over the use of that word.

"Come on, I have to, it's too damn good not to."

She laughed. "Fair enough."

There were only a few seconds of dead air between them before Jim was back on. "Caution. Evan just spun out into the infield."

Even as she reacted automatically to the information, keeping her car under control and assessing what was going on around her, Kendall's heart plummeted in her chest. "He okay?"

"Yep. He's heading to the garage with a message for you to kick some ass."

She grinned inside her helmet. "Tell him I'm on it."

"If I have to start relaying love messages back and forth I'm going to puke in my mouth" was Jim's opinion.

So just to screw with him Kendall made kiss-kiss sounds.

He laughed.

"Now leave me alone, I'm working here."

With extreme effort, she forced Evan out of her mind and her focus back to the task at hand.

"WHAT the hell?"

Evan glanced over at his sister. "I don't have time, Eve. I'm trying to get back out there." His crew was pounding away on his car, trying to repair the damage he'd done when he'd spun out into the infield.

But Eve touched his arm. "Are you okay? For real? That was a weird accident, Evan. It's like you just forgot to pay attention for a second."

"You guys are doing awesome. Give me five," he told his crew and walked Eve to the other side of the garage, where no one could hear. "Look, if I tell you this, promise not to yell at me. Just help me figure out what the fuck I'm supposed to do, okay?"

Her eyes widened. "Okay. What's going on?"

"You remember Nikki Strickland, Jonas's wife?"

"No one can forget her. She has the intelligence of a sock puppet."

"Well, she has a friend, Sara." Evan pulled off his glove, suddenly feeling the need to gnaw on his fingernail. "And she's just like Nikki, only maybe a little angrier, a little smarter."

"Yeah? What about her? I see her with Nikki all the time. Who's she dating, by the way, because she's clearly pregnant."

Evan spit out the nail he'd just ripped off of his finger. So much for his hopes that she wasn't really pregnant. "How do you know she's pregnant?"

"She weighs like seventy-three pounds. A pregnant belly is totally obvious on a woman built like that . . . Oh, my Lord in heaven." Eve's hand went up to her mouth. "You aren't saying . . ."

He was. Evan felt the need to puke again. "They came up when we were camping last fall at Lake Norman. I'd been drinking, she'd really been drinking. I tried to say no, but then she was relentless, and it had been a long time since I'd had sex . . ."

God, it sounded even worse out loud than it did in his head. He went at his nail again.

Eve grabbed his hand and shoved it to his side. "You're making yourself bleed, get ahold of yourself. So she's pregnant. You slept with her. What makes you think you're the father?"

"Because she said I am. Today. She's been sending me text messages, but I told her I wasn't interested in seeing her again. Then . . . bam. Today she says she's pregnant."

"Why would she wait like five months to tell you?"

"I don't know!"

"Well, I'm going to go find her and ask her. I saw her in the boxes with Nikki not ten minutes ago."

"What is she doing in Phoenix? We're two thousand miles from Charlotte."

"How the hell should I know? But I imagine she came with Nikki."

"You're going to talk to her? Shouldn't I talk to her? Are pregnant women even supposed to fly?"

"I think they can. I mean, obviously she did. But yes, I'm going to talk to her. I'm going to arrange for the two of you to meet somewhere completely private where no one will see you. We're keeping this totally quiet until that baby is born and we can do a DNA test."

His sister's face had gone mulish. "I don't want to be an asshole, Eve . . . she's pregnant." She'd already gone through half the pregnancy alone, he couldn't see giving her the cold shoulder until some test proved it was his. Unless she'd slept with another guy a week before or after him, it was looking highly likely this kid was his, and even if it wasn't, he had to give her the benefit of the doubt and some support. It just seemed like the right thing to do.

He had been there in that tent that night, too. He'd been as irresponsible as she had.

"No one says you have to be an asshole. But for the love of God, do not sign *anything* without me and our lawyer."

"What would I be signing?" His own death certificate, when Kendall found out what a goddamn idiot he was? "What am I going to say to my wife?"

There was a pause, then Eve rushed to his defense, which he had to say he totally appreciated. "What can she say? This happened long before the two of you were back together. Accidents happen. Sex happens. It's awkward and awful and not exactly a great newlywed discovery, but what are you going to do? It will all work out."

"You're right. We'll just deal with it. Okay. I'm going back out there to finish this race for whatever points I can get. I'll talk to you later."

"Don't worry about it." Eve gave him a smile, even if it looked somewhat maniacal. "We'll figure it out."

KENDALL zoomed past the checkered flag, less than two seconds behind Jack Daniel Davidson, in an unbelievable second-place finish. She yelled into her radio as she could hear her crew all giving shouts and whoops of excitement. When she flew into pit road, they were jumping up and down and fist pumping, which is exactly how she felt. As soon as she could, she was out of the car and jumping up and down with them, joy making her feel like she might burst.

When she got her helmet out, her crew chief put his hands on the back of her head and shook her around a little. "Damn, girl, being a bride done you good!"

She laughed, a sweaty strand of hair escaping her ponytail and sticking to her cheek. Swiping at it, she gave high fives to each of the guys on her team and gratefully accepted a bottle of water.

This was possibly the most absolutely perfect week of her life.

Even more so when her father called twenty minutes later.

"Hello?" Kendall stepped away from the noise of the track.

"Congratulations, baby, we're all very proud of you."

Those words meant more to her than he could imagine. "Thanks, Dad, I appreciate it."

"When you and your husband get home, we'll celebrate."

"Sounds good!" Kendall was having a hard time hearing him, so she told him she would call him back later when she was in the RV.

When she hung up, her crew showered her with beer. Laughing, Kendall grabbed a bottle from her jackman and took a swig. After a head rubbing from Jim, Kendall pushed him away, flushed and as proud as she had ever been. "Get off me, you big lug."

"Have you seen Evan?" she asked.

"No."

"I'll be back in five."

She wanted to find her husband.

What she didn't want to find was her husband standing outside their motor home with a blonde. Her excitement instantly deflated as she wondered just who in the hell that woman was.

As Kendall approached them, she saw that Evan looked more nauseous than flirty, but nonetheless, she wasn't liking some other woman cornering her husband. Especially given the expression on his face. He looked . . . upset.

And Eve was there, too, her shoulders tense, gesturing towards the motor home like she wanted them to take this conversation inside.

Evan looked up and spotted her. "Kendall! Sweetheart." His voice was panicked, guilty.

Guilty of what?

The blonde swung around to face her, tears streaking her pretty face. She was cute and buxom, and very thin . . . except for the perky pregnant belly tucked into a clinging T-shirt.

Feeling a sour taste building up inside her mouth, Kendall sped up her footsteps. "What's going on?" Her voice sounded shrill even to her own ears.

Evan reached to take her hand, but Kendall avoided his touch. She had a really goddamn bad feeling about this.

"This is Sara, Nikki Strickland's friend." Evan jerked his thumb in the girl's direction. "Sara, this is my wife, Kendall Holbrook."

They both stared at each other. If Evan thought they were going to do some bullshit nice-to-meet-you exchange, he was an idiot.

"I'll be in in a minute," he told her. "Just give me two seconds and I'll be right inside. Why don't you and Eve go on and crack open a bottle of champagne to celebrate your finish."

The hell with that. "I'll go in after you explain to me what is going on here."

"Can we not do this here?" Eve whispered urgently. "Seriously."

Everyone ignored her.

"I'm pregnant," Sara told her, nose in the air, sniffling primly.

"I can see that. Congratulations." Yes, that was sarcasm, because without a doubt Kendall knew what was coming next.

"Sara says there is a possibility that I may be the father."

Yep. That was it. The little bomb that exploded in Kendall's face. "Really? Is it a possibility?"

"You are the father!" Sara rounded on Evan. "You're the only guy I had sex with that whole month and the only guy in the last year I didn't use a condom with."

Judging from the expression on Evan's face, she was telling the truth about not using a condom.

Jesus. "Screw champagne. I think I'll have some whiskey now."

"Kendall, wait . . ."

Without another word, she went into the motor home, letting the door slam behind her.

Eve followed her. "Kendall, I don't know what to say . . . guys do stupid things. Hell, women do, too. I think all of us have had lapsed judgment when it comes to birth control at one point or another."

Yanking open the fridge, Kendall stared in, the contents blurring as her eyes filled with tears. "I don't want to talk about this right now."

In fact, what she wanted to do was listen. Slamming the fridge shut again, she went back to the main room of the motor home and stood by the door. The windows were open, and even though their words were muffled slightly, she could still hear Evan and Sara talking.

"Why didn't you say something sooner?" he asked.

"Because at first I wasn't sure I was even going to keep it. Then I realized I couldn't just . . . you know. I decided I want this baby. I texted you and you blew me off and that was the only way I had to get ahold of you."

"I didn't know you needed to talk to me about something important. I just thought you wanted to flirt, and my heart just wasn't in it. I didn't want to lead you on by sleeping with you again. Then a month ago, I started seeing my wife again."

His wife. Kendall grabbed a throw pillow off the couch and hugged it.

"I don't think you should listen to this," Eve told her, an open beer in each of her hands.

Kendall gratefully took the beer and drank deeply. "I have to. You would, too, you know."

"I know."

"I didn't think it was cool to tell you you're going to be a father in a text message. That's just not fair to unload something so major like that in such an impersonal way."

The girl looked barely out of high school, but so far she seemed to have a reasonable head on her shoulders.

"But when you said you couldn't talk, I didn't have a choice. I mean, what was I going to do, like stalk you or something?"

Kendall squeezed the pillow tighter, clutching it with the beer bottle tucked into it, waiting for Evan's response.

"I'm sorry. I didn't know, Sara. I'm sorry that I was so irresponsible and didn't use protection. And I'm sorry that you've had to go it alone so far. What can I do to help you?"

There it was. Her husband's acceptance of his guilt and responsibility. Kendall jammed her eyes closed and sighed. Good Lord . . . another woman was going to give birth to her husband's child.

"I just need some help with my doctor's bills, that's all. I'm not stupid, I don't expect you to be super involved or anything. Okay, I admit, I was kind of hoping we could like date or whatever, but then I heard about your marriage from Nikki and I knew that was a big forget it."

"It was spontaneous," he murmured.

"And I'm not some bitch who wants to ruin your life or anything, but I'm just a nursing school student and I don't have any money. I can't even afford maternity jeans, let alone a thousand-dollar sonogram."

"Of course I'll help you. I'll pay for everything, don't worry about it."

Eve made a sound that was something like a growl.

"What the hell? He needs to let her know that we're having a DNA test done the minute she pushes that baby out. I don't trust this chick."

But even as it splintered her heart and hollowed her soul to know that she wouldn't be the first woman to give her husband a baby, his own flesh and blood, Kendall knew she wouldn't love him if he were the kind of man who would give this girl the cold shoulder. Who demanded a DNA test five minutes after getting the news of his possible paternity. He was doing the right thing, and she was pleased with that at the same time that she was appalled at the situation.

"Where are you staying? If you need money for rent, let me know. Was it safe to fly out here, by the way?"

"It's fine for another two months. It was Nikki's idea. She's sick of me crying all the time." Sara sniffled. "I can't seem to stop, sorry."

"Hey, hey, it's okay. I think you're handling this great."

That concern in his voice, that gentle tenderness, turned Kendall's heart to stone.

"Have you been eating enough? You're super skinny, you know. Maybe I should take you to a nutritionist."

Kendall dropped the pillow. Eve was right. She didn't want to hear this. Setting the beer down on the coffee table, she headed for the bedroom.

"Kendall . . ."

But she ignored Eve, shut the door behind her, and locked it.

EVAN didn't know what to think, to feel, to do. He had sent Sara back to Nikki's with the eighty bucks he'd had in his wallet, which at best was paltry, at worst insulting. But she looked so desperately like she needed lunch, and while he knew Nikki was sponsoring her trip, he wasn't sure how much Sara was willing to ask Nikki for.

The truth was, he didn't know squat about Sara. He had only met her that one night, and he'd been buzzed and she'd been loaded.

Now they were having a baby. Jesus.

Going into his motor home, he headed straight for the kitchen cabinet that held the whiskey. He needed a drink, desperately. Eve was leaning on the counter drinking a beer. Actually, she was sucking the last drops down and going to the fridge for another.

"Helluva day, huh?" she asked.

"That is the biggest understatement of the decade." He splashed the amber whiskey into a juice glass. "I don't even know what to say. Where's Kendall?"

He wanted to explain to her, he wanted her advice and her opinion on what the hell he was supposed to do.

"She's in the bedroom with the door locked and she won't come out."

Great. He took a liberal swallow of liquor, gritting his teeth against the burn. "I'm going to go talk to her. Thanks for helping."

"I meant to arrange for a private meeting. I didn't expect the girl to ambush you at the gate."

"It's okay." He shrugged. "We needed to talk."

"But not standing around outside. This is going to get out, you know."

Evan couldn't even think about that. All he cared about was his wife and that baby.

"At least when that chick tried to pin paternity on Elec I

knew it wasn't his kid. But this is trickier. We won't know until she gives birth if you're really the father or not."

"Why would she lie about that?"

Eve gave him an incredulous look. "Um, because let's see . . . if the possible daddies are you or a guy she hooked up with at a bar, which one do you think she's going to go with?"

He knew Eve had a point, but how could Sara look him in the eye and lie about something as important as this? He was inclined to believe her.

"I guess we can ask her to keep it on the down low until the baby's born. But I need to do something to help her."

"What you need to do is go talk to your wife. I don't think she appreciated for one minute hearing you fawn all over that girl."

"Fawn over her?" Evan took another sip of the whiskey. "I wasn't doing that!"

"Word to the wise, no woman wants to hear her husband worrying over what some other woman is eating." With that, Eve set her beer down on the counter and said, "I'll call you tomorrow."

Evan got what Eve was saying, but what the hell was he supposed to do? Sara was pregnant. Wasn't it right and appropriate and all that to be concerned about her, and the baby's health? And he didn't know what he was doing here. This was all brand-new, shocking information he'd just gotten. He was bound to do or say something wrong as he bumbled his way through this.

So he went to his bedroom door and knocked gently, trying the handle. It was locked. "Kendall? Can I come in, baby?"

Her voice was muffled and hoarse, like she'd been crying. "Can you just go away please? I need to be alone right now."

He didn't like that answer. He wanted to hold her, to reassure her, hell, to have her reassure *him* that this was all going to be okay. "We need to talk about this."

"Talk about what? The fact that you're having a baby with someone else? The single most important bond two people can share?"

Evan sighed, resting his head on the door. He tried the knob again, like somehow it would magically open. "What about the bond of marriage? That's equally as important."

She didn't answer him.

The nausea he'd been fighting all day was now a burning hole in his gut. "You have a past. I have a past. What if I told you I had herpes or something? Would you refuse to speak to me?"

"It's not the same thing!"

Maybe it wasn't. But everyone made mistakes. They'd both made their fair share. This wasn't ideal, not by any stretch of the imagination, but the result of this mistake was a child, and even in his horror, Evan had to admit he was a little awed at that prospect. He also firmly believed that this baby shouldn't be punished for the mistakes her parents had made.

"Well, explain to me what it is. Let's talk about it, get our feelings out. Figure out what we're going to do."

"What you're going to do is sleep in the other motor home tonight."

That was definitely not the way to deal with it. But alright, Evan got it. Kendall needed time. This was a big deal.

"I'll sleep on the couch here. I'm not leaving. If you want to talk, just wake me up."

Not that he was going to sleep one freaking wink.

"By the way, congratulations again on your awesome finish, babe. I'm really proud of you."

"Whatever."

Yeah, she wasn't going to be coming to talk to him anytime soon.

Evan passed the couch and went right back to the whiskey.

CHAPTER
EIGHTEEN

KENDALL couldn't believe it. That girl was on the same flight as they were back to Charlotte. Granted, it made sense given the time of day and that Jonas Strickland was on the flight, but really? Did she really have to be subjected to the sight of that virtual teenager bopping down the aisle, all perky and cute and smiling now that she had gotten what she wanted?

Sitting in first class, avoiding Evan next to her, like she had for the last twelve hours, Kendall felt mean and volatile and angry. It wasn't fair. This was supposed to be the happiest time of her life—she was a newlywed and her career was taking off. But it had been marred by this skinny and extremely feminine woman, who was going to nursing school of all things. It was like everything that gave Kendall doubts about her own sexiness, her own worth as a woman, all rolled into one.

When she dug through the anger and was being rational, she realized that she wasn't mad at Sara. Sara was only doing what anyone in her circumstances would do, and she seemed reasonable. There had been nothing hateful or manipulative about her words. Nor could Kendall begrudge her her happiness over having a baby. Even though she wasn't sure if and when she wanted one herself, Kendall loved kids, understood the joy they brought, and could never think of a child as a mistake in any way.

But a small, pathetic part of her looked at Sara and thought that was the kind of woman Evan should have married—a traditional and beautiful woman who would stay at home and raise his children.

Which just made her feel like shit.

Pulling her travel blanket up tighter around her shoulders, she leaned on the window, not caring if it was dirty.

"You going to take a nap?" Evan asked her, his hand rubbing up and down on her thigh in a soothing gesture.

She moved her leg so his hand fell away. She didn't want him to touch her. "Yes."

"Sleep tight," he said, but even as he did, his head was turning and his eyes were drifting back behind them, she had to assume to check on Sara's progress.

Everything else Kendall thought would be possible to work through. They were her fears, her issues, and with time and concerted effort, she could get over her insecurities.

But this?

Watching her husband show concern for another woman? Having basically a third party inserted into their marriage, someone who needed him more than she did?

It hurt so bad she felt like she couldn't breathe. Like a hand had reached up and cut off her windpipe.

"Damn it," Evan said, frowning at his phone.

Part of her was feeling so petty and childish she didn't

even want to ask what was wrong, but curiosity got the better of her. "What?"

He held his phone out to her. There was a text from Eve.

It's out already. Got a call from Carl to confirm. Call when you land.

Wonderful. Everyone knew already that another woman was having her husband's baby. Great. Just utterly fabulous.

"I'm sorry, Kendall. I really am." He tried to hold her hand but she jerked away again. "Will you just talk to me? This was an accident. I didn't plan this."

Well, duh. That was just a stupid thing to say. Feeling the tears in her eyes, Kendall knew she should stay silent, that this was neither the time nor the place to discuss the situation, but she couldn't hold back her emotion. "I know that. I know that we were nowhere near dating at the time of conception. It doesn't change the fact that in four months you're going to be a father to a child and I won't be any part of that. It doesn't change the fact that today I am about to be thoroughly humiliated when everyone finds out. It doesn't change the fact that I am about to become fodder for the gossip mill and no one will give a shit that I finished second on Sunday. They'll just want to snicker at my situation."

"No one will be snickering at you. It's not like I cheated on you."

"You know what? Just don't try to put a pretty bow on this right now, okay? I don't want to hear it." She was snappish and she knew it. She knew he wasn't hurting her intentionally, but he was still hurting her.

Maybe a better woman could have accepted the situation, embraced Sara and her baby with open arms, but Kendall wasn't sure she could do that.

"We have to deal with this, whether we want to or not."

She knew they did. But at the moment, all she wanted to do was bury her head under her fleece blanket and weep.

"YES, I did have a relationship with Miss Parker," Evan said, trying to sound matter-of-fact and nothing more as he stared out into a room full of reporters, their pens moving across their notebooks, flashbulbs going off. "It ended approximately in late November."

That was a polite exaggeration of what he and Sara had shared, but he was trying to put a positive spin on it for everyone involved, including his wife, who had refused to attend this press conference. Had refused in fact to speak to him for the last three days.

"Is the baby yours?"

Forcing himself not to fidget, Evan answered the question exactly the way he and Eve had rehearsed. "If that is the case, I am fully prepared to live up to my emotional and financial responsibilities as a parent."

"So you're saying there's a possibility the child is not yours? That Miss Parker is lying?"

"I have no reason to believe Sara is lying."

"Is it true that Untamed Deodorant has pulled all ads with your image?"

"That is true." For which Evan was more than a little put out. It wasn't like he had cheated on his wife. This was not a scandal of epic proportions. A little shocking, sure, and definitely a case of extremely poor judgment on his part, but it wasn't like he'd kept a harem. Yet everyone was making it out to be a huge deal, and Evan actually suspected part of the reason was because of Kendall's stone silence on the matter. It made him look guilty of more than he was.

While he knew why she was devastated, he couldn't help

but be hurt himself. He needed her, desperately. Both her moral support and her love, and she was shutting him out completely.

"Are you planning to drive this weekend in Richmond?"

"Of course. I have no intention of letting my team down. The Untamed Chevrolet is running extremely well and we're looking for a good race on Sunday."

They grilled him for another ten minutes then Eve indicated one more question.

Unfortunately, it was a doozy.

"How does your wife feel about this? Quite a wedding present you gave her."

Nice. The woman smirked at him, her lips a horrible coral color.

"My wife was as surprised as I was, obviously. But she completely supports me in doing the right thing."

If she did or not was a big question mark, but it had to be said. "I just ask that you respect my wife's privacy at this time, and if you want to talk to her, focus on the fact that she's having an amazing rookie season."

Then Evan excused himself, stood up, and left the room, hoping that he looked way calmer than he felt. Within minutes he and Eve were pulling away in her SUV and Evan was feeling like he needed to hurl and have a drink, two feelings that were starting to become awfully familiar.

"That was fucking horrible," he said to his sister. "But thank you for being here and coaching me through this."

"You might have been stupid enough to fire me, but I wasn't going to leave you totally hanging out to dry." She gave him a rueful smile as she pulled out onto the main road. "I think it went well."

"Went well, huh? My whole life is exploding in front of my eyes. I can't believe my stupidity has subjected Kendall to this. God, I suck." Evan banged his head back against the headrest and wished he could write music. There was a country song waiting to be sung out of this mess.

"But you know what? Say you and Kendall didn't get back together last month . . . then you'd just be a guy who screwed up and got someone pregnant. Either way it still was an accident and you couldn't predict that you and Kendall would get back together. You couldn't predict that five months after the fact Sara would trot her pregnant butt out and make waves. So stop kicking your own ass and just deal with it."

"Just deal with it, huh? Alright, just like that. Easy enough. Sure." He groaned out loud. "If Kendall loses her sponsorship over this, man, how can I make that up to her?"

"She's not going to lose her sponsorship . . . Shit."

"What?" he asked, but he already saw what had prompted the curse. When they pulled into Kendall's driveway, she was standing in it with Tuesday and they were loading two large suitcases into her trunk. Twenty bucks said those suitcases were filled with his stuff. "Shit. Shit, shit, shit."

Evan opened the car door before Eve even came to a stop. "What's going on here?" he demanded.

Kendall froze and turned to him, her eyes focused on his shoulder. "I was going to take some of your stuff back to your condo. I think that maybe it would be good if we had some time apart."

"To do what?" he said, his voice rising louder than he intended. "Ignore the problem as long as possible? Sweep more issues under the rug? I don't think so!"

Her hands were still on his suitcase, her face pale, dark circles under her eyes. "I just can't . . . Don't you get it? I just can't."

Evan turned to Tuesday, who was standing there looking

incredibly uncomfortable. "How can you let her do this?" It wasn't remotely fair to drag her into it, but Evan was so horrified, so hurt and outraged, that he wanted a reaction from someone, anyone.

Tuesday's hands came up. "Hey, don't look at me. This isn't my marriage."

Exactly. It was their marriage, their whole future. Not something to ignore and discard. "Kendall, look at me, damn it!" he said in frustration.

But she just pulled his suitcases back out of her trunk and set them in the driveway. "I need time. You need to respect that."

"This is a marriage!" And yes, he was shouting. "Ten days ago you stood in front of me and you pledged to be my partner. Not to run away."

She rounded on him, her eyes snapping. "I am not running away. I'm just asking you for some space so I can process what the hell this means in my life. This is not something small, this is a child!"

As if he didn't know that. "I am well aware of that fact. Which is why I want to discuss how we—you and me—are going to deal with this situation. It may be my biological child, but as my wife you're going to be spending a lot of time with her, too."

"Her?"

"It's a girl." Evan didn't know what else to say. How could he force her to talk about her feelings with him?

He couldn't. That was obvious when she started to back up, tears in her eyes.

"I can't do this," she said.

"Kendall!" Evan reached for her, but she was already running for the town house.

Tuesday looked shocked, but Evan barely saw her.

All he could think was that Kendall had lacerated his heart into bloody ribbons once again.

KENDALL stood in her foyer, back on the door, tears streaming down her face. Evan was pounding on her front door, but she couldn't turn around. Couldn't answer it.

She knew she was being irrational, but she couldn't help it. She got hurt, she shut down. She needed time to work this through on her own, to process her feelings.

Evan was having a baby girl with Sara.

A child that he would look at and see himself and another woman in.

A child that to Kendall just exemplified all her failings as a woman.

She couldn't be all things to all people, she knew that. But she wanted to be all things to Evan.

"Kendall! Open this fucking door!"

She jumped at the force with which he pounded on her front door. But his anger didn't sway her. She couldn't deal with it, any of it, not right now. Why couldn't he understand that?

"Kendall, don't do this . . . I love you." His words trailed off on a sob. "Kendall!"

Okay, that reached into her chest and squeezed her heart.

She loved him, too.

But maybe their wedding had been too spontaneous. Maybe they had needed to work out some things first, like how they problem-solved and whether they were planning to have children someday. They had talked about patterns, her shutting down, his impulsiveness, but after the fact . . .

She pressed her fingers to her temples, not sure what to do, what to think, how to feel.

He pounded again, a harsh thump, thump, thump that echoed the rhythm of her racing heart. "Kendall!"

Maybe she should open the door. Maybe she should let him see her vulnerabilities and insecurities . . . maybe she should trust him. Trust herself. Maybe she should learn from the past and not repeat her same mistakes.

Maybe she should believe that Evan could love her just as she was, that she had nothing to fear from a woman like Sara.

Maybe . . .

Swiping her hands across her damp cheeks, she turned and opened her front door, prepared to both burst into tears and to fling herself into her husband's arms and have it be all better.

Except he wasn't there.

Evan had left.

"No, damn it," she whispered. She would just go after him. He couldn't be that far.

But when she stepped out onto the stoop to see if he and Eve were still in the driveway, her ankle rolled as she stepped on something. Moving her foot with a wince, she glanced down to see what had caused her to lose her footing.

It was the band she had put on Evan's finger on their wedding night.

He had thrown it on the ground.

Like it was nothing.

She supposed, as her eyes blurred, that it was.

ENGINE CHECK
by Tuesday Talladega

WTF!! People, people, what is going on in the world of racing? Evan Monroe announced this morning that at the

end of this season he will be retiring from the series. Retiring. At twenty-nine years old. No indication from his
camp what he will be doing post-driving, but I strongly
suspect changing diapers will be on his agenda. Since he
is in the midst of some heavy-duty personal issues, I pre-
fer to think of this exit as a temporary one . . . a paternity
leave, if you will.

Please tell us, Evan, that you'll be back on the track.
It just won't be the same without you.

EVAN sat on the old dirt track off Route 3 and stared into
space. It was the first of May already and grass and weeds
were growing like crazy in the damp spring weather. His
thoughts were hopeless, his heart aching.

Walking away from driving was the right thing to do. He
was at peace with that. Maybe, if anything, the hell of the
last two weeks had forced his hand. He didn't have the passion or the dedication he needed to go out there anymore.
Hell, maybe he'd never had it. Time to step aside and let the
new guard take his spot.

That had definitely factored into his decision.

He had also stepped back to distance himself from Kendall personally and professionally. He couldn't force her to
talk to him, he couldn't take back the past and the outcome
of that night with Sara, but he could ensure that Kendall
wouldn't lose her sponsorship with Untamed. He could take
the fallout with the gossip mongers and with Carl and cut
her free of an association with him.

He could give her the divorce she was clearly going to
want.

But not yet. He couldn't bring himself to do that quite yet.
Glancing down at his bare left hand, he regretted for

the thousandth time taking that ring off. It had been stupid and petty to leave it on her stoop. But he had been devastated that she wouldn't even open the door. It had seemed a good way to hurt her as much as he'd been hurt, but he now completely regretted it. That wasn't what their relationship was about and he wasn't nineteen anymore.

He wanted both the ring and her back.

The sounds of tires on the brush and gravel behind him made him sigh as he leaned against the hood of the car. He wanted to sit awhile longer, but if someone else was coming around, he was going to leave. He didn't want to make small talk with a stranger.

Only it wasn't a stranger who got out of the truck after parking it next to Evan's. It was Ryder Jefferson.

"What are you doing here?" Evan asked him, put out that he was going to have to talk. He didn't want to talk to anyone. He just wanted to sit and stare. For the next ten years or so.

"Thought maybe you'd want to go for a mani/pedi with me."

"Very funny. How did you know I was out here?"

"Eve told me. Your sister is really worried about you."

He might have been touched if he wasn't totally numb. "I'm fine. I'll be fine. And no, I don't want to talk about it."

"Alright." Ryder leaned on the truck with him, staring out at the track like he was. "I'll just do the talking. They say men are terrible communicators, but you know, some women don't exactly do a fabulous job at expressing their emotions."

Evan fought the urge to roll his eyes. He was starting to get irritated with Ryder. Couldn't the guy see he just wanted to wallow in his own misery?

"I should know, I was married to a woman like that. And you see, I didn't push her to talk to me, so she didn't. And we wound up divorced. Is this sounding at all like something you've experienced?"

Evan wasn't going to talk about it. He wasn't. But then he couldn't help himself. He needed someone to know, to acknowledge that damn it, he had wanted to work this through. "Except I've tried to force Kendall to talk about it. She won't do it."

"So you just give up? Or do you keep trying?"

"You want me to beat my head against a wall? Eventually my brains will just spill." Evan bent down and picked up a rock. He tossed it up and down in the palm of his hand.

"Or maybe you'll work things out. I wish I had tried harder to talk to Suzanne three years ago. I might not have lost two years. And the truth is, I'm damn lucky we wound up back together. The odds were stacked against us. Once you file for divorce, it's hard to turn back."

"Who said anything about filing for divorce?" Evan hurled the rock forward twenty feet, watching it hit and bounce across the track. "Do you know something I don't know?"

"No. I'm just telling you I understand how much it hurts. And trust me, fixing it is worth whatever you have to go through to get there."

"I'd fix it in a heartbeat if I could," Evan told Ryder. "I just don't know what to do."

"Well, you either do nothing and sit here and feel sorry for yourself for a couple of years like I did. Or you can think of something to try." Ryder pushed off of the truck and pulled his keys out of his pocket. "Just remember that sometimes a grand gesture is needed."

"What, like flowers?"

Ryder frowned. "Are you serious? Flowers aren't a grand

gesture, flowers are for scoring a little weeknight sex, not repairing serious damage. Grand. Like billboard-sized."

Evan hated the fact that he felt a little flicker of hope sparking to life. "So you and Suzanne are really happy now, huh?"

Ryder grinned. "So happy it'll make you sick."

Grand gesture. Huh.

Maybe, just maybe, that might work.

And if it didn't, what was one more head butt into the wall?

CHAPTER NINETEEN

"YOU can't let Evan just quit driving." Kendall stared across the desk at Carl. "He doesn't deserve to be forced out."

The news, which had come to her through Eve, had made Kendall sick to her stomach. Nothing about what was going down between them or between Sara and Evan was anyone's business in racing. This was his career, his life, and while Kendall still couldn't bring herself to talk to him, she couldn't stand the thought of him losing everything.

"No one forced him out." Carl leaned back in his chair, his expression impassive, eyes slightly narrowed. "He came to me all on his own."

That just didn't make any sense. Carl had been gunning for Evan for months. He had to be the impetus behind Evan's decision. "Why would he do that?"

"Why don't you ask your husband that question?" Carl said.

Confused, Kendall felt her anger and indignation deflate. She had stormed into Carl's office, determined to get Evan his spot back, and now she was hearing he didn't want that spot?

"So you're saying that Evan still has a car with Hinder Motors?"

"If he wants it, yes." Carl shrugged. "Look, Kendall, I am not going to deny I'm pissed that you and Evan are out there creating drama. But you were right—personal lives are personal lives, and I'd hate to lose a damn fine driver just because he's had sex with a woman he shouldn't have. Hell, I'd lose my whole team if that were the case."

No doubt that was true. Kendall wasn't sure what to say, so she just nodded. "Exactly. Thanks, Carl. Glad we're on the same page."

"Sounds like you and me are, it's just Evan that needs to be brought around."

As she stood up, Kendall wondered how to do that, or if she were even the woman with the right to do it anyway.

"ARE you okay to drive?" Jim asked her an hour before race time.

Kendall frowned at him. "Of course I'm fine, why wouldn't I be?"

He held his hand up. "You just look like shit, that's all. Like you haven't slept in two weeks."

That would be because she hadn't. Not one freaking wink, it felt like. Spinning her helmet around in her hands, Kendall lifted up and down on the balls of her feet. "I'm fine."

"If you're not, don't you dare get behind that wheel, ya hear me? I'm not having you jeopardizing your safety or someone else's."

"I said I'm fine," she snapped. "Don't question my judgment."

Jim sighed. "I'm not. I'm just worried about you. Don't you think you ought to at least talk to Evan?"

She did. But what was she supposed to say now that she'd retrieved his wedding ring off her concrete stoop? Now that she'd learned he had just walked away from racing without even consulting her on it?

Of course, she had given him no option to talk to her.

Damn it.

"Mind your own business." Kendall moved towards her car to check on it. Then suddenly stopped when she glanced up and saw Evan on the jumbo screen, standing on the stage they used for introductions. "What the hell is he doing on the stage?" she asked out loud, to no one in particular.

"I just want to dedicate this to my wife, Kendall Holbrook Monroe, who is going to win the Chase in the not too distant future."

"Oh, my God." She couldn't breathe. What was he doing?

"What is he doing?" Jim stood next to her and gawked up at the screen.

Her entire pit crew was craning their necks as well, all curious, all confused.

"What's he gonna do?" Kenny, her jackman asked.

"I have no idea." None whatsoever. Evan was impulsive, but what on earth was he going to say up there?

But then the first notes came out over the infield and she knew. He wasn't going to talk. "Holy shit . . ." She didn't know whether to be horrified or deeply touched.

It was Rod Stewart's "Have I Told You Lately That I Love You?"

And Evan opened his mouth and started singing it.

"Holy shit is right," Jim said. "That boy can't sing."

No, he couldn't. Evan was off-key and warbling, but he

was standing up there, mic in hand, belting his heart out. For her.

Good God.

"I'm so embarrassed right now," Jim added.

"I think it's highly romantic," the jackman said. "I'm kinda wishing I was Kendall right now."

"That's the freakiest damn thing you've ever said." Jim made a face. "Between Evan and you, I'm getting the willies all the way around."

Their words were registering in her brain, but Kendall couldn't respond to them. She could only stare up at the screen. At her husband. He was making a total fool out of himself. For her. Because she had told him that she had always wanted a man to serenade her, though in her fantasies it had been someone more along the lines of Keith Urban, or at the very least in tune.

But she had to admit this was even better.

Tears filled her eyes.

"You're crying," Jim said accusingly. "Fuck, fuck, fuck. We're fucked. Why is he doing this now?"

"I'm not crying!" Kendall refused to lift her hand and wipe the tears that were now in fact rolling down her cheeks.

She wished Jim would go away. She just wanted to be alone, with Evan.

She wanted to look into his eyes and just see that he loved her.

When Evan finished the song, he said, "If that doesn't prove I love my wife I just don't know what does."

The announcer, who had been standing slightly offstage, walked up next to Evan. "Whew, I'll say. That was, uh, something else, Evan." He smiled towards the crowd. "Wasn't that something else, folks?"

There was a roar of approval up from the fans.

"So how about we get your wife on up here, just for a smile and a wave together?"

Instantly Kendall froze. She couldn't do that. Just couldn't do that.

"I'm sure she's busy at the moment, but how about after the race? Now that I'm done embarrassing myself, I have a car to hop into." Evan gave a bow and a wave, and the audience cheered loudly again.

Kendall stood there, not sure what she was feeling or thinking.

"You'd better go and talk to him after the race."

She turned and saw Tuesday standing next to her, tears in her eyes as well. "Tuesday? What's wrong? What are you doing here?"

Normally her friend was in the media room for the races, if she bothered to attend at all. Tuesday only made race day about once a month.

"Remember I told you I was coming to Virginia to visit my parents and take my dad to the race?"

"Oh, yeah, I'm sorry, I forgot. And I don't know . . . I'm not sure I can go up there with Evan after the race. I'm so confused."

"What you are is insecure," Tuesday said vehemently, rounding on her. "And I just don't see why. Do you realize how fucking lucky you are?"

Stunned, Kendall just stared at her, her cheeks going hot. "What do you mean?"

"I mean, look at you. You are so successful. You're at the top of your field! Do you know how many women struggle to achieve success in their careers, and here you are, yet you never think you're good enough. You have this guy who is so sweet and so amazing and so completely in love with you that he's willing to make an ass out of himself, and you hesitate?"

With no idea where this was coming from, and stunned at the anger in Tuesday's voice, Kendall just shook her head. "You don't understand."

"I do! I understand that you're afraid. Well, big fucking whoop. Go ahead, be afraid, and spend your life alone. What a waste."

Given that Tuesday's voice hitched and she was now crying full force, Kendall knew this wasn't just about her marriage. "Tuesday, what's wrong?"

"My parents just told me my dad has cancer."

"Oh, my God, I'm so sorry." She reached out and wrapped her arms around her friend. "It will be okay, though. I know it's scary but cancer is so beatable now."

Tuesday stayed in the hug briefly, then pulled away, putting her arms across her chest. "Not in this case. It's stage four. They've given him six months."

"Sweetie, oh, I'm so sorry . . ." Kendall was horrified. She didn't know what to say.

Jim came up to them. "Sorry to interrupt, but we need you, kiddo."

"Go." Tuesday waved her off. "I'll be fine. But think about what I said. Life is too short, Kendall. It's a total cliché, but damn, it's the truth."

Worried about her friend, Kendall told her, "I'll be here after the race. Just let me know what you need."

"You know what I need? Is for you to recognize what's in front of you. Love. Happiness."

Kendall didn't know what to say. Cancer. God, what would she do if she got that news about her father? It suddenly made everything seem all so insignificant. What would she have done if something had happened to her father after she had stomped out on Easter?

So he hadn't been a perfect father. Who was?

He did love her.

As did Evan.

With all his heart.

Suddenly, without warning or any real awareness of what she was doing, Kendall took off running.

"What the hell are you doing?" Jim asked, sounding freaked out and angry.

She just put her finger up to indicate one minute and ran like the wind, weaving around people towards the stage, her heart in her throat.

Tuesday was right. She was a complete and total fool. Was she really going to throw away the greatest love she'd ever known because she was insecure and afraid?

No wins on the track could ever make up for the loss of her marriage, and no life would ever be full and complete without Evan by her side.

Hadn't she spent the last ten years learning that lesson?

She spotted him strolling towards pit road, looking handsome and adorable and maybe just a little embarrassed. A little worried.

But then he spotted her and he smiled. "I'm not much of a singer," he started to say.

Kendall just leaped up into his arms and wrapped herself around him like a monkey, interrupting him. "I'm sorry, I'm sorry. I don't want to lose you."

When his arms held her tight and he looked into her eyes and said, "Oh, baby, I don't want to lose you either," Kendall knew it was going to be okay.

And she vowed that they were going to cross that finish line together.

EVAN sat on the grass on the edge of the lake, next to Kendall, her head on his shoulder. He sighed deeply with contentment. It had been a twisting road, with a few caution laps along the way, but they'd made it to the end.

Or more accurately, the beginning.

It was a gorgeous Monday in Charlotte, spring in full bloom, the morning after his impromptu and badly done Rod Stewart serenade. "I'm never going to be able to go on YouTube again," he said. "I'm sure someone has posted me singing and I'm equally sure everyone has slammed me for it."

Not that he cared. It had gotten Kendall to talk to him and that was all that mattered.

Kendall laughed. "Don't listen to haters. I think it was beautiful."

"That's because you love me."

"I do."

He turned and looked into her rich amber eyes. "You do, don't you?" He knew she did, but he wanted to hear it again. And again. Every day for the rest of his life.

"Yes. I do. I love you, Evan Roscoe Monroe."

Without his stupid middle name would have been nice, but he was feeling so smug in love, he'd take it. "I love you, too, Kendall Carolina."

After they shared a deep kiss, intimate and tender, Kendall ran her fingers across his lips. Evan instantly went hard, sure she was coming on to him.

But instead she gave him another kiss on the lips and said,

"Mmm, you taste good. But don't ruin the sentiment with my middle name. It's so singsongy."

"You said my middle name first, sweetheart. Besides, yours is cute, like you."

She made a face. "Thanks."

"What's wrong with cute?"

"It's just so . . . cute."

"Actually, I think you're cute and drop dead gorgeous and sinfully sexy and pinup worthy, but I don't want to swell your head."

He was trying to make light, but she studied him searchingly. "I'm insecure, do you know that? Have I ever mentioned that?"

"I know you are." He did. He saw that now in a way he hadn't before. "I'll do my best to reassure you."

"And I'll do my best to trust who I am and what I have."

Evan kissed the top of her head. "I know this won't be easy for you. I'm sorry that you have to deal with this pregnancy. But I thank you for sticking with me."

"I love you," she said simply. "And I'll love your baby."

His throat was suddenly tight. "After this season, it's just going to be all about you and that baby. I want to support your career and be there for my daughter. Then I'm thinking about team ownership a few years down the road. Or maybe a driving school. For girls. What do you think?"

"I think that's a great idea. But only if you're sure about leaving driving."

He was. It had actually been something of a relief. "I am. Carl didn't even have a heart attack when I told him. I think he's glad to see me go."

"That's not true. I went to Carl and talked to him yesterday. He said you'll always have a car at Hinder if you want one."

Evan pulled back to look at her. "You went to Carl? For what?"

His wife shrugged sheepishly. "I went to chew him out for letting you go, only he informed me you weren't forced out, you quit."

That gave him a great deal of satisfaction and he held her closer. Knowing she had his back meant everything to him. "Thanks for doing that."

"It was the least I could do after the horrible way I handled the pregnancy news. I'm always going to support you, you know. From here on out."

That meant everything to him. "Likewise."

"So what are they doing with our commercial, by the way?"

Evan shrugged. "They're airing it. Going to milk our marriage and my last season for all they're worth. They did invest a fair amount of money, so it's only fair."

Not that he really cared much about any of that at the moment. And considering that Kendall made a noncommittal sound, he didn't think she really did either. They were just enjoying the day and each other.

"Can I have my ring back?" he asked her. That had been bothering him, and he wanted that symbol of their marriage back on his finger.

"Let's get you a new one. I didn't like that cheap one anyway. And maybe we should have a wedding reception for our friends. A party."

"Now you're talking. That would be nice, to celebrate with our families and our friends."

Kendall's finger came out and she pointed. "Hey look, the ducks are back. And they have babies . . . how cute."

The family of ducks was swimming in the lake, the mother and father and four fuzzy, awkward little ducklings.

"They're kind of goofy looking," Evan remarked. He'd never really understand the attraction humans had to those noisy things.

"Sometimes families don't always look perfect. That doesn't mean they don't work."

Well, that was the truth.

And it was their future.

"I bet that momma duck can change a tire faster than the daddy duck."

Kendall grinned. "I bet she can."

Turn the page for a special preview of
Erin McCarthy's next Fast Track Novel,

Slow Ride

Coming October 2011 from Berkley Sensation!

TUESDAY Jones was feeling both grateful that her toast as maid of honor was·behind her and that her orange bridesmaid dress looked remarkably better under the muted ballroom lights. Heading for the bar, because one glass of champagne clearly wasn't enough, she veered at the last second to the dessert table. She was supposed to meet Evan Monroe, the man who had been smart enough to marry her best friend, Kendall, and throw her a big old wedding reception four months after their impulsive elopement. When Evan had commented during dinner that women couldn't do shots of whiskey, Tuesday felt it was her duty, orange dress and all, to stand up for her gender.

But first she wanted a piece of cake.

To coat her stomach for the liquor.

Or maybe just because she liked cake.

She had to admit she was feeling weird—happy for Kendall, but also like she still wasn't totally enjoying herself. Like she couldn't. Yet for the first time in the three weeks since her dad had died, she didn't feel like she might burst into tears at any given moment, so that was progress. Baby steps. Little tiny almost nonexistent baby steps, because there was nothing easy about losing her father. Death sucked. Grief sucked.

Grabbing a piece of cake from the assortment displayed on the table, she crammed it into her mouth on that very unpleasant thought.

And discovered that she had chosen the damn coconut slice, one of her very least favorite foods ever. There was good, there was bad, and then there was coconut. Her mouth automatically opening in horror, she looked around for a napkin, the flavor invading and offending every single one of her taste buds. Feeling like she might gag, she worked the cake forward with her tongue, debating just chucking it out of her mouth and into her champagne glass.

A hand shot out in front of her mouth and Evan said, "Just spit it out."

She only paused for a second before depositing the vile waxy coconut hunk into Evan's hand. "Oh, my God, thank you. That was so freaking gross—"

Tuesday forgot the rest of her sentence when she realized that it wasn't Evan next to her. It was Diesel Lange. Retired driver. The man she had cried on at her father's funeral.

And the man whose outstretched palm she had now just spit chewed-up cake into.

Oh. My. God. She felt heat flood her face as she stared at him, trying to think of something, anything to say. "Sorry" was the best she could manage. "I thought you were Evan."

It was a lame explanation, but how did you really explain regurgitation onto total strangers?

His eyebrows furrowed. "Why would you think I was Evan?"

"Because I was meeting Evan." Tuesday licked her lips, still tasting the coconut, still feeling like an ass. "I don't usually just spit out food into random people's hands, you know." Food she realized he was still holding. "God, that's so gross, I'm sorry."

She reached out and grabbed the cold, mushy, spit-filled blob off his hand. It left a slimey smear across his skin. "Crap, sorry." She was tempted to lick it off, but figured that would make it worse. A lot worse. She didn't imagine any man wanted a woman to just lick him at a wedding reception.

Then again, maybe men did.

The oven her face had become burned a little hotter.

But he just gave her a lopsided smile. "Quit apologizing. I'm the one who stuck my hand out. I don't like coconut either, so I'm glad I could help. The texture makes me want to hurl."

She felt slightly better, or at least she would when that saliva trail across his hand was gone. First she snotted on his dress shirt at the funeral, now she spit on him. Classy.

"Let me get you a napkin." Which, now that she was glancing around, she saw there were plenty of on the corner of the table, but they were blending into the tablecloth, creating this moment of horror for her. "Here." She grabbed several off the top of the stack and scrubbed at his hand with them. "I can't believe I spit on you."

His other hand reached out and stilled her, wrapping loosely around her wrist. "Stop. A little saliva never killed anyone."

"I don't have any communicable diseases, just so you know." Oh, God, did she really just say that? Tuesday downed the rest of her glass of champagne.

Diesel burst out laughing. "That is good to know. But I wasn't worried."

Then he just . . . looked at her. Tuesday wondered if he remembered who she was. Wondered if she was supposed to acknowledge that she had cried on him. But what if she said something and he didn't recognize her? She glanced ruefully into the bottom of her empty glass.

What was the most disconcerting thing of all was that she had never been the type of woman who worried about things like this. She was no stranger to voicing her opinion and she had never lacked for confidence. You couldn't be missing either quality if you wanted to be successful in the field of sports reporting. So why she was standing there wide-eyed and mute like a Precious Moments figurine she did not understand. That shit had to stop.

"I was meeting Evan at the bar, I should head on over there," she said. "Come with me and I'll buy you a drink."

"It's an open bar."

She grinned. "I know. But it's the thought that counts."

He smiled back, a crooked smile that sent a shiver racing up her spine. Hello. She'd just felt the first jolt of sexual interest she'd had in months. It had been instantaneous when the corner of his mouth rose slowly and slyly, and Tuesday cleared her throat, suddenly unnerved. He was tall, with shaggy dark blond hair and some short facial hair that she felt the urge to touch to test its softness.

She knew he was single.

And she knew herself well enough to know that she needed to get the hell away from him as soon as possible.

But he held his arm out for her. Like a gentleman does to escort a woman somewhere. "Lead the way, Tuesday," he told her.

There was no way to avoid slipping her own arm through his without being totally rude, so she did, clutching the empty glass in her free hand and trying not to look up at him.

He had used her name. Did that mean he did remember her or he had just heard her name announced as maid of honor at the beginning of dinner?

She decided that she was Tuesday Jones, damn it, and even though she hadn't felt stronger than a wet napkin the last few months, she needed to at least thank this man. "By the way," she told him, forcing her head to lift to look at him. "Thanks for letting me bawl on you in the cemetery. I appreciate you tolerating the crazy girl."

He sidled a look down at her that she couldn't read. It was sympathetic, yes, but there didn't seem to be any pity in it. It was something else, another emotion, but then again, maybe it was just the light playing off his pale blue eyes.

"No problem. I'm glad I could be there for you. Your dad was a good guy, and I'm really sorry for your loss."

Tuesday drew up short a foot from the bar. He knew her dad? Well, duh, of course he knew her father. Over the years her dad had probably interviewed him a dozen times. Her brain wasn't firing at full neurons lately. "Thanks," she murmured, setting the champagne glass down on the bar before it slipped from her sweaty palm.

"What the hell took you so long?" Evan asked, grinning from ear to ear, his tie askew. "Change your mind, wimp out on me?"

Tuesday's emotions were swirling close to the surface, thoughts of her father's extensive career as a sports journalist suddenly thrust in front of her by Diesel Lange, and she wiped her hand down the front of her pumpkin-colored dress. Who thought of pumpkins in August? It made no sense. But the orange color scheme was what Kendall had wanted, and Tuesday guessed maybe it was supposed to be more tropical than fall foliage.

Evan's grin started to slip. "Are you okay?"

No, no, not really. She was feeling far from okay. And that feeling like she might cry at any given second had returned full force. "Yeah, of course I am. Bring it on, Monroe." She turned to Diesel. "Do you want to do a shot with us?"

He shook his head. "No, thanks."

Why was he looking at her like that? Those eyes just bored into her, like he was seeing something she didn't want anyone to see. Tuesday was intensely aware of how close he was standing to her, how tall he was even though she was five-foot-eight. There weren't a lot of men who towered over her, but he did. He had a presence, too, that seemed to surround her, that made her want to both lean on his chest for comfort and strip him naked and get thrown against a wall.

Neither of which were appropriate to do at the moment.

"Don't be a wuss." Evan tried to hand Diesel a shot glass filled with whiskey. "It's my wedding and I never see you anymore, so I say you owe me."

"Seriously, no thanks. I take pain meds, and trust me, it ain't a good combination." Diesel shrugged. "I'll take a Coke though."

Tuesday thought about the limp she had seen Diesel walking with at the cemetery. For some reason, she had assumed that's all it was, that there wouldn't actually be pain anymore. It had been at least two years since his accident, if she was remembering correctly. But if he limped, she imagined it was because he was in pain.

Yet he always looked so calm.

Suddenly confused, her emotions pinging in multiple directions, Tuesday turned to the bartender. "Can we get a Coke please?" She took the shot of whiskey Evan was holding out to her. God knew the last thing she needed was to throw back some Jack, but the truth was, she was a little afraid of the direction her thoughts and feelings were going in. Maybe the liquor would take the edge off.

"Are you sure your wife doesn't want a shot?" Tuesday asked Evan.

"Are you kidding? Kendall can't hold her liquor. She's not drinking at all tonight because she doesn't want to wind up trashed and doing the worm on the dance floor."

Tuesday sniffed her drink. "So that's what you have me for, right? I'll be the one making an ass out of myself in a few hours."

Evan grinned. "We can only hope."

Unfortunately, given the way she was feeling, Tuesday thought it might not be that far from the truth. For a split second, she hesitated. Maybe the whiskey was a bad idea on top of the champagne. But then Evan lifted his glass and tossed it back and she was just competitive enough that she had to follow suit, taking it cleanly and quickly. As the burn raced down her throat, she tried not to wince.

Diesel raised his eyebrow, his Coke lifted to his lips. "You don't play around."

No, she didn't. And she wasn't going to let this night descend into melancholy for her. It was Kendall and Evan's wedding, for crying out loud. New beginnings, a celebration of hope and love and the future. She needed to shake it off.

"Hell, no," she told him. "You have to take drinking seriously, you know. You want to dance?"

He shook his head. "No."

It was amazing how fast alcohol could loosen her limbs. She ought to be worried, but the truth was, she was glad the knots in her shoulders had unfurled just a bit. "What Well, that's just rude. Why wouldn't you want to dance wit me?"

"I can't dance."

"Pfft." She looked at Evan. "You can't dance, and you do it anyway."

"I can so dance. I own that dance floor. If Lange won't dance with you, I will."

Tuesday would rather spend more time with Diesel, but he was shaking his head. She ought to be offended, but there was something about the way he looked at her; she couldn't believe it was that he didn't want to be with her. There was that something . . . There was a word for it but she was starting to suspect she was drunk, because she couldn't figure out what it was.

"Okay. Let's polka."

"But they're playing Donna Summer," Evan protested.

"Perfect. We'll polka and hustle at the same time. It's all about creating your own path, my friend." Tuesday leaned over the bar. "Another champagne, *s'il vous plaît*." Oh, yeah, she was drunk. Busting out high school French was always a sure sign of that.

"See you later," she said to Diesel, taking her drink from the bartender. "Stay away from coconut."

Did that make sense? She wasn't really sure, but he just nodded. "Have fun."

"Always." Not exactly true, but if she stated it often enough, maybe it would become true.

Fun. Yeah. That's what she was having.

Tuesday grabbed Evan by the arm and went to prove it.

From the national bestselling author of
FLAT-OUT SEXY

Erin McCarthy

HARD *AND* FAST

He has what it takes to set her heart racing . . .

Praise for Erin McCarthy's novels

"Sizzling hot."
—*Romance Junkies*

"Funny, charming, and very entertaining."
—*Romance Reviews Today*

M517T0609

**Love Shifts into High Gear in
the First Fast Track Novel**

FROM *USA TODAY* BESTSELLING AUTHOR

ERIN McCARTHY

FLAT-OUT SEXY

The last place widowed single mother Tamara Briggs
wanted to find a man was at the racetrack. Been
there, done that. But rookie driver Elec Monroe sure
does get her heart racing . . .

"Steamy . . . fast-paced and red hot."
—*Publishers Weekly*

penguin.com

ALSO FROM *USA TODAY* BESTSELLING AUTHOR

ERIN McCARTHY

THE TAKING

Heiress Regan Henry knows that passion can be an illusion, and she keeps her emotions in check—until she falls under the spell of the beguiling Felix Leblanc. He knows the rumors that her mansion is haunted are true, and that he's the only one who can save her from the spirits residing there. But the only way he can free her is by sacrificing his last chance at redemption . . . or risk a love that could consign them both to an eternity of evil.

M660T0310

It's a...

Total Rush

Free spirit Gemma Dante wishes her love life were going as well as her New Age business. So she casts a spell to catch her Mr. Right. But when the cosmic wires get crossed, into her life walks a clean-cut fireman who's anything but her type.

Sean Kennealy doesn't know what to make of his pretty neighbor who burns incense. He only knows that being near her sparks a fire in him that even the guys at Ladder 29, Engine 31 can't put out.

From
New York Times Bestselling Author

Deirdre Martin

M205T0209